I0749253

The Best Psychic Stories

Joseph Lewis French

The Best Psychic Stories

The present edition is a reproduction of previous publication of this classic work. Minor typographical errors may have been corrected without note; however, for an authentic reading experience the spelling, punctuation, and capitalization have been retained from the original text.

ISBN: 978-1-63637-273-0

CONTENTS

PREFACE

The case for the "psychic" element in literature rests on a very old foundation; it reaches back to the ancient masters,—the men who wrote the Greek tragedies. Remorse will ever seem commonplace alongside the furies. Ever and always the shadow of the supernatural invites, pursues us. As the art of literature has progressed it has grown along with it. To-day there is a whole new school of writers of Ghost-Stories, and the domain of the invisible is being invaded by explorers in many paths. We do not believe so much more, perhaps, that is, we do not so openly express a belief, but art has finally and frankly claimed the supernatural for its own. One discerning authority even goes so far as to assert that the borders of its domain will be greatly enlarged in the wonderful new field of the screen.

There is no motive in a story, no image in poetry, that can give us quite the thrill of a supernatural idea. If we were formally charged with this we might resent the imputation, but the evidence has persisted from the beginning, lives on every hand, and multiplies daily. What we have been in the habit of calling the "machinery" of the old Greek drama—its supernatural effects—has come finally to be an art cultivated with care at the present hour, and has given us some wonderful new writers. In fact, few of the best masters for a generation now have been able to resist its persistent and abiding charm. Every writer of true imagination, almost without exception, including even certain realists, has given us at least one story, long or short, in which the central motive is purely psychical in the Greek sense of the word.

The whole subject opens up a virgin field which has after all only begun to be tilled. Within the coming generation we may look for great artists to devote their whole powers to it, as Algernon Blackwood is doing to-day. A simple underlying reason is enough to account for it all—the new field imposes simply no limit on the imagination. In addition to all that science has taught us, there is illimitable store of myth and legend to aid, to draw from, to work in, to work over, as Lord Dunsany has shown us. It is the most significant movement in literature at the present hour, and whether it is supported by a special background of interest—as at present in spiritism—or not, the assertion is logical that it is creating a new body of fictional literature of permanent importance for the first time in the history of literature. The human comedy seems to have been exploited to its final limits; as the art of the novel, the art of the stage, but too sadly prove to-day. We have turned outward for new thrills to the supernatural and we are getting them.

It only remains to be added that the present great interest in spiritualism and allied phenomena has made necessary the addition of certain material of a "literal" character which we believe will be found quite as interesting by the general reader as the purely literary portion of the book.

JOSEPH LEWIS FRENCH

INTRODUCTION

THE PSYCHIC IN LITERATURE

War, that relentless disturber of boundaries and of traditions in a spiritual as well as a material sense, has brought a tremendous revival of interest in the life after death and the possibility of communication between the living and the dead. As France became nearer to millions over here because our soldiers lived there for a few months, as French soil will forever be holy ground because our dead rest there, so the far country of the soul likewise seems nearer because of those young adventurers. The conflict which changed the map of Europe has in the minds of many effaced the boundaries between this world and the world beyond. Winifred Kirkland, in her book, The New Death, discusses the new concept of death, and the change in our standards that it is making. "We are used to speaking of this or that friend's philosophy of life; the time has now come when every one of us who is to live at peace with his own brain must possess also a philosophy of death." This New Death, she says, is so far mainly an immense yearning receptivity, an unprecedented humility of brain and of heart toward all implications of survival. She believes that it is an influence which is entering the lives of the people as a whole, not a movement of the intellectuals, nor the result of psychical research propaganda, but arising from the simple, elemental emotions of the soul, from human love and longing for reassurance of continued life.

"If a man die, shall he live again?" has been propounded ever since Job's agonized inquiry. Now numbers are asking in addition, "Can we have communication with the dead?" Science, long derisive, is sympathetic to the questioning, and while many believe and many doubt, the subject is one that interests more people than ever before. Professor James Hyslop, Secretary of the American Society for Psychical Research, believes that the war has had great influence in arousing new interest in psychical subjects and that tremendous spiritual discoveries may come from it.

Literature, always a little ahead of life, or at least in advance of general thinking, has in the more recent years been acutely conscious of this new influence. Poetry, the drama, the novel, the short story, have given affirmative answer to the question of the soul's survival after death. No other element has so largely entered into the tissue of recent literature as has the supernatural, which now we meet in all forms in the writings of all lands. And no aspect of the ghostly art is more impressive or more widely used than the introduction of the spirit of the dead seeking to manifest itself to the living. No thoughtful person can fail to be interested in a theme which has so affected literature as has the ghostly, even though he may disbelieve what the Psychical Researchers hold to be established.

Man's love for the supernatural, which is one of the most natural things about him, was never more marked than now. Man's imagination, ever vaster than his environment, overleaps the barriers of time and space and claims all worlds as eminent domain, so that literature, which he has the power to create, as he cannot create his material surroundings, possesses a dramatic intensity and an epic sweep unknown in actuality. Literature shows what humanity really is and longs to be. Man, feeling belittled by his petty round of uninspiring days, longs for a larger life. He yearns for traffic with immortal beings that can augment his wisdom, that can bring comfort to his soul dismayed and bewildered by life. He reaches out for a power beyond his puny strength. Aware how relentlessly time ticks away his little hour, he craves companionship with the eternal spirits. Ignorant of what lies before him in the life to which he speeds so fast, he would take counsel of those who know, would ask about the customs of the country where presently he will be a citizen. He feels so terribly alone that he cries out like a child in the dark for supermortal companionship.

Literature, which is both a cause and an effect of man's interest in the supernatural as in anything else, reflects his longings and records his cries. And when we read the imaginings of the different generations, we find that the spirit of the dead is represented almost everywhere. Before poetry and fiction were recorded, there were singers and story-tellers by the fire to give to their listeners the thrill that comes from art. And what thrill is comparable to that which comes from contact with the supermortal? The earliest literature relates the appearance of the spirits of those who have died as coming back to comfort or to take vengeance on the living, but always as sentient, intelligent, and with an interest in the earth they have left. All through the centuries the wraith has survived in literature, has flitted pallidly across the pages of poetry, story and play, with a sad wistfulness, a forlorn dignity.

A double relation exists between the literature and the records of the Psychical Research Society. Lacy Collison-Morley, in his Greek and Roman Ghost Stories, speaks of the similarity between ancient tales of spirits and records of recent instances. "There are in the Fourth Book of Gregory the Great's Dialogues a number of stories of the passing of souls which are curiously like some of those collected by the Psychical Research Society," he says. Possibly human personality is much the same in all lands and all times.

Conversely, some of the best examples of ghostly literature have had their inspiration in the records of the society, Henry James's The Turn of the Screw being a notable example. Algernon Blackwood, that extraordinary adapter of psychic material to fiction, makes frequent mention of the Psychical Research Society, and uses many aspects of the psychical in his fiction. Innumerable stories, novels, plays and poems have been written to show the nearness of the dead to the living, and the thinness of the veil that separates the two worlds. There is deep pathos in the concept of the longing felt by the dead and living alike to speak with each other, to rend the dividing veil, which adds a poignancy to literature, even for readers incredulous of the possibility of such communication. There are many who are unconvinced of the reality of the messages in Raymond, for instance,—yet who could fail to be touched by the delicate art with which Barrie suggests the dead son's return in his play, The Well-Remembered Voice? While one may be repelled by what he feels is fraud and trickery in some of the psychic records, it is impossible not to be moved by such an impressive piece of symbolism as Granville Barker's Souls on Fifth, where the lonely, futile spirits of the dead are represented as hovering near the place they knew the best, seeking piteously to win some recognition from the living. The repulsive aspects of spirit manifestations have been treated many times and with power, as in Joseph Hergesheimer's The Meeker Ritual, to give one very recent example. The subject has interested the minds of many writers who have dealt with it satirically or sympathetically, or with a curious mixture of scoffing and respect, as did Browning in Sludge, the Medium. Even such pronounced realists as William Dean Howells and Hamlin Garland have written novels dealing with attempts at spirit communication.

Any subject that has won so incontestable a place in our literature as this has, possesses a right to our thought, whatever be our attitude of acceptance or rejection of its claims to actuality. No person wishes to be ignorant of what the world is thinking with reference to a matter so important as the spirit. Hence this volume, The Best Psychic Stories, in presenting these studies in the occult, will have interest for a wide range of readers, and Mr. French, the editor, has shown critical discrimination and extensive knowledge of the subject. Many who are already interested in psychic phenomena will be glad to be informed concerning recent and startling manifestations recounted by special investigators. The sincerity of a man like W. T. Stead, well known and respected on both sides of the Atlantic, cannot be doubted, so that his article on

Photographing Invisible Beings will have unusual weight. Hereward Carrington, author of various books on psychic subjects, and considered an authority in his field, gives in The Phantom Armies Seen in France a report of occult phenomena widely believed in during the war.

Helena Blavatsky, author of A Witch's Den, will be remembered as the sensational medium who mystified experimenters in various lands a few years ago. While most of us can be content not to touch a ghost, we may find subject for surprise and wonder in Gambier Bolton's Ghosts in Solid Form, describing spirits that can be weighed and put to material tests, while Dr. Walter H. Prince, well known as a psychic investigator, relates remarkable experiments of famous persons, that challenge explanation on purely physical bases. These accounts show that modern scientific investigation of spiritual manifestations can be made as enthralling as fiction or drama. Hamlin Garland remarks in a recent article, The Spirit-World on Trial, "When the medium consented to enter the laboratory of the physicist, a new era in the study of psychic phenomena began."

Even those who refuse credence to spirit manifestations in fact, but who appreciate the art with which they are shown in literature, should read with interest the stories given here. The genius of Edgar Allan Poe was never more impressive than in his studies of the supernatural, and Ligeia has a dramatic art unsurpassed even by Poe. The tense economy with which Ambrose Bierce could evoke a dreadful spirit is evident in The Eyes of the Panther, and the haunting symbolism of Fiona Macleod's The Sin-Eater is unforgetable. Lafcadio Hearn, author of A Ghost, held the belief that there was no great artist in any land, and certainly no Anglo-Saxon writer, who had not distinguished himself in his use of the supernatural. The subject of the soul's survival after death and its attempts to reveal itself to those still in the folding flesh is of interest to every rational person, whether as a matter of scientific concern or merely as an aspect of literary art. And the possibilities for further use of the psychic in literature are as alluring as they are illimitable.

Dorothy Scarborough
New York City March 29, 1920

WHEN THE WORLD WAS YOUNG[1]

By Jack London

I

He was a very quiet, self-possessed sort of man, sitting a moment on top of the wall to sound the damp darkness for warnings of the dangers it might conceal. But the plummet of his hearing brought nothing to him save the moaning of wind through invisible trees and the rustling of leaves on swaying branches. A heavy fog drifted and drove before the wind, and though he could not see this fog, the wet of it blew upon his face, and the wall on which he sat was wet.

Without noise he had climbed to the top of the wall from the outside, and without noise he dropped to the ground on the inside. From his pocket he drew an electric night-stick, but he did not use it. Dark as the way was, he was not anxious for light. Carrying the night-stick in his hand, his finger on the button, he advanced through the darkness. The ground was velvety and springy to his feet, being carpeted with dead pine-needles and leaves and mold which evidently had been undisturbed for years. Leaves and branches brushed against his body, but so dark was it that he could not avoid them. Soon he walked with his hand stretched out gropingly before him, and more than once the hand fetched up against the solid trunks of massive trees. All about him he knew were these trees; he sensed the loom of them everywhere; and he experienced a strange feeling of microscopic smallness in the midst of great bulks leaning toward him to crush him. Beyond, he knew, was the house, and he expected to find some trail or winding path that would lead easily to it.

Once, he found himself trapped. On every side he groped against trees and branches, or blundered into thickets of underbrush, until there seemed no way out. Then he turned on his light, circumspectly, directing its rays to the ground at his feet. Slowly and carefully he moved it about him, the white brightness showing in sharp detail all the obstacles to his progress. He saw an opening between huge-trunked trees, and advanced through it, putting out the light and treading on dry footing as yet protected

[1] By permission of The Century Co.

from the drip of the fog by the dense foliage overhead. His sense of direction was good, and he knew he was going toward the house.

And then the thing happened—the thing unthinkable and unexpected. His descending foot came down upon something that was soft and alive, and that arose with a snort under the weight of his body. He sprang clear, and crouched for another spring, anywhere, tense and expectant, keyed for the onslaught of the unknown. He waited a moment, wondering what manner of animal it was that had arisen from under his foot and that now made no sound nor movement and that must be crouching and waiting just as tensely and expectantly as he. The strain became unbearable. Holding the night-stick before him, he pressed the button, saw, and screamed aloud in terror. He was prepared for anything, from a frightened calf or fawn to a belligerent lion, but he was not prepared for what he saw. In that instant his tiny searchlight, sharp and white, had shown him what a thousand years would not enable him to forget—a man, huge and blond, yellow-haired and yellow-bearded, naked except for soft-tanned moccasins and what seemed a goat-skin about his middle. Arms and legs were bare, as were his shoulders and most of his chest. The skin was smooth and hairless, but browned by sun and wind, while under it heavy muscles were knotted like fat snakes.

Still, this alone, unexpected as it well was, was not what had made the man scream out. What had caused his terror was the unspeakable ferocity of the face, the wild-animal glare of the blue eyes scarcely dazzled by the light, the pine-needles matted and clinging in the beard and hair, and the whole formidable body crouched and in the act of springing at him. Practically in the instant he saw all this, and while his scream still rang, the thing leaped, he flung his night-stick full at it, and threw himself to the ground. He felt its feet and shins strike against his ribs, and he bounded up and away while the thing itself hurled onward in a heavy crashing fall into the underbrush.

As the noise of the fall ceased, the man stopped and on hands and knees waited. He could hear the thing moving about, searching for him, and he was afraid to advertise his location by attempting further flight. He knew that inevitably he would crackle the underbrush and be pursued. Once he drew out his revolver, then changed his mind. He had recovered his composure and hoped to get away without noise. Several times he heard the thing beating up the thickets for him, and there were moments when it, too, remained still and listened. This gave an idea to the man. One of his hands was resting on a chunk of dead wood. Carefully, first feeling about him in the darkness to know that the full swing of his arm was clear, he raised the chunk of wood and threw it. It was not a large piece, and it went far, landing noisily in a bush. He heard the thing bound into the bush, and at the same time himself crawled steadily away. And on hands and knees, slowly and cautiously, he crawled on, till his knees were wet on the soggy mold. When he listened he heard naught but the moaning wind and the drip-drip of the fog from the branches. Never abating his caution, he stood erect and went on to the stone wall, over which he climbed and dropped down to the road outside.

Feeling his way in a clump of bushes, he drew out a bicycle and prepared to mount. He was in the act of driving the gear around with his foot for the purpose of getting the opposite pedal in position, when he heard the thud of a heavy body that landed lightly and evidently on its feet. He did not wait for more, but ran, with hands on the handles of his bicycle, until he was able to vault astride the saddle, catch the pedals, and start a spurt. Behind he could hear the quick thud-thud of feet on the dust of the road, but he drew away from it and lost it.

Unfortunately, he had started away from the direction of town and was heading higher up into the hills. He knew that on this particular road there were no cross roads. The only way back was past that terror, and he could not steel himself to face it. At the end of half an hour, finding himself on an ever increasing grade, he dismounted. For still greater safety, leaving the wheel by the roadside, he climbed through a fence into what he decided was a hillside pasture, spread a newspaper on the ground, and sat down.

"Gosh!" he said aloud, mopping the sweat and fog from his face.

And "Gosh!" he said once again, while rolling a cigarette and as he pondered the problem of getting back.

But he made no attempt to go back. He was resolved not to face that road in the dark, and with head bowed on knees, he dozed, waiting for daylight.

How long afterward he did not know, he was awakened by the yapping bark of a young coyote. As he looked about and located it on the brow of the hill behind him, he noted the change that had come over the face of the night. The fog was gone; the stars and moon were out; even the wind had died down. It had transformed into a balmy California summer night. He tried to doze again, but the yap of the coyote disturbed him. Half asleep, he heard a wild and eery chant. Looking about him, he noticed that the coyote had ceased its noise and was running away along the crest of the hill, and behind it, in full pursuit, no longer chanting, ran the naked creature he had encountered in the garden. It was a young coyote, and it was being overtaken when the chase passed from view. The man trembled as with a chill as he started to his feet, clambered over the fence, and mounted his wheel. But it was his chance and he knew it. The terror was no longer between him and Mill Valley.

He sped at a breakneck rate down the hill, but in the turn at the bottom, in the deep shadows, he encountered a chuck-hole and pitched headlong over the handle bar.

"It's sure not my night," he muttered, as he examined the broken fork of the machine.

Shouldering the useless wheel, he trudged on. In time he came to the stone wall, and, half disbelieving his experience, he sought in the road for tracks, and found them—moccasin tracks, large ones, deep-bitten into the dust at the toes. It was while bending over them, examining, that again he heard the eery chant. He had seen the thing pursue the coyote, and he knew he had no chance on a straight run. He did not attempt it, contenting himself with hiding in the shadows on the off side of the road.

And again he saw the thing that was like a naked man, running swiftly and lightly and singing as it ran. Opposite him it paused, and his heart stood still. But instead of coming toward his hiding-place, it leaped into the air, caught the branch of a roadside tree, and swung swiftly upward, from limb to limb, like an ape. It swung across the wall, and a dozen feet above the top, into the branches of another tree, and dropped out of sight to the ground. The man waited a few wondering minutes, then started on.

II

Dave Slotter leaned belligerently against the desk that barred the way to the private office of James Ward, senior partner of the firm of Ward, Knowles & Co. Dave was angry. Every one in the outer office had looked him over suspiciously, and the man who faced him was excessively suspicious.

"You just tell Mr. Ward it's important," he urged.

"I tell you he is dictating and cannot be disturbed," was the answer. "Come to-morrow."

"To-morrow will be too late. You just trot along and tell Mr. Ward it's a matter of life and death."

The secretary hesitated and Dave seized the advantage.

"You just tell him I was across the bay in Mill Valley last night, and that I want to put him wise to something."

"What name?" was the query.

"Never mind the name. He don't know me."

When Dave was shown into the private office, he was still in the belligerent frame of mind, but when he saw a large fair man whirl in a revolving chair from dictating to a stenographer to face him, Dave's demeanor abruptly changed. He did not know why it changed, and he was secretly angry with himself.

"You are Mr. Ward?" Dave asked with a fatuousness that still further irritated him. He had never intended it at all.

"Yes," came the answer. "And who are you?"

"Harry Bancroft," Dave lied. "You don't know me, and my name don't matter."

"You sent in word that you were in Mill Valley last night?"

"You live there, don't you?" Dave countered, looking suspiciously at the stenographer.

"Yes. What do you mean to see me about? I am very busy."

"I'd like to see you alone, sir."

Mr. Ward gave him a quick, penetrating look, hesitated, then made up his mind.

"That will do for a few minutes, Miss Potter."

The girl arose, gathered her notes together, and passed out. Dave looked at Mr. James Ward wonderingly, until that gentleman broke his train of inchoate thought.

"Well?"

"I was over in Mill Valley last night," Dave began confusedly.

"I've heard that before. What do you want?"

And Dave proceeded in the face of a growing conviction that was unbelievable.

"I was at your house, or in the grounds, I mean."

"What were you doing there?"

"I came to break in," Dave answered in all frankness. "I heard you lived all alone with a Chinaman for cook, and it looked good to me. Only I didn't break in. Something happened that prevented. That's why I'm here. I come to warn you. I found a wild man loose in your grounds—a regular devil. He could pull a guy like me to pieces. He gave me the run of my life. He don't wear any clothes to speak of, he climbs trees like a monkey, and he runs like a deer. I saw him chasing a coyote, and the last I saw of it, by God, he was gaining on it."

Dave paused and looked for the effect that would follow his words. But no effect came. James Ward was quietly curious, and that was all.

"Very remarkable, very remarkable," he murmured. "A wild man, you say. Why have you come to tell me?"

"To warn you of your danger. I'm something of a hard

proposition myself, but I don't believe in killing people ... that is, unnecessarily. I realized that you was in danger. I thought I'd warn you. Honest, that's the game. Of course, if you wanted to give me anything for my trouble, I'd take it. That was in my mind, too. But I don't care whether you give me anything or not. I've warned you anyway, and done my duty."

Mr. Ward meditated and drummed on the surface of his desk. Dave noticed that his hands were large, powerful, withal well-cared for despite their dark sunburn. Also, he noted what had already caught his eye before—a tiny strip of flesh-colored courtplaster on the forehead over one eye. And still the thought that forced itself into his mind was unbelievable.

Mr. Ward took a wallet from his inside coat pocket, drew out a greenback, and passed it to Dave, who noted as he pocketed it that it was for twenty dollars.

"Thank you," said Mr. Ward, indicating that the interview was at an end. "I shall have the matter investigated. A wild man running loose is dangerous."

But so quiet a man was Mr. Ward, that Dave's courage returned. Besides, a new theory had suggested itself. The wild man was evidently Mr. Ward's brother, a lunatic privately confined. Dave had heard of such things. Perhaps Mr. Ward wanted it kept quiet. That was why he had given him the twenty dollars.

"Say," Dave began, "now I come to think of it that wild man looked a lot like you—"

That was as far as Dave got, for at that moment he witnessed a transformation and found himself gazing into the same unspeakably ferocious blue eyes of the night before, at the same clutching talon-like hands, and at the same formidable bulk in the act of springing upon him. But this time Dave had no night-stick to throw, and he was caught by the biceps of both arms in a grip so terrific that it made him groan with pain. He saw the large white teeth exposed, for all the world as a dog's about to bite. Mr. Ward's beard brushed his face as the teeth went in for the grip of his throat. But the bite was not given. Instead, Dave felt the other's body stiffen as with an iron restraint, and then he was flung aside, without effort but with such force that only the wall stopped his momentum and dropped him gasping to the floor.

"What do you mean by coming here and trying to blackmail me?" Mr. Ward was snarling at him. "Here, give me back that money."

Dave passed the bill back without a word.

"I thought you came here with good intentions. I know you

now. Let me see and hear no more of you, or I'll put you in prison where you belong. Do you understand?"

"Yes, sir," Dave gasped.

"Then go."

And Dave went, without further word, both his biceps aching intolerably from the bruise of that tremendous grip. As his hand rested on the door knob, he was stopped.

"You were lucky," Mr. Ward was saying, and Dave noted that his face and eyes were cruel and gloating and proud. "You were lucky. Had I wanted, I could have torn your muscles out of your arms and thrown them in the waste basket there."

"Yes, sir," said Dave; and absolute conviction vibrated in his voice.

He opened the door and passed out. The secretary looked at him interrogatively.

"Gosh!" was all Dave vouchsafed, and with this utterance passed out of the offices and the story.

III

James G. Ward was forty years of age, a successful business man, and very unhappy. For forty years he had vainly tried to solve a problem that was really himself and that with increasing years became more and more a woeful affliction. In himself he was two men, and, chronologically speaking, these men were several thousand years or so apart. He had studied the question of dual personality probably more profoundly than any half dozen of the leading specialists in that intricate and mysterious psychological field. In himself he was a different case from any that had been recorded. Even the most fanciful flights of the fiction-writers had not quite hit upon him. He was not a Dr. Jekyll and Mr. Hyde, nor was he like the unfortunate young man in Kipling's Greatest Story in the World. His two personalities were so mixed that they were practically aware of themselves and of each other all the time.

His one self was that of a man whose rearing and education were modern and who had lived through the latter part of the nineteenth century and well into the first decade of the twentieth. His other self he had located as a savage and a barbarian living under the primitive conditions of several thousand years before. But which self was he, and which was the other, he could never tell. For he was both selves, and both selves all the time. Very rarely indeed did it happen that one self did not know what the other was doing. Another thing was that he had no visions nor memories of the past in which that early self had lived. That early self lived in the present; but while it lived in the present, it was under the compulsion to live the way of life that must have been in that distant past.

In his childhood he had been a problem to his father and mother, and to the family doctors, though never had they come within a thousand miles of hitting upon the clue to his erratic conduct. Thus, they could not understand his excessive somnolence in the forenoon, nor his excessive activity at night. When they found him wandering along the hallways at night, or climbing over giddy roofs, or running in the hills, they decided he was a somnambulist. In reality he was wide-eyed awake and merely under the night-roaming compulsion of his early life. Questioned by an obtuse medico, he once told the truth and suffered the ignominy of having the revelation contemptuously labeled and dismissed as "dreams."

The point was, that as twilight and evening came on he became wakeful. The four walls of a room were an irk and a restraint. He heard a thousand voices whispering to him through the darkness. The night called to him, for he was, for that period of the twenty-four hours, essentially a night-prowler. But nobody understood, and never again did he attempt to explain. They classified him as a sleep-walker and took precautions accordingly—precautions that very often were futile. As his childhood advanced, he grew more cunning, so that the major portion of all his nights were spent in the open at realizing his other self. As a result, he slept in the forenoons. Morning studies and schools were impossible, and it was discovered that only in the afternoons, under private teachers, could he be taught anything. Thus was his modern self educated and developed.

But a problem, as a child, he ever remained. He was known as a little demon of insensate cruelty and viciousness. The family medicos privately adjudged him a mental monstrosity and a degenerate. Such few boy companions as he had, hailed him as a wonder, though they were all afraid of him. He could outclimb, outswim, outrun, outdevil any of them; while none dared fight with him. He was too terribly strong, too madly furious.

When nine years of age he ran away to the hills, where he flourished, night-prowling, for seven weeks before he was discovered and brought home. The marvel was how he had managed to subsist and keep in condition during that time. They did not know, and he never told them, of the rabbits he had killed, of the quail, young and old, he had captured and devoured, of the farmers' chicken-roosts he had raided, nor of the cave-lair he had made and carpeted with dry leaves and grasses and in which he had slept in warmth and comfort, through the forenoons of many days.

At college he was notorious for his sleepiness and stupidity during the morning lectures and for his brilliance in the afternoon. By collateral reading and by borrowing the notebook of his fellow students he managed to scrape through the detestable morning courses, while his afternoon courses were triumphs. In football he proved a giant and a terror, and, in almost every form of track athletics, save for strange Berserker rages that were sometimes displayed, he could be depended upon to win. But his fellows were afraid to box with him, and he signalized his last wrestling bout by sinking his teeth into the shoulder of his opponent.

After college, his father, in despair, sent him among the cow-punchers of a Wyoming ranch. Three months later the doughty cowmen confessed he was too much for them and telegraphed his father to come and take the wild man away. Also, when the father arrived to take him away, the cowmen allowed that they would vastly prefer chumming with howling cannibals, gibbering lunatics, cavorting gorillas, grizzly bears, and man-eating tigers than with this particular young college product with hair parted in the middle.

There was one exception to the lack of memory of the life of his early self, and that was language. By some quirk of atavism, a certain portion of that early self's language had come down to him as a racial memory. In moments of happiness, exaltation, or battle, he was prone to burst out in wild barbaric songs or chants. It was by this means that he located in time and space that strayed half of him who should have been dead and dust for thousands of years. He sang, once, and deliberately, several of the ancient chants in the presence of Professor Wertz, who gave courses in old Saxon and who was a philologist of repute and passion. At the first one, the professor pricked up his ears and demanded to know what mongrel tongue or hog-German it was. When the second chant was rendered, the professor was highly excited. James Ward then concluded the performance by giving a song that always irresistibly rushed to his lips when he was engaged in fierce struggling or fighting. Then it was that Professor Wertz proclaimed it no hog-German, but early German, or early Teuton, of a date that must far precede anything that had ever been discovered and handed down by the scholars. So early was it that it was beyond him; yet it was filled with haunting reminiscences of word-forms he knew and which his trained intuition told him were true and real. He demanded the source of the songs, and asked to borrow the previous book that contained them. Also, he demanded to know why young Ward had always posed as being profoundly ignorant of the German language. And Ward could neither explain his ignorance nor lend the book. Whereupon, after pleadings and entreaties that extended through weeks, Professor Wertz took a dislike to the young man, believed him a liar, and classified him as a man of monstrous selfishness for not giving him a glimpse of this wonderful screed that was older than the oldest any philologist had ever known or dreamed.

But little good did it do this much-mixed young man to know that half of him was late American and the other half early Teuton. Nevertheless, the late American in him was no weakling, and he (if he were a he and had a shred of existence outside of these two) compelled an adjustment or compromise between his one self that was a night-prowling savage that kept his other self sleepy of mornings, and that other self that was cultured and refined and that wanted to be normal and love and prosecute business like other people. The afternoons and early evenings he gave to the one, the nights to the other; the forenoons and parts of the nights were devoted to sleep for the twain. But in the mornings he slept in bed like a civilized man. In the night time he slept like a wild animal, as he had slept the night Dave Slotter stepped on him in the woods.

Persuading his father to advance the capital, he went into business, and keen and successful business he made of it, devoting his afternoons whole-souled to it, while his partner devoted the mornings. The early evenings he spent socially, but, as the hour grew to nine or ten, an irresistible restlessness overcame him and he disappeared from the haunts of men until the next afternoon. Friends and acquaintances thought that he spent much of his time in sport. And they were right, though they never would have dreamed of the nature of the sport, even if they had seen him running coyotes in night-chases over the hills of Mill Valley. Neither were the schooner captains believed when they reported seeing, on cold winter mornings, a man swimming in the tide-rips of Raccoon Straits or in the swift currents between Goat Island and Angel Island miles from shore.

In the bungalow at Mill Valley he lived alone, save for Lee Sing, the Chinese cook and factotum, who knew much about the strangeness of his master, who was paid well for saying nothing, and who never did say anything. After the satisfaction of his nights, a morning's sleep, and a breakfast of Lee Sing's, James Ward crossed the bay to San Francisco on a midday ferryboat and went to the club and on to his office, as normal and conventional a man of business as could be found in the city. But as the evening lengthened, the night called to him. There came a quickening of all his perceptions and a restlessness. His hearing was suddenly acute; the myriad night-noises told him a luring and familiar story; and, if alone, he would begin to pace up and down the narrow room like any caged animal from the wild.

Once, he ventured to fall in love. He never permitted himself that diversion again. He was afraid. And for many a day the young lady, scared at least out of a portion of her young ladyhood, bore on her arms and shoulders and wrists divers black-and-blue bruises—tokens of caresses which he had bestowed in all fond gentleness but too late at night. There was the mistake. Had he ventured love-making in the afternoon, all would have been well, for it would have been as the quiet gentleman that he would have made love—but at night it was the uncouth, wife-stealing savage of the dark German forests. Out of his wisdom, he decided that afternoon love-making could be prosecuted successfully; but out of the same wisdom he was convinced that marriage would prove a ghastly failure. He found it appalling to imagine being married and encountering his wife after dark.

So he had eschewed all love-making, regulated his dual life, cleaned up a million in business, fought shy of match-making mamas and bright- and eager-eyed young ladies of various ages, met Lilian Gersdale and made it a rigid observance never to see her later than eight o'clock in the evening, ran of nights after his coyotes, and slept in forest lairs—and through it all had kept his secret save for Lee Sing ... and now, Dave Slotter. It was the latter's discovery of both his selves that frightened him. In spite of the counter fright he had given the burglar, the latter might talk. And even if he did not, sooner or later he would be found out by some one else.

Thus it was that James Ward made a fresh and heroic effort to control the Teutonic barbarian that was half of him. So well did he make it a point to see Lilian in the afternoons and early evenings, that the time came when she accepted him for better or worse, and when he prayed privily and fervently that it was not for worse. During this period no prize-fighter ever trained more harshly and faithfully for a contest than he trained to subdue the wild savage in him. Among other things, he strove to exhaust himself during the day, so that sleep would render him deaf to the call of the night. He took a vacation from the office and went on long hunting trips, following the deer through the most inaccessible and rugged country he could find—and always in the daytime. Night found him indoors and tired. At home he installed a score of exercise machines, and where other men might go through a particular movement ten times, he went hundreds. Also, as a compromise, he built a sleeping porch on the second story. Here he at least breathed the blessed night air. Double screens prevented him from escaping into the woods, and each night Lee Sing locked him in and each morning let him out.

The time came, in the month of August, when he engaged additional servants to assist Lee Sing and dared a house party in his Mill Valley bungalow. Lilian, her mother and brother, and half a dozen mutual friends, were the guests. For two days and nights all went well. And on the third night, playing bridge till eleven o'clock, he had reason to be proud of himself. His restlessness he successfully hid, but as luck would have it, Lilian Gersdale was his opponent on his right. She was a frail delicate flower of a woman, and in his night-mood her very frailty incensed him. Not that he loved her less, but that he felt almost irresistibly impelled to reach out and paw and maul her. Especially was this true when she was engaged in playing a winning hand against him.

He had one of the deer-hounds brought in, and, when it seemed he must fly to pieces with the tension, a caressing hand laid on the animal brought him relief. These contacts with the hairy coat gave him instant easement and enabled him to play out the evening. Nor did any one guess the terrible struggle their host was making, the while he laughed so carelessly and played so keenly and deliberately.

When they separated for the night, he saw to it that he parted from Lilian in the presence of the others. Once on his sleeping porch, and safely locked in, he doubled and tripled and even quadrupled his exercises until, exhausted, he lay down on the couch to woo sleep and to ponder two problems that especially troubled him. One was this matter of exercise. It was a paradox. The more he exercised in this excessive fashion, the stronger he became. While it was true that he thus quite tired out his night-running Teutonic self, it seemed that he was merely setting back the fatal day when his strength would be too much for him and overpower him, and then it would be a strength more terrible than he had yet known. The other problem was that of his marriage and of the stratagems he must employ in order to avoid his wife after dark. And thus fruitlessly pondering he fell asleep.

Now, where the huge grizzly bear came from that night was long a mystery, while the people of the Springs Brothers' Circus, showing at Sausalito, searched long and vainly for "Big Ben, the Biggest Grizzly in Captivity." But Big Ben escaped, and, out of the mazes of half a thousand bungalows and country estates, selected the grounds of James J. Ward for visitation. The first Mr. Ward knew was when he found himself on his feet, quivering and tense, a surge of battle in his breast and on his lips the old war-chant. From without came a wild baying and bellowing of the hounds. And sharp as a knife-thrust through the pandemonium came the agony of a stricken dog—his dog, he knew.

Not stopping for slippers, pajama-clad, he burst through the door Lee Sing had so carefully locked, and sped down the stairs and out into the night. As his naked feet struck the graveled driveway, he stopped abruptly, reached under the steps to a hiding-place he knew well, and pulled forth a huge knotty club—his old companion on many a mad night adventure on the hills. The frantic hullabaloo of the dogs was coming nearer, and, swinging the club, he sprang straight into the thickets to meet it.

The aroused household assembled on the wide veranda. Somebody turned on the electric lights, but they could see nothing but one another's frightened faces. Beyond the brightly illuminated driveway the trees formed a wall of impenetrable blackness. Yet somewhere in that blackness a terrible struggle was going on. There was an infernal outcry of animals, a great snarling and growling, the sound of blows being struck, and a smashing and crashing of underbrush by heavy bodies.

The tide of battle swept out from among the trees and upon the driveway just beneath the onlookers. Then they saw. Mrs. Gersdale cried out and clung fainting to her son. Lilian, clutching the railing so spasmodically that a bruising hurt was left in her finger-ends for days, gazed horror-stricken at a yellow-haired, wild-eyed giant whom she recognized as the man who was to be her husband. He was swinging a great club, and fighting furiously and calmly with a shaggy monster that was bigger than any bear she had ever seen. One rip of the beast's claws had dragged away Ward's pajama-coat and streaked his flesh with blood.

While most of Lilian Gersdale's fright was for the man beloved, there was a large portion of it due to the man himself. Never had she dreamed so formidable and magnificent a savage lurked under the starched shirt and conventional garb of her betrothed. And never had she had any conception of how a man battled. Such a battle was certainly not modern; nor was she there beholding a modern man, though she did not know it. For this was not Mr. James J. Ward, the San Francisco business man, but one unnamed and unknown, a crude, rude savage creature who, by some freak of chance, lived again after thrice a thousand years.

The hounds, ever maintaining their mad uproar, circled about the fight, or dashed in and out, distracting the bear. When the animal turned to meet such flanking assaults, the man leaped in and the club came down. Angered afresh by every such blow, the bear would rush, and the man, leaping and skipping, avoiding the dogs, went backwards or circled to one side or the other. Whereupon the dogs, taking advantage of the opening, would again spring in and draw the animal's wrath to them.

The end came suddenly. Whirling, the grizzly caught a hound with a wide sweeping cuff that sent the brute, its ribs caved in and its back broken, hurtling twenty feet. Then the human brute went mad. A foaming rage flecked the lips that parted with a wild inarticulate cry, as it sprang in, swung the club mightily in both hands, and brought it down full on the head of the uprearing grizzly. Not even the skull of a grizzly could withstand the crushing force of such a blow, and the animal went down to meet the worrying of the hounds. And through their scurrying leaped the man, squarely upon the body, where, in the white electric light, resting on his club, he chanted a triumph in an unknown tongue—a song so ancient that Professor Wertz would have given ten years of his life for it.

His guests rushed to possess him and acclaim him, but James Ward, suddenly looking out of the eyes of the early Teuton, saw the fair frail Twentieth Century girl he loved, and felt something snap in his brain. He staggered weakly toward her, dropped the club, and nearly fell. Something had gone wrong with him. Inside his brain was an intolerable agony. It seemed as if the soul of him were flying asunder. Following the excited gaze of the others, he glanced back and saw the carcass of the bear. The sight filled him with fear. He uttered a cry and would have fled, had they not restrained him and led him into the bungalow.

James J. Ward is still at the head of the firm of Ward, Knowles & Co. But he no longer lives in the country; nor does he run of nights after the coyotes under the moon. The early Teuton in him died the night of the Mill Valley fight with the bear. James J. Ward is now wholly James J. Ward, and he shares no part of his being with any vagabond anachronism from the younger world. And so wholly is James J. Ward modern, that he knows in all its bitter fullness the curse of civilized fear. He is now afraid of the dark, and night in the forest is to him a thing of abysmal terror. His city house is of the spick and span order, and he evinces a great interest in burglar-proof devices. His home is a tangle of electric wires, and after bed-time a guest can scarcely breathe without setting off an alarm. Also, he has invented a combination keyless door-lock that travelers may carry in their vest pockets and apply immediately and successfully under all circumstances. But his wife does not deem him a coward. She knows better. And, like any hero, he is content to rest on his laurels. His bravery is never questioned by those of his friends who are aware of the Mill Valley episode.

THE RETURN[2]

By Algernon Blackwood

It was curious—that sense of dull uneasiness that came over him so suddenly, so stealthily at first he scarcely noticed it, but with such marked increase after a time that he presently got up and left the theater. His seat was on the gangway of the dress circle, and he slipped out awkwardly in the middle of what seemed to be the best and jolliest song of the piece. The full house was shaking with laughter; so infectious was the gaiety that even strangers turned to one another as much as to say, "Now, isn't that funny?"

It was curious, too, the way the feeling first got into him at all, and in the full swing of laughter, music, light-heartedness; for it came as a vague suggestion, "I've forgotten something—something I meant to do—something of importance. What in the world was it, now?" And he thought hard, searching vainly through his mind; then dismissed it as the dancing caught his attention. It came back a little later again, during a passage of long-winded talk that bored him and set his attention free once more, but came more strongly this time, insisting on an answer. What could it have been that he had overlooked, left undone, omitted to see to? It went on nibbling at the subconscious part of him. Several times this happened, this dismissal and return, till at last the thing declared itself more plainly—and he felt bothered, troubled, distinctly uneasy.

He was wanted somewhere. There was somewhere else he ought to be. That describes it best, perhaps. Some engagement of moment had entirely slipped his memory—an engagement that involved another person, too. But where, what, with whom? And, at length, this vague uneasiness amounted to positive discomfort, so that he felt unable to enjoy the piece, and left abruptly. Like a man to whom comes suddenly the horrible idea that the match he lit his cigarette with and flung into the waste-paper basket on leaving was not really out—a sort of panic distress—he jumped into a taxicab and hurried to his flat to find everything in order, of course; no smoke, no fire, no smell of burning.

But his evening was spoiled. He sat smoking in his armchair at home, this business man of forty, practical in mind, of character some called stolid, cursing himself for an imaginative fool. It was

---

[2] From Pan's Garden, by Algernon Blackwood—Permission of the Macmillan Company.

now too late to go back to the theater; the club bored him; he spent an hour with the evening papers, dipping into books, sipping a long cool drink, doing odds and ends about the flat. "I'll go to bed early for a change," he laughed, but really all the time fighting—yes, deliberately fighting—this strange attack of uneasiness that so insidiously grew upwards, outwards from the buried depths of him that sought so strenuously to deny it. It never occurred to him that he was ill. He was not ill. His health was thunderingly good. He was as robust as a coal-heaver.

The flat was roomy, high up on the top floor, yet in a busy part of town, so that the roar of traffic mounted round it like a sea. Through the open windows came the fresh night air of June. He had never noticed before how sweet the London night air could be, and that not all the smoke and dust could smother a certain touch of wild fragrance that tinctured it with perfume—yes, almost perfume—as of the country. He swallowed a draught of it as he stood there, staring out across the tangled world of roofs and chimney-pots. He saw the procession of the clouds; he saw the stars; he saw the moonlight falling in a shower of silver spears upon the slates and wires and steeples. And something in him quickened—something that had never stirred before.

He turned with a horrid start, for the uneasiness had of a sudden leaped within him like an animal. There was some one in the flat.

Instantly, with action—even this slight action—the fancy vanished; but, all the same, he switched on the electric lights and made a search. For it seemed to him that some one had crept up close behind him while he stood there watching the night—some one, whose silent presence fingered with unerring touch both this new thing that had quickened in his heart and that sense of original deep uneasiness. He was amazed at himself—angry—indignant that he could be thus foolishly upset over nothing, yet at the same time profoundly distressed at this vehement growth of a new thing in his well-ordered personality. Growth? He dismissed the word the moment it occurred to him—but it had occurred to him. It stayed. While he searched the empty flat, the long passages, the gloomy bedroom at the end, the little hall where he kept his overcoats and golf sticks, it stayed. Growth! It was oddly disquieting. Growth to him involved, though he neither acknowledged nor recognized the truth perhaps, some kind of undesirable changeableness, instability, unbalance.

Yet singular as it all was, he realized that the uneasiness and the sudden appreciation of beauty that was so new to him had both entered by the same door into his being. When he came back to the front room he noticed that he was perspiring. There were little drops of moisture on his forehead. And down his spine ran chills, little, faint quivers of cold. He was shivering.

He lit his big meerschaum pipe, and left the lights all burning. The feeling that there was something he had overlooked, forgotten, left undone, had vanished. Whatever the original cause of this absurd uneasiness might be—he called it absurd on purpose because he now realized in the depths of him that it was really more vital than he cared about—it was much nearer to discovery than before. It dodged about just below the threshold of discovery. It was as close as that. Any moment he would know what it was; he would remember. Yes, he would remember. Meanwhile, he was in the right place. No desire to go elsewhere afflicted him, as in the theater. Here was the place, here in the flat.

And then it was with a kind of sudden burst and rush—it seemed to him the only way to phrase it—memory gave up her dead.

At first he only caught her peeping round the corner at him, drawing aside a corner of an enormous curtain, as it were; striving for more complete entrance as though the mass of it were difficult to move. But he understood, he knew, he recognized. It was enough for that. As an entrance into his being—heart, mind, soul—was being attempted and the entrance because of his stolid temperament was difficult of accomplishment, there was effort, strain. Something in him had first to be opened up, widened, made soft and ready as by an operation, before full entrance could be effected. This much he grasped though for the life of him he could not have put it into words. Also he knew who it was that sought an entrance. Deliberately from himself he withheld the name. But he knew as surely as though Straughan stood in the room and faced him with a knife saying, "Let me in, let me in. I wish you to know I'm here. I'm clearing a way! You recall our promise?"

He rose from his chair and went to the open window again, the strange fear slowly passing. The cool air fanned his cheeks. Beauty till now had scarcely ever brushed the surface of his soul. He had never troubled his head about it. It passed him by indifferent; and he had ever loathed the mouthy prating of it on others' lips. He was practical; beauty was for dreamers, for women, for men who had means and leisure. He had not exactly scorned it; rather it had never touched his life, to sweeten, to cheer, to uplift. Artists for him were like monks—another sex almost—useless beings who never helped the world go round. He was for action always, work, activity, achievement as he saw them. He remembered Straughan vaguely—Straughan, the ever impecunious friend of his youth, always talking of color and sound—mysterious, ineffectual things. He even forgot what they had quarreled about, if they had quarreled at all even; or why they had gone apart all these years ago. And certainly he had forgotten any promise. Memory as yet only peeped at him round the corner of that huge curtain tentatively, suggestively, yet—he was obliged to admit it—somewhat winningly. He was conscious of this gentle, sweet seductiveness that now replaced his fear.

And as he stood now at the open window peering over huge London, beauty came close and smote him between the eyes. She came blindingly, with her train of stars and clouds and perfumes. Night, mysterious, myriad-eyed, and flaming across her sea of haunted shadows invaded his heart and shook him with her immemorial wonder and delight. He found no words of course to clothe the new unwonted sensations. He only knew that all his former dread, uneasiness, distress, and with them this idea of growth that had seemed so repugnant to him were merged, swept up, and gathered magnificently home into a wave of beauty that enveloped him. "See it, and understand," ran a secret inner whisper across his mind. He saw. He understood....

He went back and turned the lights out. Then he took his place again at that open window, drinking in the night. He saw a new world; a species of intoxication held him. He sighed, as his thoughts blundered for expression among words and sentences that knew him not. But the delight was there, the wonder, the mystery. He watched with heart alternately tightening and expanding the transfiguring play of moon and shadow over the sea of buildings. He saw the dance of the hurrying clouds, the open patches into outer space, the veiling and unveiling of that ancient silvery face; and he caught strange whispers of the hierophantic, sacerdotal power that has echoed down the world since Time began and dropped strange magic phrases into every poet's heart, since first "God dawned on Chaos"—the Beauty of the Night.

A long time passed—it may have been one hour, it may have been three—when at length he turned away and went slowly to his bedroom. A deep peace lay over him. Something quite new and blessed had crept into his life and thought. He could not quite understand it all. He only knew that it uplifted. There was no longer the least sign of affliction or distress. Even the inevitable reaction that set in could not destroy that.

And then as he lay in bed nearing the borderland of sleep, suddenly and without any obvious suggestion to bring it, he remembered another thing. He remembered the promise. Memory got past the big curtain for an instant and showed her face. She looked into his eyes. It must have been a dozen years ago when

Straughan and he had made that foolish solemn promise, that whoever died first should show himself if possible to the other.

He had utterly forgotten it—till now. But Straughan had not forgotten it. The letter came three weeks later from India. That very evening Straughan had died—at nine o'clock. And he had come back—in the Beauty that he loved.

THE SECOND GENERATION[3]

By Algernon Blackwood

Sometimes, in a moment of sharp experience, comes that vivid flash of insight that makes a platitude suddenly seem a revelation—its full content is abruptly realized. "Ten years is a long time, yes," he thought, as he walked up the drive to the great Kensington house where she still lived.

Ten years—long enough, at any rate, for her to have married and for her husband to have died. More than that he had not heard, in the outlandish places where life had cast him in the interval. He wondered whether there had been any children. All manner of thoughts and questions, confused a little, passed across his mind. He was well-to-do now, though probably his entire capital did not amount to her income for a single year. He glanced at the huge, forbidding mansion. Yet that pride was false which had made of poverty an insuperable obstacle. He saw it now. He had learned values in his long exile.

But he was still ridiculously timid. This confusion of thought, of mental images rather, was due to a kind of fear, since worship ever is akin to awe. He was as nervous as a boy going up for a viva voce; and with the excitement was also that unconquerable sinking—that horrid shrinking sensation that excessive shyness brings. Why in the world had he come? Why had he telegraphed the very day after his arrival in England? Why had he not sent a tentative, tactful letter, feeling his way a little?

Very slowly he walked up the drive, feeling that if a reasonable chance of escape presented itself he would almost take it. But all the windows stared so hard at him that retreat was really impossible now and though no faces were visible behind the curtains, all had seen him, possibly she herself—his heart beat absurdly at the extravagant suggestion. Yet it was odd—he felt so certain of being seen, and that someone watched him. He reached the wide stone steps that were clean as marble, and shrank from the mark his boots must make upon their spotlessness. In desperation, then, before he could change his mind, he touched the bell. But he did not hear it ring—mercifully; that irrevocable sound must have paralyzed him altogether. If no one came to answer, he might still leave a card in the letter-box and slip away. Oh, how utterly he despised himself for

---

[3] From Ten-Minute Stories, published by E. P. Dutton & Co.

such a thought! A man of thirty with such a chicken heart was not fit to protect a child, much less a woman. And he recalled with a little stab of pain that the man she married had been noted for his courage, his determined action, his inflexible firmness in various public situations, head and shoulders above lesser men. What presumption on his own part ever to dream!... He remembered, too, with no apparent reason in particular, that this man had a grown-up son already, by a former marriage.

And still no one came to open that huge, contemptuous door with its so menacing, so hostile air. His back was to it, as he carelessly twirled his umbrella, but he felt its sneering expression behind him while it looked him up and down. It seemed to push him away. The entire mansion focused its message through that stern portal: Little timid men are not welcomed here.

How well he remembered the house! How often in years gone by had he not stood and waited just like this, trembling with delight and anticipation, yet terrified lest the bell should be answered and the great door actually swung wide! Then, as now, he would have run, had he dared. He was still afraid—his worship was so deep. But in all these years of exile in wild places, farming, mining, working for the position he had at last attained, her face and the memory of her gracious presence had been his comfort and support, his only consolation, though never his actual joy. There was so little foundation for it all, yet her smile and the words she had spoken to him from time to time in friendly conversation had clung, inspired, kept him going—for he knew them all by heart. And more than once in foolish optimistic moods, he had imagined, greatly daring, that she possibly had meant more....

He touched the bell a second time—with the point of his umbrella. He meant to go in, carelessly as it were, saying as lightly as might be, "Oh, I'm back in England again—if you haven't quite forgotten my existence—I could not forego the pleasure of saying 'How-do-you-do?' and hearing that you are well ...," and the rest; then presently bow himself easily out—into the old loneliness again. But he would at least have seen her; he would have heard her voice, and looked into her gentle, amber eyes; he would have touched her hand. She might even ask him to come in another day and see her! He had rehearsed it all a hundred times, as certain feeble temperaments do rehearse such scenes. And he came rather well out of that rehearsal, though always with an aching heart, the old great yearnings unfulfilled. All the way across the Atlantic he had thought about it, though with lessening confidence as the time drew near. The very night of his arrival in London he wrote, then, tearing up the letter (after sleeping over it), he had telegraphed next morning, asking if she would be in. He signed his surname—such a very common name, alas! but surely she would know—and her reply, "Please call 4:30," struck him as rather oddly worded. Yet here he was.

There was a rattle of the big door knob, that aggressive, hostile knob that thrust out at him insolently like a fist of bronze. He started, angry with himself for doing so. But the door did not open. He became suddenly conscious of the wilds he had lived in for so long; his clothes were hardly fashionable; his voice probably had a twang in it, and he used tricks of speech that must betray the rough life so recently left. What would she think of him, now? He looked much older, too. And how brusque it was to have telegraphed like that! He felt awkward, gauche, tongue-tied, hot and cold by turns. The sentences, so carefully rehearsed, fled beyond recovery.

Good heavens—the door was open! It had been open for some minutes. It moved noiselessly on big hinges. He acted automatically; he heard himself asking if her ladyship was at home, though his voice was nearly inaudible. The next moment he was standing in the great, dim hall, so poignantly familiar, and the remembered perfume almost made him sway. He did not hear the door close, but he knew. He was caught. The butler betrayed an instant's surprise—or was it over-wrought imagination again?—when he gave his name. It seemed to him—though only later did he grasp the significance of that curious intuition—that the man had expected another caller instead. The man took his card respectfully and disappeared. These flunkeys were so marvellously trained. He was too long accustomed to straight question and straight answer, but here, in the Old Country, privacy was jealously guarded with such careful ritual.

And almost immediately the butler returned, still expressionless, and showed him into the large drawing-room on the ground floor that he knew so well. Tea was on the table—tea for one. He felt puzzled. "If you will have tea first, sir, her ladyship will see you afterwards," was what he heard. And though his breath came thickly, he asked the question that forced itself out. Before he knew what he was saying he asked it, "Is she ill?" "Oh, no, her ladyship is quite well, thank you, sir. If you will have tea first, sir, her ladyship will see you afterwards." The horrid formula was repeated, word for word. He sank into an armchair and mechanically poured out his own tea. What he felt he did not exactly know. It seemed so unusual, so utterly unexpected, so unnecessary, too. Was it a special attention, or was it merely casual? That it could mean anything else did not occur to him. How was she busy, occupied—not here to give him tea? He could not understand it. It seemed such a farce having tea alone like this—it was like waiting for an audience, it was like a doctor's or a dentist's room. He felt bewildered, ill at ease, cheap.... But after ten years in primitive lands perhaps London usages had changed in some extraordinary manner. He recalled his first amazement at the motor-omnibuses, taxicabs, and electric tubes. All were new. London was otherwise than when he left it. Piccadilly and the Marble Arch themselves had altered. And, with his reflection, a shade more confidence stole in. She knew that he was there and presently she would come in and speak with him, explaining everything by the mere fact of her delicious presence. He was ready for the ordeal, he would see her—and drop out again. It was worth all manner of pain, even of mortification. He was in her house, drinking her tea, sitting in a chair she used herself perhaps. Only he would never dare to say a word or make a sign that might betray his changeless secret. He still felt the boyish worshipper, worshipping in dumbness from a distance, one of a group of many others like himself. Their dreams had faded, his had continued, that was the difference. Memories tore and raced and poured upon him. How sweet and gentle she had always been to him! He used to wonder sometimes.... Once, he remembered, he had rehearsed a declaration, but while rehearsing the big man had come in and captured her, though he had only read the definite news long after by chance in an Arizona paper.

He gulped his tea down. His heart alternately leaped and stood still. A sort of numbness held him most of that dreadful interval, and no clear thought came at all. Every ten seconds his head turned towards the door that rattled, seemed to move, yet never opened. But any moment now it must open, and he would be in her very presence, breathing the same air with her. He would see her, charge himself with her beauty once more to the brim, and then go out again into the wilderness—the wilderness of life—without her, and not for a mere ten years but for always. She was so utterly beyond his reach. He felt like a backwoodsman, he was a backwoodsman.

For one thing only was he duly prepared, though he thought about it little enough—she would, of course, have changed. The photograph he owned, cut from an illustrated paper, was not true now. It might even be a little shock perhaps. He must remember that. Ten years cannot pass over a woman without—

Before he knew it the door was open, and she was advancing quietly towards him across the thick carpet that deadened sound. With both hands outstretched she came, and with the sweetest welcoming smile upon her parted lips he had seen in any human face. Her eyes were soft with joy. His whole heart leaped within him; for the instant he saw her it all flashed clear as sunlight—that she knew and understood. She had always known, had always understood. Speech came easily to him in a flood, had he needed it, but he did not need it. It was all so adorably easy, simple, natural, and true. He just took her hands—those welcoming, outstretched hands—in both of his own, and led her to the nearest sofa. He was not even surprised at himself. Inevitably, out of depths of truth, this meeting came about. And he uttered a little foolish commonplace, because he feared the huge revulsion that his sudden glory brought, and loved to taste it slowly:

"So you live here still?"

"Here, and here," she answered softly, touching his heart, and then her own. "I am attached to this house, too, because you used to come and see me here, and because it was here I waited so long for you, and still wait. I shall never leave it—unless you change. You see, we live together here."

He said nothing. He leaned forward to take and hold her. The abrupt knowledge of it all somehow did not seem abrupt—it was as though he had known it always; and the complete disclosure did not seem disclosure either—rather as though she told him something he had inexplicably left unrealized, yet not forgotten. He felt absolutely master of himself, yet, in a curious sense, outside of himself at the same time. His arms were already open—when she gently held her hands up to prevent. He heard a faint sound outside the door.

"But you are free," he cried, his great passion breaking out and flooding him, yet most oddly well controlled, "and I—"

She interrupted him in the softest, quietest whisper he had ever heard:

"You are not free, as I am free—not yet."

The sound outside came suddenly closer. It was a step. There was a faint click on the handle of the door. In a flash, then, came the dreadful shock that overwhelmed him—the abrupt realization of the truth that was somehow horrible—that Time, all these years, had left no mark upon her and that she had not changed. Her face was as young as when he saw her last.

With it there came cold and darkness into the great room. He shivered with cold, but an alien, unaccountable cold. Some great shadow dropped upon the entire earth, and though but a second could have passed before the handle actually turned, and the other person entered, it seemed to him like several minutes. He heard her saying this amazing thing that was question, answer, and forgiveness all in one—this, at least, he divined before the ghastly interruption came—"But, George—if you had only spoken—!"

With ice in his blood he heard the butler saying that her ladyship would be "pleased" to see him if he had finished his tea and would be "so good as to bring the papers and documents upstairs with him." He had just sufficient control of certain muscles to stand upright and murmur that he would come. He rose from a sofa that held no one but himself. All at once he staggered. He really did not know exactly what happened, or how he managed to stammer out the medley of excuses and semi-explanations that battered their way through his brain and issued somehow in definite words from his lips. Somehow or other he accomplished it. The sudden attack, the faintness, the collapse!... He vaguely remembered afterwards—with amazement too—the suavity of the butler as he suggested telephoning for a doctor, and that he just managed to forbid it, refusing the offered glass of brandy as well, remembered contriving to stumble into the taxicab and give his hotel address with a final explanation that he would call another day and "bring the papers." It was quite clear that his telegram had been attributed to someone else, someone "with papers"—perhaps a solicitor or architect. His name was such an ordinary one, there were so many Smiths. It was also clear that she whom he had come to see and had seen, no longer lived here in the flesh....

And just as he left the hall he had the vision—mere fleeting glimpse it was—of a tall, slim, girlish figure on the stairs asking if anything was wrong, and realized vaguely through his atrocious pain that she was, of course, the wife of the son who had inherited....

JOSEPH: A STORY

By Katherine Rickford

They were sitting round the fire after dinner—not an ordinary fire—one of those fires that has a little room all to itself with seats at each side of it to hold a couple of people or three.

The big dining room was paneled with oak. At the far end was a handsome dresser that dated back for generations. One's imagination ran riot when one pictured the people who must have laid those pewter plates on the long, narrow, solid table. Massive medieval chests stood against the walls. Arms and parts of armor hung against the panelling; but one noticed few of these things, for there was no light in the room save what the fire gave.

It was Christmas Eve. Games had been played. The old had vied with the young at snatching raisins from the burning snapdragon. The children had long since gone to bed; it was time their elders followed them, but they lingered round the fire, taking turns at telling stories. Nothing very weird had been told; no one had felt any wish to peep over his shoulder or try to penetrate the darkness of the far end of the room; the omission caused a sensation of something wanting. From each one there this thought went out, and so a sudden silence fell upon the party. It was a girl who broke it—a mere child; she wore her hair up that night for the first time, and that seemed to give her the right to sit up so late.

"Mr. Grady is going to tell one," she said.

All eyes were turned to a middle-aged man in a deep armchair placed straight in front of the fire. He was short, inclined to be fat, with a bald head and a pointed beard like the beards that sailors wear. It was plain that he was deeply conscious of the sudden turning of so much strained yet forceful thought upon himself. He was restless in his chair as people are in a room that is overheated. He blinked his eyes as he looked round the company. His lips twitched in a nervous manner. One side of him seemed to be endeavoring to restrain another side of him from a feverish desire to speak.

"It was this room that made me think of him," he said thoughtfully.

There was a long silence, but it occurred to no one to prompt him. Every one seemed to understand that he was going to speak, or rather that something inside him was going to speak, some force that craved expression and was using him as a medium.

The little old man's pink face grew strangely calm, the animation that usually lit it was gone. One would have said that the girl who had started him already regretted the impulse, and now wanted to stop him. She was breathing heavily, and once or twice made as though she would speak to him, but no words came. She must have abandoned the idea, for she fell to studying the company. She examined them carefully, one by one. "This one," she told herself, "is so-and-so, and that one there just another so-and-so." She stared at them, knowing that she could not turn them to herself with her stare. They were just bodies kept working, so to speak, by some subtle sort of sentry left behind by the real selves that streamed out in pent-up thought to the little old man in the chair in front of the fire.

"His name was Joseph; at least they called him Joseph. He dreamed, you understand—dreams. He was an extraordinary lad in many ways. His mother—I knew her very well—had three children in quick succession, soon after marriage; then ten years went by and Joseph was born. Quiet and reserved he always was, a self-contained child whose only friend was his mother. People said things about him, you know how people talk. Some said he was not Clara's child at all, but that she had adopted him; others, that her husband was not his father, and these put her change of manner down to a perpetual struggle to keep her husband comfortably in the dark. I always imagined that the boy was in some way aware of all this gossip, for I noticed that he took a dislike to the people who spread it most."

The little man rested his elbows on the arms of his chair and let the tips of his fingers meet in front of him. A smile played about his mouth. He seemed to be searching among his reminiscences for the one that would give the clearest portrait of Joseph.

"Well, anyway," he said at last, "the boy was odd, there is no gainsaying the fact. I suppose he was eleven when Clara came down here with her family for Christmas. The Coningtons owned the place then—Mrs. Conington was Clara's sister. It was Christmas Eve, as it is now, many years ago. We had spent a normal Christmas Eve; a little happier, perhaps, than usual by reason of the family re-union and because of the presence of so many children. We had eaten and drank, laughed and played and gone to bed.

"I woke in the middle of the night from sheer restlessness. Clara, knowing my weakness, had given me a fire in my room. I lit a cigarette, played with a book, and then, purely from curiosity, opened the door and looked down the passage. From my door I could see the head of the staircase in the distance; the opposite wing of the house, or the passage rather beyond the stairs, was in darkness. The reason I saw the staircase at all was that the window you pass coming downstairs allowed the moon to throw an uncertain light upon it, a weird light because of the stained glass. I was arrested by the curious effect of this patch of light in so much darkness when suddenly someone came into it, turned, and went downstairs. It was just like a scene in a theater; something was about to happen that I was going to miss. I ran as I was, barefooted, to the head of the stairs and looked over the banister. I was excited, strung up, too strung up to feel the fright that I knew must be with me. I remember the sensation perfectly. I knew that I was afraid, yet I did not feel fright.

"On the stairs nothing moved. The little hall down here was lost in darkness. Looking over the banister I was facing the stained glass window. You know how the stairs run around three sides of the hall; well, it occurred to me that if I went halfway down and stood under the window I should be able to keep the top of the stairs in sight and see anything that might happen in the hall. I crept down very cautiously and waited under the window. First of all, I saw the suit of empty armor just outside the door here. You know how a thing like that, if you stare at it in a poor light, appears to move; well, it moved sure enough, and the illusion was enhanced by clouds being blown across the moon. By the fire like this one can talk of these things rationally, but in the dead of night it is a different matter, so I went down a few steps to make sure of that armor, when suddenly something passed me on the stairs. I did not hear it, I did not see it, I sensed it in no way, I just knew that something had passed me on its way upstairs. I realized that my retreat was cut off, and with the knowledge fear came upon me.

"I had seen someone come down the stairs; that, at any rate, was definite; now I wanted to see him again. Any ghost is bad enough, but a ghost that one can see is better than one that one can't. I managed to get past the suit of armor, but then I had to feel my way to these double doors here."

He indicated the direction of the doors by a curious wave of his hand. He did not look toward them nor did any of the party. Both men and women were completely absorbed in his story; they seemed to be mesmerized by the earnestness of his manner. Only the girl was restless; she gave an impression of impatience with the slowness with which he came to his point. One would have said that she was apart from her fellows, an alien among strangers.

"So dense was the darkness that I made sure of finding the first door closed, but it was not, it was wide open, and, standing between them, I could feel that the other was open, too. I was standing literally in the wall of the house, and as I peered into the room, trying to make out some familiar object, thoughts ran through my mind of people who had been bricked up in walls and left there to die. For a moment I caught the spirit of the inside of a thick wall. Then suddenly I felt the sensation I have often read about but never experienced before: I knew there was some one in the room. You are surprised, yes, but wait! I knew more: I knew that some one was conscious of my presence. It occurred to me that whoever it was might want to get out of the door. I made room for him to pass. I waited for him, made sure of him, began to feel giddy, and then a man's voice, deep and clear:

"'There is some one there; who is it?'

"I answered mechanically, 'George Grady.'

"'I'm Joseph.'

"A match was drawn across a matchbox, and I saw the boy bending over a candle waiting for the wick to catch. For a moment I thought he must be walking in his sleep, but he turned to me quite naturally and said in his own boyish voice:

"'Lost anything?'

"I was amazed at the lad's complete calm. I wanted to share my fright with some one, instead I had to hide it from this boy. I was conscious of a curious sense of shame. I had watched him grow, taught him, praised him, scolded him, and yet here he was waiting for an explanation of my presence in the dining room at that odd hour of the night.

"Soon he repeated the question, 'Lost anything?'

"'No,' I said, and then I stammered, 'Have you?'

"'No,' he said with a little laugh. 'It's that room, I can't sleep in it.'

"'Oh,' I said. 'What's the matter with the room?'

"'It's the room I was killed in,' he said quite simply.

"Of course I had heard about his dreams, but I had had no direct experience of them; when, therefore, he said that he had been killed in his room I took it for granted that he had been dreaming again. I was at a loss to know quite how to tackle him; whether to treat the whole thing as absurd and laugh it off as such, or whether to humor him and hear his story. I got him upstairs to my room, sat him in a big armchair, and poked the fire into a blaze.

"'You've been dreaming again,' I said bluntly.

"'Oh, no I haven't. Don't you run away with that idea.'

"His whole manner was so grown up that it was quite unthinkable to treat him as the child he really was. In fact, it was a little uncanny, this man in a child's frame.

"'I was killed there,' he said again.

"'How do you mean, killed?' I asked him.

"'Why, killed—murdered. Of course it was years and years ago, I can't say when; still I remember the room. I suppose it was the room that reminded me of the incident.'

"'Incident?' I exclaimed.

"'What else? Being killed is only an incident in the existence of any one. One makes a fuss about it at the time, of course, but really when you come to think of it....'

"'Tell me about it,' I said, lighting a cigarette. He lit one too, that child, and began.

"'You know my room is the only modern one in this old house. Nobody knows why it is modern. The reason is obvious. Of course it was made modern after I was killed there. The funny thing is that I should have been put there. I suppose it was done for a purpose, because I—I——'

"He looked at me so fixedly I knew he would catch me if I lied.

"'What?' I asked.

"'Dream.'

"'Yes,' I said, 'that is why you were put there.'

"'I thought so, and yet of all the rooms—but then, of course, no one knew. Anyhow I did not recognize the room until after I was in bed. I had been asleep some time and then I woke suddenly. There is an old wheel-back chair there—the only old thing in the room. It is standing facing the fire as it must have stood the night I was killed. The fire was burning brightly, the pattern of the back of the chair was thrown in shadow across the ceiling. Now the night I was murdered the conditions were exactly the same, so directly I saw that pattern on the ceiling I remembered the whole thing. I was not dreaming, don't think it, I was not. What happened that night was this: I was lying in bed counting the parts of the back of that chair in shadow on the ceiling. I probably could not get to sleep, you know the sort of thing, count up to a thousand and remember in the morning where you got to. Well, I was counting those pieces when suddenly they were all obliterated, the whole back became a shadow, some one was sitting in the chair. Now, surely, you understand that directly I saw the shadow of that chair on the ceiling to-night I realized that I had not a moment to lose. At any moment that same person might come back to that same chair and escape would be impossible. I slipped from my bed as quickly as I could and ran downstairs.'

"'But were you not afraid,' I asked, 'downstairs?'

"'That she might follow me? It was a woman, you know. No, I don't think I was. She does not belong downstairs. Anyhow she didn't.'

"'No,' I said. 'No.'

"My voice must have been out of control, for he caught me up at once.

"'You don't mean to say you saw her?' he said vehemently.

"'Oh, no.'

"'You felt her?'

"'She passed me as I came downstairs,' I said.

"'What can I have done to her that she follows me so?' He buried his face in his hands as though searching for an answer to his thought. Suddenly he looked up and stared at me.

"'Where had I got to? Oh yes, the murder. I can remember how startled I was to see that shadow in the chair—startled, you know, but not really frightened. I leaned up in bed and looked at the chair, and sure enough a woman was sitting in it—a young woman. I watched her with a profound interest until she began to turn in her chair, as I felt, to look at me; when she did that I shrank back in bed. I dared not meet her eyes. She might not have had eyes, she might not have had a face. You know the sort of pictures that one sees when one glances back at all one's soul has ever thought.

"'I got back in the bed as far as I could and peeped over the sheets at the shadow on the ceiling. I was tired; frightened to death; I grew weary of watching. I must have fallen asleep, for suddenly the fire was almost out, the pattern of the chair barely discernible, the shadow had gone. I raised myself with a sense of huge relief. Yes, the chair was empty, but, just think of it, the woman was on the floor, on her hands and knees, crawling toward the bed.

"'I fell back stricken with terror.

"'Very soon I felt a gentle pull at the counterpane. I thought I was in a nightmare but too lazy or too comfortable to try to wake myself from it. I waited in an agony of suspense, but nothing seemed to be happening, in fact I had just persuaded myself that the movement of the counterpane was fancy when a hand brushed softly over my knee. There was no mistaking it, I could feel the long, thin fingers. Now was the time to do something. I tried to rouse myself, but all my efforts were futile, I was stiff from head to foot.

"'Although the hand was lost to me, outwardly, it now came within my range of knowledge, if you know what I mean. I knew that it was groping its way along the bed feeling for some other part of me. At any moment I could have said exactly where it had got to. When it was hovering just over my chest another hand knocked lightly against my shoulder. I fancied it lost, and wandering in search of its fellow.

"'I was lying on my back staring at the ceiling when the hands met; the weight of their presence brought a feeling of oppression to my chest. I seemed to be completely cut off from my body; I had no sort of connection with any part of it, nothing about me would respond to my will to make it move.

"'There was no sound at all anywhere.

"'I fell into a state of indifference, a sort of patient indifference that can wait for an appointed time to come. How long I waited I cannot say, but when the time came it found me ready. I was not taken by surprise.

"'There was a great upward rush of pent-up force released; it was like a mighty mass of men who have been lost in prayer rising to their feet. I can't remember clearly, but I think the woman must have got on to my bed. I could not follow her distinctly, my whole attention was concentrated on her hands. At the time I felt those fingers itching for my throat.

"'At last they moved; slowly at first, then quicker; and then a long-drawn swish like the sound of an over-bold wave that has broken too far up the beach and is sweeping back to join the sea.'

"The boy was silent for a moment, then he stretched out his hand for the cigarettes.

"'You remember nothing else?' I asked him.

"'No,' he said. 'The next thing I remember clearly is deliberately breaking the nursery window because it was raining and mother would not let me go out.'"

There was a moment's tension, then the strain of listening passed and every one seemed to be speaking at once. The Rector was taking the story seriously.

"Tell me, Grady," he said. "How long do you suppose elapsed between the boy's murder and his breaking the nursery window?"

But a young married woman in the first flush of her happiness broke in between them. She ridiculed the whole idea. Of course the boy was dreaming. She was drawing the majority to her way of thinking when, from the corner where the girl sat, a hollow-sounding voice:

"And the boy? Where is he?"

The tone of the girl's voice inspired horror, that fear that does not know what it is it fears; one could see it on every face; on every face, that is, but the face of the bald-headed little man; there was no horror on his face; he was smiling serenely as he looked the girl straight in the eyes.

"He's a man now," he said.

"Alive?" she cried.

"Why not?" said the little old man, rubbing his hands together.

She tried to rise, but her frock had got caught between the chairs and pulled her to her seat again. The man next her put out his hand to steady her, but she dashed it away roughly. She looked round the party for an instant for all the world like an animal at bay, then she sprang to her feet and charged blindly. They crowded round her to prevent her falling; at the touch of their hands she stopped. She was out of breath as though she had been running.

"All right," she said, pushing their hands from her. "All right. I'll come quietly. I did it."

They caught her as she fell and laid her on the sofa watching the color fade from her face.

The hostess, an old woman with white hair and a kind face, approached the little old man; for once in her life she was roused to anger.

"I can't think how you could be so stupid," she said. "See what you have done."

"I did it for a purpose," he said.

"For a purpose?"

"I have always thought that girl was the culprit. I have to thank you for the opportunity you have given me of making sure."

THE CLAVECIN, BRUGES[4]

By George Wharton Edwards

A silent, grass-grown market-place, upon the uneven stones of which the sabots of a passing peasant clatter loudly. A group of sleepy-looking soldiers in red trousers lolling about the wide portal of the Belfry, which rears aloft against the pearly sky

All the height it has
Of ancient stone.

As the chime ceases there lingers for a space a faint musical hum in the air; the stones seem to carry and retain the melody; one is loath to move for fear of losing some part of the harmony.

I feel an indescribable impulse to climb the four hundred odd steps; incomprehensible, for I detest steeple-climbing, and have no patience with steeple-climbers.

Before I realize it, I am at the stairs. "Hold, sir!" from behind me. "It is forbidden." In wretched French a weazen-faced little soldier explains that repairs are about to be made in the tower, in consequence of which visitors are forbidden. A franc removes this military obstacle, and I press on.

At the top of the stairs is an old Flemish woman shelling peas, while over her shoulder peeps a tame magpie. A savory odor of stewing vegetables fills the air.

"What do you wish, sir?" Many shrugs, gesticulations, and sighs of objurgation, which are covered by a shining new five-franc piece, and she produces a bunch of keys. As the door closes upon me the magpie gives a hoarse, gleeful squawk.

... A huge, dim room with a vaulted ceiling. Against the wall lean ancient stone statues, noseless and disfigured, crowned and sceptered effigies of forgotten lords and ladies of Flanders. High up on the wall two slitted Gothic windows, through which the violet light of day is streaming. I hear the gentle coo of pigeons. To the right a low door, some vanishing steps of stone, and a hanging hand-rope. Before I have taken a dozen steps upward I am lost in the darkness; the steps are worn hollow and sloping, the rope is slippery—seems to have been waxed, so smooth has it become by handling. Four hundred steps and over; I have lost track of the

---

4 By permission of The Century Co.

number, and stumble giddily upward round and round the slender stone shaft. I am conscious of low openings from time to time—openings to what? I do not know. A damp smell exhales from them, and the air is cold upon my face as I pass them. At last a dim light above. With the next turn a blinding glare of light, a moment's blankness, then a vast panorama gradually dawns upon me. Through the frame of stonework is a vast reach of grayish green bounded by the horizon, an immense shield embossed with silvery lines of waterways, and studded with clustering red-tiled roofs. A rim of pale yellow appears—the sand-dunes that line the coast—and dimly beyond a grayish film, evanescent, flashing—the North Sea.

Something flies through the slit from which I am gazing, and following its flight upward, I see a long beam crossing the gallery, whereon are perched an array of jackdaws gazing down upon me in wonder.

I am conscious of a rhythmic movement about me that stirs the air, a mysterious, beating, throbbing sound, the machinery of the clock, which some one has described as a "heart of iron beating in a breast of stone."

I lean idly in the narrow slit, gazing at the softened landscape, the exquisite harmony of the greens, grays, and browns, the lazily turning arms of far-off mills, reminders of Cuyp, Van der Velde, Teniers, shadowy, mysterious recollections. I am conscious of uttering aloud some commonplaces of delight. A slight and sudden movement behind me, a smothered cough. A little old man in a black velvet coat stands looking up at me, twisting and untwisting his hands. There are ruffles at his throat and wrists, and an amused smile spreads over his face, which is cleanly shaven, of the color of wax, with a tiny network of red lines over the cheek-bones, as if the blood had been forced there by some excess of passion and had remained. He has heard my sentimental ejaculation. I am conscious of the absurdity of the situation, and move aside for him to pass. He makes a courteous gesture with one ruffled hand.

There comes a prodigious rattling and grinding noise from above—then a jangle of bells, some half-dozen notes in all. At the first stroke the old man closes his eyes, throws back his head, and follows the rhythm with his long white hands, as though playing a piano. The sound dies away; the place becomes painfully silent; still the regular motion of the old man's hands continues. A creepy, shivery feeling runs up and down my spine; a fear of which I am ashamed seizes upon me.

"Fine pells, sare," says the little old man, suddenly dropping his hands, and fixing his eyes upon me. "You sall not hear such pells in your countree. But stay not here; come wis me, and I will show you the clavecin. You sall not see the clavecin yet? No?"

I had not, of course, and thanked him.

"You sall see Melchior, Melchior t'e Groote, t'e magnif'."

As he spoke we entered a room quite filled with curious machinery, a medley of levers, wires, and rope above; below, two large cylinders studded with shining brass points.

He sprang among the wires with a spidery sort of agility, caught one, pulled and hung upon it with, all his weight. There came a r-r-r-r-r-r of fans and wheels, followed by a shower of dust; slowly one great cylinder began to revolve; wires and ropes reaching into the gloom above began to twitch convulsively; faintly came the jangle of far-off bells. Then came a pause, then a deafening boom, that well nigh stunned me. As the waves of sound came and went, the little old man twisted and untwisted his hands in delight, and ejaculated, "Melchior you haf heeard, Melchior t'e Groote—t'e bourdon."

I wanted to examine the machinery, but he impatiently seized my arm and almost dragged me away saying, "I will skow you—I will skow you. Come wis me."

From a pocket he produced a long brass key and unlocked a door covered with red leather, disclosing an up-leading flight of steps to which he pushed me. It gave upon an octagon-shaped room with a curious floor of sheet-lead. Around the wall ran a seat under the diamond-paned Gothic windows. From their shape I knew them to be the highest in the tower. I had seen them from the square below many times, with the framework above upon which hung row upon row of bells.

In the middle of the room was a rude sort of keyboard, with pedals below, like those of a large organ. Fronting this construction sat a long, high-backed bench. On the rack over the keyboard rested some sheets of music, which, upon examination, I found to be of parchment and written by hand. The notes were curious in shape, consisting of squares of black and diamonds of red upon the lines. Across the top of the page was written, in a straggling hand, "Van den Gheyn Nikolaas." I turned to the little old man with the ruffles. "Van den Gheyn!" I said in surprise, pointing to the parchment. "Why, that is the name of the most celebrated of carillonneurs, Van den Gheyn of Louvain." He untwisted his hands and bowed. "Eet ees ma name, mynheer—I am the carillonneur."

I fancied that my face showed all too plainly the incredulity I felt, for his darkened, and he muttered, "You not belief, Engelsch? Ah, I show you; then you belief, parehap," and with astounding agility seated himself upon the bench before the clavecin, turned up the ruffles at his wrists, and literally threw himself upon the keys. A sound of thunder accompanied by a vivid flash of lightning filled the air, even as the first notes of the bells reached my ears. Involuntarily I glanced out of the diamond-leaded window—dark clouds were all about us, the housetops and surrounding country were no longer to be seen. A blinding flash of lightning seemed to fill the room; the arms and legs of the little old man sought the keys and pedals with inconceivable rapidity; the music crashed about us with a deafening din, to the accompaniment of the thunder, which seemed to sound in unison with the boom of the bourdon. It was grandly terrible. The face of the little old man was turned upon me, but his eyes were closed. He seemed to find the pedals intuitively, and at every peal of thunder, which shook the tower to its foundations, he would open his mouth, a toothless cavern, and shout aloud. I could not hear the sounds for the crashing of the bells. Finally, with a last deafening crash of iron rods and thunderbolts, the noise of the bells gradually died away. Instinctively I had glanced above when the crash came, half expecting to see the roof torn off.

"I think we had better go down," I said. "This tower has been struck by lightning several times, and I imagine that discretion—"

I don't know what more I said, for my eyes rested upon the empty bench, and the bare rack where the music had been. The clavecin was one mass of twisted iron rods, tangled wires, and decayed, worm-eaten woodwork; the little old man had disappeared. I rushed to the red leather-covered door; it was fast. I shook it in a veritable terror; it would not yield. With a bound I reached the ruined clavecin, seized one of the pedals, and tore it away from the machine. The end was armed with an iron point. This I inserted between the lock and the door. I twisted the lock from the worm-eaten wood with one turn of the wrist, the door opened, and I almost fell down the steep steps. The second door at the bottom was also closed. I threw my weight against it once, twice; it gave, and I half slipped, half ran down the winding steps in the darkness.

Out at last into the fresh air of the lower passage! At the noise I made in closing the ponderous door came forth the old custode.

In my excitement I seized her by the arm, saying, "Who was the little old man in the black velvet coat with the ruffles? Where is he?"

She looked at me in a stupid manner. "Who is he," I repeated—"the little old man who played the clavecin?"

"Little old man, sir? I don't know," said the crone. "There has been no one in the tower to-day but yourself."

LIGEIA

By Edgar Allan Poe

"And the will therein lieth, which dieth not. Who knoweth the mysteries of the will, with its vigor? For God is but a great will prevading all things by nature of its intentness. Man doth not yield himself to the angels, nor unto death utterly, save only through the weakness of his feeble will."—

Joseph Glanvill

I cannot, for my soul, remember how, when, or even precisely where, I first became acquainted with the lady Ligeia. Long years have since elapsed, and my memory is feeble through much suffering. Or, perhaps, I cannot now bring these points to mind, because, in truth, the character of my beloved, her rare learning, her singular yet placid caste of beauty, and the thrilling and enthralling eloquence of her low musical language, made their way into my heart by paces so steadily and stealthily progressive, that they have been unnoticed and unknown. Yet I believe that I met her first and most frequently in some large, old, decaying city near the Rhine. Of her family I have surely heard her speak. That it is of a remotely ancient date cannot be doubted. Ligeia! Ligeia! Buried in studies of a nature more than all else adapted to deaden impressions of the outward world, it is by that sweet word alone—by Ligeia—that I bring before mine eyes in fancy the image of her who is no more. And now, while I write, a recollection flashes upon me that I have never known the paternal name of her who was my friend and my betrothed, and who became the partner of my studies, and finally the wife of my bosom. Was it a playful charge on the part of my Ligeia? Or was it a test of my strength of affection, that I should institute no inquiries upon this point? Or was it rather a caprice of my own—a wildly romantic offering on the shrine of the most passionate devotion? I but indistinctly recall the fact itself—what wonder that I have utterly forgotten the circumstances which originated or attended it? And, indeed, if ever that spirit which is entitled Romance—if ever she, the wan and the misty-winged Ashtophet of idolatrous Egypt—presided, as they tell, over marriages ill-omened, then most surely she presided over mine.

There is one dear topic, however, on which my memory fails

me not. It is the person of Ligeia. In stature she was tall, somewhat slender, and, in her latter days, even emaciated. I would in vain attempt to portray the majesty, the quiet ease of her demeanor, or the incomprehensible lightness and elasticity of her footfall. She came and departed as a shadow. I was never made aware of her entrance into my closed study, save by the dear music of her low sweet voice, as she placed her marble hand upon my shoulder. In beauty of face no maiden ever equalled her. It was the radiance of an opium-dream—an airy and spirit-lifting vision more wildly divine than the fantasies which hovered about the slumbering souls of the daughters of Delos. Yet her features were not of that regular mould which we have been falsely taught to worship in the classical labors of the heathen. "There is no exquisite beauty," says Bacon, Lord Verulam, speaking truly of all the forms and genera of beauty, "without some strangeness in the proportion." Yet, although I saw that the features of Ligeia were not of a classic regularity—although I perceived that her loveliness was indeed exquisite and felt that there was much of strangeness pervading it—yet I have tried in vain to detect the irregularity and to trace home my own perception of "the strange." I examined the contour of the lofty and pale forehead; it was faultless—how cold indeed that word when applied to a majesty so divine—the skin rivalling the purest ivory; the commanding extent and repose, the gentle prominence of the regions above the temples; and then the raven-black, the glossy, the luxuriant and naturally-curling tresses, setting forth the full force of the Homeric epithet, "hyacinthine"! I looked at the delicate outlines of the nose, and nowhere but in the graceful medallions of the Hebrews had I beheld a similar perfection. There were the same luxurious smoothness of surface, the same scarcely perceptible tendency to the aquiline, the same harmoniously curved nostrils speaking the free spirit. I regarded the sweet mouth. Here was indeed the triumph of all things heavenly—the magnificent turn of the short upper lip, the soft, voluptuous slumber of the under, the dimples which sported, and the color which spoke, the teeth glancing back, with a brilliancy almost startling, every ray of the holy light which fell upon them in her serene and placid, yet most exultingly radiant of all smiles. I scrutinized the formation of the chin, and here, too, I found the gentleness of breadth, the softness and the majesty, the fulness and the spirituality of the Greek—the contour which the god Apollo revealed but in a dream, to Cleomenes, the son of the Athenian. And then I peered into the large eyes of Ligeia.

For eyes we have no models in the remotely antique. It might have been, too, that in these eyes of my beloved lay the secret to which Lord Verulam alludes. They were, I must believe, far larger than the ordinary eyes of our own race. They were even fuller than the fullest of the gazelle eyes of the tribe of the valley of Nourjahad. Yet it was only at intervals—in moments of intense excitement—that this peculiarity became more than slightly noticeable in Ligeia. And at such moments was her beauty—in my heated fancy thus it appeared perhaps—the beauty of beings either above or apart from the earth—the beauty of the fabulous Houri of the Turk. The hue of the orbs was the most brilliant of black, and far over them hung jetty lashes of great length. The brows, slightly irregular in outline, had the same tint. The "strangeness," however, which I found in the eyes, was of a nature distinct from the formation, or the color, or the brilliancy of the features, and must, after all, be referred to the expression. Ah, word of no meaning, behind whose vast latitude of mere sound we intrench our ignorance of so much of the spiritual! The expression of the eyes of Ligeia! How for long hours have I pondered upon it! How have I, through the whole of a midsummer night, struggled to fathom it! What was it—that something more profound than the well of Democritus—which lay far within the pupils of my beloved? What was it? I was possessed with a passion to discover. Those eyes, those large, those shining, those divine orbs—they became to me twin stars of Leda, and I to them devoutest of astrologers.

There is no point, among the many incomprehensible anomalies of the science of mind, more thrillingly exciting than the fact—never, I believe, noticed in the schools—that in our endeavors to recall to memory something long forgotten, we often find ourselves upon the very verge of remembrance, without being able, in the end, to remember. And thus how frequently, in my intense scrutiny of Ligeia's eyes, have I felt approaching the full knowledge of their expression—felt it approaching, yet not quite be mine—and so at length entirely depart! And (strange, oh strangest mystery of all!) I found in the commonest objects of the universe, a circle of analogies to that expression. I mean to say that, subsequently to the period when Ligeia's beauty passed into my spirit, there dwelling as in a shrine, I derived from many existences in the material world a sentiment such as I felt always around, within me, by her large and luminous orbs. Yet not the more could I define that sentiment, or analyze, or even steadily view it. I recognized it, let me repeat, sometimes in the survey of a rapidly-growing vine, in the contemplation of a moth, a butterfly, a chrysalis, a stream of running water. I have felt it in the ocean, in the falling of a meteor. I have felt it in the glances of unusually aged people. And there are one or two stars in heaven, (one especially, a star of the sixth magnitude, double and changeable, to be found near the large star in Lyra) in a telescopic scrutiny of which I have been made aware of the feeling. I have been filled with it by certain sounds from stringed instruments, and not unfrequently by passages from books. Among innumerable other instances, I well remember something in a volume of Joseph Glanvill, which (perhaps merely from its quaintness—who shall say?) never failed to inspire me with the sentiment: "And the will therein lieth, which dieth not. Who knoweth the mysteries of the will, with its vigor? For God is but a great will pervading all things by nature of its intentness. Man doth not yield him to the angels, nor unto death utterly, save only through the weakness of his feeble will."

Length of years and subsequent reflection have enabled me to trace, indeed, some remote connection between this passage in the English moralist and a portion of the character of Ligeia. An intensity in thought, action, or speech was possibly, in her, a result or at least an index of that gigantic volition which, during our long intercourse, failed to give other and more immediate evidence of its existence. Of all the women whom I have ever known, she—the outwardly calm, the ever-placid Ligeia—was the most violently a prey to the tumultuous vultures of stern passion. And of such passion I could form no estimate, save by the miraculous expansion of those eyes which at once so delighted and appalled me, by the almost magical melody, modulation, distinctness, and placidity of her very low voice, and by the fierce energy (rendered doubly effective by contrast with her manner of utterance) of the wild words which she habitually uttered.

I have spoken of the learning of Ligeia; it was immense, such as I have never known in woman. In the classical tongues was she deeply proficient, and as far as my own acquaintance extended in regard to the modern dialects of Europe, I have never known her at fault. Indeed upon any theme of the most admired, because simply the most abstruse of the boasted erudition of the academy, have I ever found Ligeia at fault? How singularly, how thrillingly, this one point in the nature of my wife has forced itself, at this late period only, upon my attention! I said her knowledge was such as I have never known in woman—but where breathes the man who has traversed, and successfully, all the wide areas of moral, physical, and mathematical science? I saw not then what I now clearly perceive, that the acquisitions of Ligeia were gigantic, were astounding; yet I was sufficiently aware of her infinite supremacy to resign myself, with a child-like confidence, to her guidance through the chaotic world of metaphysical investigation at which I was most busily occupied during the earlier years of our marriage. With how vast a triumph, with how vivid a delight, with how much of all that is ethereal in hope, did I feel, as she bent over me in studies but little sought—but less known—that delicious vista by slow degrees expanding before me, down whose long, gorgeous, and all untrodden path I might at length pass onward to the goal of a wisdom too divinely precious not to be forbidden!

How poignant, then, must have been the grief with which, after some years, I beheld my well-grounded expectations take wings to themselves and fly away! Without Ligeia I was but as a child groping benighted. Her presence, her readings alone, rendered vividly luminous the many mysteries of the transcendentalism in which we were immersed. Wanting the radiant luster of her eyes, letters, lambent and golden, grew duller than Saturnian lead. And now those eyes shone less and less frequently upon the pages over which I pored. Ligeia grew ill. The wild eyes blazed with a too, too glorious effulgence; the pale fingers became of the transparent waxen hue of the grave; and the blue veins upon the lofty forehead swelled and sank impetuously with the tides of the most gentle emotion. I saw that she must die—and I struggled desperately in spirit with the grim Azrael. And the struggles of the passionate wife were, to my astonishment, even more energetic than my own. There had been much in her stern nature to impress me with the belief that, to her, death would have come without its terrors; but not so. Words are impotent to convey any just idea of the fierceness of resistance with which she wrestled with the Shadow. I groaned in anguish at the pitiable spectacle. I would have soothed, I would have reasoned, but, in the intensity of her wild desire for life—for life—but for life—solace and reason were alike the uttermost of folly. Yet not until the last instance, amid the most convulsive writhings of her fierce spirit, was shaken the external placidity of her demeanor. Her voice grew more gentle—grew more low—yet I would not wish to dwell upon the wild meaning of the quietly uttered words. My brain reeled as I hearkened, entranced, to a melody more than mortal, to assumptions and aspirations which mortality had never before known.

That she loved me I should not have doubted, and I might have been easily aware that, in a bosom such as hers, love would have reigned no ordinary passion. But in death only was I fully impressed with the strength of her affection. For long hours, detaining my hand, would she pour out before me the overflowing of a heart whose more than passionate devotion amounted to idolatry. How had I deserved to be so blessed by such confessions? How had I deserved to be so cursed with the removal of my beloved in the hour of her making them? But upon this subject I cannot bear to dilate. Let me say only, that in Ligeia's more than womanly abandonment to a love, alas! all unmerited, all unworthily bestowed, I at length recognized the principle of her longing, with so wildly earnest a desire, for the life which was now fleeing so rapidly away. It is this wild longing—it is this eager vehemence of desire for life—but for life—that I have no power to portray, no utterance capable of expressing.

At high noon of the night in which she departed, beckoning me peremptorily to her side, she bade me repeat certain verses composed by herself not many days before. I obeyed her. They were these:

Lo! 'tis a gala night Within the lonesome latter years!
An angel throng, bewinged, bedight
In veils, and drowned in tears,
Sit in a theater, to see
A play of hopes and fears,
While the orchestra breathes fitfully
The music of the spheres.

Mimes, in the form of God on high,
Mutter and mumble low,
And hither and thither fly;
Mere puppets they, who come and go
At bidding of vast formless things
That shift the scenery to and fro,
Flapping from out their condor wings
Invisible Woe!

That motley drama!—oh, be sure
It shall not be forgot!
With its Phantom chased for evermore,
By a crowd that seize it not,
Through a circle that ever returneth in
To the self-same spot;
And much of Madness, and more of Sin
And Horror, the soul of the plot!

But see, amid the mimic rout
A crawling shape intrude!
A blood-red thing that writhes from out
The scenic solitude!
It writhes!—it writhes!—with mortal
The mimes become its food,

And the seraphs sob at vermin fangs
In human gore imbued.

Out—out are the lights—out all!
And over each quivering form,
The curtain, a funeral pall,
Comes down with the rush of a storm—
And the angels, all pallid and wan,
Uprising, unveiling, affirm
That the play is the tragedy, "Man,"
And its hero, the Conqueror Worm.

"O God!" half-shrieked Ligeia, leaping to her feet and extending her arms aloft with a spasmodic movement, as I made an end of these lines, "O God! O Divine Father! Shall these things be undeviatingly so? Shall this conqueror be not once conquered? Are we not part and parcel in Thee? Who—who knoweth the mysteries of the will with its vigor? Man doth not yield him to the angels, nor unto death utterly, save only through the weakness of his feeble will."

And now, as if exhausted with emotion, she suffered her white arms to fall, and returned solemnly to her bed of death. And as she breathed her last sighs, there came mingled with them a low murmur from her lips. I bent to them my ear, and distinguished again, the concluding words of the passage in Glanvill: "Man doth not yield him to the angels, nor unto death utterly, save only through the weakness of his feeble will."

She died, and I, crushed into the very dust with sorrow, could no longer endure the lonely desolation of my dwelling in the dim and decaying city by the Rhine. I had no lack of what the world calls wealth. Ligeia had brought me far more, very far more than ordinarily falls to the lot of mortals. After a few months, therefore, of weary and aimless wandering, I purchased and put in some repair an abbey which I shall not name in one of the wildest and least frequented portions of fair England. The gloomy and dreary grandeur of the building, the almost savage aspect of the domain, the many melancholy and time-honored memories connected with both, had much in unison with the feelings of utter abandonment which had driven me into that remote and unsocial region of the country. Yet, although the external abbey with its verdant decay hanging about it suffered but little alteration, I gave way with a child-like perversity, and perchance with a faint hope of alleviating my sorrows, to a display of more than regal magnificence within. For such follies, even in childhood, I had imbibed a taste, and now they came back to me as if in the dotage of grief. Alas, I feel how much even of incipient madness might have been discovered in the gorgeous and fantastic draperies, in the solemn carvings of Egypt, in the wild cornices and furniture, in the Bedlam patterns of the carpets of tufted gold! I had become a bounden slave in the trammels of opium, and my labors and my orders had taken a coloring from my dreams. But these absurdities I must not pause to detail. Let me speak only of that one chamber, ever accursed, whither in a moment of mental alienation, I led from the altar as my bride—as the successor of the unforgotten Ligeia—the fair-haired and blue-eyed Lady Rowena Trevanion, of Tremaine.

There is no individual portion of the architecture and decoration of that bridal chamber which is not now visibly before me. Where were the souls of the haughty family of the bride, when, through thirst of gold, they permitted to pass the threshold of an apartment so bedecked, a maiden and a daughter so beloved? I have said that I minutely remember the details of the chamber, yet I am sadly forgetful on topics of deep moment; and here there was no system, no keeping, in the fantastic display, to take hold upon the memory. The room lay in a high turret of the castellated abbey, was pentagonal in shape, and of capacious size. Occupying the whole southern face of the pentagon was the sole window—an immense sheet of unbroken glass from Venice—a single pane, and tinted of a leaden hue, so that the rays of either the sun or moon passing through it fell with a ghastly luster on the objects within. Over the upper portion of this huge window extended the trellis-work of an aged vine which clambered up the massy walls of the turret. The ceiling, of gloomy-looking oak, was excessively lofty, vaulted, and elaborately fretted with the wildest and most grotesque specimens of a semi-Gothic, semi-Druidical device. From out the most central recess of this melancholy vaulting depended, by a single chain of gold with long links, a huge censer of the same metal, Saracenic in pattern, and with many perforations so contrived that there writhed in and out of them, as if endued with a serpent vitality, a continual succession of parti-colored fires.

Some few ottomans and golden candelabra of Eastern figure were in various stations about; and there was the couch, too—the bridal couch—of an Indian model, and low, and sculptured of solid ebony, with a pall-like canopy above. In each of the angles of the chamber stood on end a gigantic sarcophagus of black granite, from the tombs of the kings over against Luxor, with their aged lids full of immemorial sculpture. But in the draping of the apartment lay, alas! the chief fantasy of all. The lofty walls, gigantic in height—even unproportionably so—were hung from summit to foot in vast folds with a heavy and massive-looking tapestry—tapestry of a material which was found alike as a carpet on the floor, as a covering for the ottomans and the ebony bed, as a canopy for the bed, and as the gorgeous volutes of the curtains which partially shaded the window. The material was the richest cloth of gold. It was spotted all over, at irregular intervals, with arabesque figures, about a foot in diameter, and wrought upon the cloth in patterns of the most jetty black. But these figures partook of the true character of the arabesque only when regarded from a single point of view. By a contrivance now common, and indeed traceable to a very remote period of antiquity, they were made changeable in aspect. To one entering the room they bore the appearance of simple monstrosities, but upon a farther advance this appearance gradually departed; and, step by step as the visitor moved his station in the chamber he saw himself surrounded by an endless succession of the ghastly forms which belong to the superstition of the Norman, or arise in the guilty slumbers of the monk. The phantasmagoric effect was vastly heightened by the artificial introduction of a strong continual current of wind behind the draperies—giving a hideous and uneasy animation to the whole.

In halls such as these—in a bridal chamber such as this—I passed, with the Lady of Tremaine, the unhallowed hours of the first month of our marriage—passed them with but little disquietude. That my wife dreaded the fierce moodiness of my temper, that she shunned me, and loved me but little, I could not help perceiving; but it gave me rather pleasure than otherwise. I loathed her with a hatred belonging more to demon than to man. My memory flew back—oh, with what intensity of regret!—to Ligeia, the beloved, the august, the beautiful, the entombed. I revelled in recollections of her purity, of her wisdom, of her lofty, her ethereal nature, of her passionate, her idolatrous love. Now, then, did my spirit fully and freely burn with more than all the fires of her own. In the excitement of my opium dreams (for I was habitually fettered in the shackles of the drug) I would call aloud upon her name, during the silence of the night, or among the sheltered recesses of the glens by day, as if, through the wild eagerness, the solemn passion, the consuming ardor of my longing for the departed, I could restore her to the pathway she had abandoned—ah, could it be for ever?—upon the earth.

About the commencement of the second month of the marriage the Lady Rowena was attacked with sudden illness, from which her recovery was slow. The fever which consumed her rendered her nights uneasy; and in her perturbed state of half-slumber she spoke of sounds and of motions in and about the chamber of the turret which I concluded had no origin save in the distemper of her fancy, or perhaps in the phantasmagoric influences of the chamber itself. She became at length convalescent—finally, well. Yet but a brief period elapsed ere a second more violent disorder again threw her upon a bed of suffering, and from this attack her frame, at all times feeble, never altogether recovered. Her illnesses were, after this epoch, of alarming character and of more alarming recurrence, defying alike the knowledge and the great exertions of her physicians. With the increase of the chronic disease, which had thus, apparently, taken too sure hold upon her constitution to be eradicated by human means, I could not fail to observe a similar increase in the nervous irritation of her temperament, and in her excitability by trivial causes of fear. She spoke again, and now more frequently and pertinaciously, of the sounds—of the slight sounds—and of the unusual motions among the tapestries, to which she had formerly alluded.

One night near the closing in of September she pressed this distressing subject with more than usual emphasis upon my attention. She had just awakened from an unquiet slumber, and I had been watching, with feelings half of anxiety, half of vague terror, the workings of her emaciated countenance. I sat by the side of her ebony bed, upon one of the ottomans of India. She partly arose, and spoke, in an earnest low whisper, of sounds which she then heard, but which I could not hear, of motions which she then saw, but which I could not perceive. The wind was rushing hurriedly behind the tapestries, and I wished to show her (what, let me confess it, I could not all believe) that those almost inarticulate breathings, and those very gentle variations of the figures upon the wall, were but the natural effects of that customary rushing of the wind. But a deadly pallor overspreading her face had proved to me that my exertions to reassure her would be fruitless. She appeared to be fainting, and no attendants were within call. I remembered where was deposited a decanter of light wine which had been ordered by her physicians, and hastened across the chamber to procure it. But as I stepped beneath the light of the censer, two circumstances of a startling nature attracted my attention. I had felt that some palpable although invisible object had passed lightly by my person; and I saw that there lay upon the golden carpet, in the very middle of the rich luster thrown from the censer, a shadow—a faint, indefinite shadow of angelic aspect, such as might be fancied for the shadow of a shade. But I was wild with the excitement of an immoderate dose of opium, and heeded these things but little, nor spoke of them to Rowena. Having found the wine, I recrossed the chamber and poured out a gobletful which I held to the lips of the fainting lady. She had now partially recovered, however, and took the vessel herself, while I sank upon an ottoman near me, with my eyes fastened upon her person. It was then that I became distinctly aware of a gentle footfall upon the carpet and near the couch; and in a second after as Rowena was in the act of raising the wine to her lips I saw, or may have dreamed that I saw, fall within the goblet, as if from some invisible spring in the atmosphere of the room, three or four large drops of a brilliant and ruby-colored fluid. If this I saw—not so Rowena. She swallowed the wine unhesitatingly, and I forbore to speak to her of a circumstance which must, after all, I considered, have been but the suggestion of a vivid imagination, rendered morbidly active by the terror of the lady, by the opium, and by the hour.

Yet I cannot conceal it from my own perception that, immediately subsequent to the fall of the ruby-drops, a rapid change for the worse took place in the disorder of my wife, so that, on the third subsequent night the hands of her menials prepared her for the tomb, and on the fourth I sat alone with her shrouded body in that fantastic chamber which had received her as my bride. Wild visions, opium-engendered, fluttered, shadow-like, before me. I gazed with unquiet eye upon the sarcophagi in the angles of the room, upon the varying figures of the drapery, and upon the writhing of the parti-colored fires in the censer overhead. My eyes then fell, as I called to mind the circumstances of a former night, to the spot beneath the glare of the censer where I had seen the faint traces of the shadow. It was there, however, no longer; and breathing with greater freedom, I turned my glances to the pallid and rigid figure upon the bed. Then rushed upon me a thousand memories of Ligeia—and then came back upon my heart with the turbulent violence of a flood the whole of that unutterable woe with which I had regarded her thus enshrouded. The night waned; and still, with a bosom full of bitter thoughts of the one only and supremely beloved, I remained gazing upon the body of Rowena.

It might have been midnight, or perhaps earlier, or later—for I had taken no note of time—when a sob, low, gentle, but very distinct, startled me from my revery. I felt that it came from the bed of ebony—the bed of death. I listened in an agony of superstitious terror—but there was no repetition of the sound. I strained my vision to detect any motion in the corpse—but there was not the slightest perceptible. Yet I could not have been deceived. I had heard the noise, however faint, and my soul was awakened within me. I resolutely and perseveringly kept my attention riveted upon the body. Many minutes elapsed before any circumstance occurred tending to throw light upon the mystery. At length it became evident that a slight, a very feeble and barely noticeable tinge of color had flushed up within the cheeks, and along the sunken small veins of the eyelids. Through a species of unutterable horror and awe, for which the language of mortality has no sufficiently energetic expression, I felt my heart cease to beat, my limbs grow rigid where I sat. Yet a sense of duty finally operated to restore my self-possession. I could no longer doubt that we had been precipitate in our preparations—that Rowena still lived. It was necessary that some immediate exertion be made, yet the turret was altogether apart from the portion of the abbey tenanted by the servants—there were none within call, and I had no means of summoning them to my aid without leaving the room for many minutes—and this I could not venture to do. I therefore struggled alone in my endeavors to call back the spirit still hovering. In a short period it was certain, however, that a relapse had taken place, the color disappeared from both eyelid and cheek, leaving a wanness even more than that of marble; the lips became doubly shrivelled and pinched up in the ghastly expression of death; a repulsive clamminess and coldness overspread rapidly the surface of the body; and all the usual rigorous stiffness immediately supervened. I fell back with a shudder upon the couch from which I had been so startlingly aroused, and again gave myself up to passionate waking visions of Ligeia.

An hour thus elapsed, when—could it be possible?—I was a second time aware of some vague sound issuing from the region of the bed. I listened—in extremity of horror. The sound came again—it was a sigh. Rushing to the corpse, I saw—distinctly saw—a tremor upon the lips. In a minute afterward they relaxed, disclosing a bright line of the pearly teeth. Amazement now struggled in my bosom with the profound awe which had hitherto reigned there alone. I felt that my vision grew dim, that my reason wandered, and it was only by a violent effort that I at length succeeded in nerving myself to the task which duty thus once more had pointed out. There was now a partial glow upon the forehead and upon the cheek and throat, a perceptible warmth pervaded the whole frame, there was even a slight pulsation at the heart. The lady lived; and with redoubled ardor I betook myself to the task of restoration. I chafed and bathed the temples and the hands and used every exertion which experience and no little medical reading could suggest. But in vain. Suddenly, the color fled, the pulsation ceased, the lips resumed the expression of the dead, and, in an instant afterward, the whole body took upon itself the icy chilliness, the livid hue, the intense rigidity, the sunken outline, and all the loathsome peculiarities of that which has been, for many days, a tenant of the tomb.

And again I sunk into visions of Ligeia—and again, (what marvel that I shudder while I write?) again there reached my ears a low sob from the region of the ebony bed. But why should I minutely detail the unspeakable horrors of that night? Why should I pause to relate how, time after time, until near the period of the gray dawn, this hideous drama of revivification was repeated; how each terrific relapse was only into a sterner and apparently more irredeemable death; how each agony wore the aspect of a struggle with some invisible foe; and how each struggle was succeeded by I know not what of wild change in the personal appearance of the corpse? Let me hurry to a conclusion.

The greater part of the fearful night had worn away, and she who had been dead, once again stirred—and now more vigorously than hitherto, although arousing from a dissolution more appalling in its utter hopelessness than any. I had long ceased to struggle or to move, and remained sitting rigidly upon the ottoman, a helpless prey to a whirl of violent emotions, of which extreme awe was perhaps the least terrible, the least consuming. The corpse, I repeat, stirred, and now more vigorously than before. The hues of life flushed up with unwonted energy into the countenance, the limbs relaxed, and, save that the eyelids were yet pressed heavily together and that the bandages and draperies of the grave still imparted their charnel character to the figure, I might have dreamed that Rowena had indeed shaken off utterly the fetters of Death. But if this idea was not even then altogether adopted, I could at least doubt no longer, when arising from the bed, tottering, with feeble steps, with closed eyes, and with the manner of one bewildered in a dream, the thing that was enshrouded advanced boldly and palpably into the middle of the apartment.

I trembled not—I stirred not—for a crowd of unutterable fancies connected with the air, the stature, the demeanor of the figure, rushing hurriedly through my brain, had paralyzed—had chilled me into stone. I stirred not—but gazed upon the apparition. There was a mad disorder in my thoughts—a tumult unappeasable. Could it, indeed, be the living Rowena who confronted me? Could it indeed be Rowena at all—the fair-haired, the blue-eyed Lady Rowena Trevanion of Tremaine? Why, why should I doubt it? The bandage lay heavily about the mouth—but then might it not be the mouth of the breathing Lady of Tremaine? And the cheeks—there were the roses as in her noon of life—yes, these might indeed be the fair cheeks of the living Lady of Tremaine. And the chin, with its dimples, as in health, might it not be hers?—but had she then grown taller since her malady? What inexpressible madness seized me with that thought! One bound, and I had reached her feet. Shrinking from my touch she let fall from her head, unloosened, the ghastly cerements which had confined it, and there streamed forth into the rushing atmosphere of the chamber huge masses of long and dishevelled hair; it was blacker than the raven wings of midnight! And now slowly opened the eyes of the figure which stood before me. "Here then, at least," I shrieked aloud, "can I never—can I never be mistaken—these are the full and the black, and the wild eyes of my lost love—of the Lady—of the Lady Ligeia."

THE SYLPH AND THE FATHER[5]

By Elsa Barker

Passing yesterday along the line where the great French army stands before its powerful opponent, and marking the spirit of courage and aspiration which makes it seem like a long line of living light, I saw a familiar face in the regions outside the physical.

I paused, highly pleased at the encounter, and the sylph—for it was a sylph whom I met—paused also with a little smile of recognition.

Do you recall in my former book the story of a sylph, Meriline, who was the companion and familiar of a student of magic who lived in the rue de Vaugirard in Paris?

It was Meriline that I met above the line of light which shows to wanderers in the astral regions where the soldiers of la belle France fight and die for the same ideal which inspired Jeanne d'Arc—to drive the foreigner out of France.

"Where is your friend and master?" I asked the sylph, and she pointed below to a trench which spoke loud its determination to conquer.

"I am here, to be still with him," she said.

"And can you speak to him here?" I asked.

"I can always speak with him," she answered. "I have been very useful to him—and to France."

"To France?" I enquired, with growing interest.

"Oh, yes! When his commanding officer wants to know what is being plotted over there, he often asks my friend, and my friend asks me."

"Truly," I thought, "the French are an inspired people, when the officers of armies ask guidance from the realm of the invisible! But had not Jeanne her visions?"

"And how do you gain the information desired?" I asked, drawing nearer to Meriline, who seemed more serious than when we met some years before in Paris.

"Why," she answered, "I go over there and look around me. I have learned what to look for, he has taught me, and when I bring him news he rewards me with more love."

"And do you love him still, as of old?"

"As of old?"

---

5 By permission of the author of War Letters of the Living Dead Man and Mitchell Kennerley.

"Yes, as you did back there in Paris."

"Time must have passed slowly with you," said the sylph, "if you call a few years ago 'as of old'."

"Are a few years, then, as nothing?"

"A few years are as nothing to me," she replied. "I have lived a long time."

"And do you know the future of your friend?" I asked.

A puzzled look came over the face of Meriline, and she said, slowly:

"I used to know everything that would happen to him, because I could read his will, and whatever he willed came to pass; but since we have been out here he seems to have lost his will."

"Lost his will!" I exclaimed, in surprise.

"Yes, lost his will; for he prays continually to a great Being whom he loves far more than me, and he always prays one prayer, 'Thy will be done!' It used to be his will which was always done; but now, as I say, he seems to have lost his will."

"Perhaps," I said, "it is true of the will as was once said of the life, and he that loses his will shall find it."

"I hope he will find it soon," she answered, "for in the old days he was always giving me interesting things to do, to help him achieve the purposes of his will, and now he only sends me over there. I don't like over there!"

"Why not?"

"Because my friend is menaced by something over there."

"And what has his will to do with that?"

"Why, even about that, he says all day to the great Being that he loves so much more than me, 'Thy will be done.'"

"Do you think you could learn to say it, too?" I asked.

"I say it after him sometimes; but I don't know what it means."

"Have you never heard of God?"

"I have heard of many gods, of Isis and Osiris and Set, and of Horus, the son of Osiris."

"And is it to one of these that he says, 'Thy will be done'?"

"Oh, no! It is not to any of the gods that he used to call upon in his magical working. This is some new god that he has found."

"Or the oldest of all gods that he has returned to," I suggested. "What does he call Him?"

"Our Father who art in heaven."

"If you also should learn to say 'Thy will be done' to our Father who is in heaven," I said, "it might help you toward the attainment of that soul you were wanting and waiting for, when last we met in Paris."

"How could our Father help me?"

"It was He who gave souls to men," I said.

The eyes of the sylph were brilliant with something almost human.

"And could He give a soul to me?"

"It is said that He can do anything."

"Then I will ask Him for a soul."

"But to ask Him for a soul," I said, "is not to pray the prayer your friend prays."

"He only says——"

"Yes, I know. Suppose you say it after him."

"I will, if you will tell me what it means. I like to do what my friend does."

"'Thy will be done,'" I said, "when addressed to the Father in heaven, means that we give up all our desires, whether for pleasure or love or happiness, or anything else, and lay all those desires at His feet, sacrificing all we have or hope for to Him, because we love Him more than ourselves."

"That is a strange way to get what one desires," she said.

"It is not done to get what one desires," I answered.

"But what is it done for?"

"For love of the Father in heaven."

"But I do not know the Father in heaven. What is He?"

"He is the Source and the Goal of the being of your friend. He is the One that your friend will re-become some day, if he can forever say to Him, Thy will be done."

"The One he will re-become?"

"Yes, for when he blends his will with that of the Father in heaven, the Father in heaven dwells in his heart and the two become one."

"Then is the Father in heaven really the Self of my friend?"

"The greatest philosopher could not have expressed it more truly," I said.

"Then indeed do I love the Father in heaven," breathed the sylph, "and I will say now every day and all day, 'Thy will be done' to Him."

"Even if it separates you from your friend?"

"How can it separate me from my friend, if the Father is the Self of him?"

"I would that all angels were your equal in learning," I said.

But Meriline had turned from me in utter forgetfulness, and was saying over and over, with joy in her uplifted face, "Thy will be done! Thy will be done!"

"Truly," I said to myself, as I passed along the line, "he who worships the Father as the Self of the beloved has already acquired a soul."

A GHOST[6]

By Lafcadio Hearn

I

Perhaps the man who never wanders away from the place of his birth may pass all his life without knowing ghosts; but the nomad is more than likely to make their acquaintance. I refer to the civilized nomad, whose wanderings are not prompted by hope of gain, nor determined by pleasure, but simply compelled by certain necessities of his being—the man whose inner secret nature is totally at variance with the stable conditions of a society to which he belongs only by accident. However intellectually trained, he must always remain the slave of singular impulses which have no rational source, and which will often amaze him no less by their mastering power than by their continuous savage opposition to his every material interest. These may, perhaps, be traced back to some ancestral habit—be explained by self-evident hereditary tendencies. Or perhaps they may not,—in which event the victim can only surmise himself the Imago of some pre-existent larval aspiration—the full development of desires long dormant in a chain of more limited lives.

Assuredly the nomadic impulses differ in every member of the class, take infinite variety from individual sensitiveness to environment—the line of least resistance for one being that of greatest resistance for another; no two courses of true nomadism can ever be wholly the same. Diversified of necessity both impulse and direction, even as human nature is diversified! Never since consciousness of time began were two beings born who possessed exactly the same quality of voice, the same precise degree of nervous impressibility, or, in brief, the same combination of those viewless force-storing molecules which shape and poise themselves in sentient substance. Vain, therefore, all striving to particularize the curious psychology of such existences; at the very utmost it is possible only to describe such impulses and preceptions of nomadism as lie within the very small range of one's own observation. And whatever in these is strictly personal can have little interest or value except in so far as it holds something in common with the great general experience of restless lives. To such

[6] From Karma (Boni & Liveright).

experience may belong, I think, one ultimate result of all those irrational partings, self-wrecking, sudden isolations, abrupt severances from all attachment, which form the history of the nomad—the knowledge that a strong silence is ever deepening and expanding about one's life, and that in that silence there are ghosts.

II

Oh! the first vague charm, the first sunny illusion of some fair city, when vistas of unknown streets all seem leading to the realization of a hope you dare not even whisper; when even the shadows look beautiful, and strange façades appear to smile good omen through light of gold! And those first winning relations with men, while you are still a stranger, and only the better and the brighter side of their nature is turned to you! All is yet a delightful, luminous indefiniteness—sensation of streets and of men—like some beautifully tinted photograph slightly out of focus.

Then the slow solid sharpening of details all about you, thrusting through illusion and dispelling it, growing keener and harder day by day through long dull seasons; while your feet learn to remember all asperities of pavements, and your eyes all physiognomy of buildings and of persons—failures of masonry, furrowed lines of pain. Thereafter only the aching of monotony intolerable, and the hatred of sameness grown dismal, and dread of the merciless, inevitable, daily and hourly repetition of things; while those impulses of unrest, which are Nature's urgings through that ancestral experience which lives in each one of us—outcries of sea and peak and sky to man—ever make wilder appeal. Strong friendships may have been formed; but there finally comes a day when even these can give no consolation for the pain of monotony, and you feel that in order to live you must decide, regardless of result, to shake forever from your feet the familiar dust of that place.

And, nevertheless, in the hour of departure you feel a pang. As train or steamer bears you away from the city and its myriad associations, the old illusive impression will quiver back about you for a moment—not as if to mock the expectation of the past, but softly, touchingly, as if pleading to you to stay; and such a sadness, such a tenderness may come to you, as one knows after reconciliation with a friend misapprehended and unjustly judged. But you will never more see those streets—except in dreams.

Through sleep only they will open again before you, steeped in the illusive vagueness of the first long-past day, peopled only by friends outstretching to you. Soundlessly you will tread those shadowy pavements many times, to knock in thought, perhaps, at doors which the dead will open to you. But with the passing of years all becomes dim—so dim that even asleep you know 'tis only a ghost-city, with streets going to nowhere. And finally whatever is left of it becomes confused and blended with cloudy memories of other cities—one endless bewilderment of filmy architecture in which nothing is distinctly recognizable, though the whole gives the sensation of having been seen before, ever so long ago.

Meantime, in the course of wanderings more or less aimless, there has slowly grown upon you a suspicion of being haunted—so frequently does a certain hazy presence intrude itself upon the visual memory. This, however, appears to gain rather than to lose in definiteness; with each return its visibility seems to increase. And the suspicion that you may be haunted gradually develops into a certainty.

III

You are haunted—whether your way lie through the brown gloom of London winter, or the azure splendor of an equatorial day—whether your steps be tracked in snows, or in the burning black sand of a tropic beach—whether you rest beneath the swart shade of Northern pines, or under spidery umbrages of palm—you are haunted ever and everywhere by a certain gentle presence. There is nothing fearsome in this haunting—the gentlest face, the kindliest voice—oddly familiar and distinct, though feeble as the hum of a bee.

But it tantalizes—this haunting—like those sudden surprises of sensation within us, though seemingly not of us, which some dreamers have sought to interpret as inherited remembrances, recollections of preëxistence. Vainly you ask yourself, "Whose voice? Whose face?" It is neither young nor old, the Face; it has a vapory indefinableness that leaves it a riddle; its diaphaneity reveals no particular tint; perhaps you may not even be quite sure whether it has a beard. But its expression is always gracious, passionless, smiling—like the smiling of unknown friends in dreams, with infinite indulgence for any folly, even a dream-folly. Except in that you cannot permanently banish it, the presence offers no positive resistance to your will; it accepts each caprice with obedience; it meets your every whim with angelic patience. It is never critical, never makes plaint even by a look, never proves irksome; yet you cannot ignore it, because of a certain queer power it possesses to make something stir and quiver in your heart—like an old vague sweet regret—something buried alive which will not die. And so often does this happen that desire to solve the riddle becomes a pain; that you finally find yourself making supplication to the Presence; addressing to it questions which it will never answer directly, but only by a smile or by words having no relation to the asking—words enigmatic, which make mysterious agitation in old forsaken fields of memory, even as a wind betimes, over wide wastes of marsh, sets all the grasses whispering about nothing. But you will question on, untiringly, through the nights and days of years:

"Who are you? What are you? What is this weird relation that you bear to me? All you say to me I feel that I have heard before, but where? But when? By what name am I to call you, since you will answer to none that I remember? Surely you do not live; yet I know the sleeping-places of all my dead, and yours I do not know! Neither are you any dream—for dreams distort and change; and you, you are ever the same. Nor are you any hallucination; for all my senses are still vivid and strong. This only I know beyond doubt—that you are of the Past; you belong to memory—but to the memory of what dead suns?"

Then, some day or night, unexpectedly, there comes to you at least, with a soft swift tingling shock as of fingers invisible, the knowledge that the Face is not the memory of any one face; but a multiple image formed of the traits of many dear faces, superimposed by remembrance, and interblended by affection into one ghostly personality—infinitely sympathetic, phantasmally beautiful—a Composite of recollections! And the Voice is the echo of no one voice, but the echoing of many voices, molten into a single utterance, a single impossible tone, thin through remoteness of time, but inexpressibly caressing.

IV

Thou most gentle Composite!—thou nameless and exquisite Unreality, thrilled into semblance of being from out the sum of all lost sympathies!—thou Ghost of all dear vanished things, with thy vain appeal of eyes that looked for my coming, and vague faint pleading of voices against oblivion, and thin electric touch of buried hands—must thou pass away forever with my passing, even as the Shadow that I cast, O thou Shadowing of Souls?

I am not sure. For there comes to me this dream—that if aught in human life hold power to pass, like a swerved sunray through interstellar spaces, into the infinite mystery, to send one sweet strong vibration through immemorial Time, might not some luminous future be peopled with such as thou? And in so far as that which makes for us the subtlest charm of being can lend one choral note to the Symphony of the Unknowable Purpose—in so much might there not endure also to greet thee, another Composite One—embodying, indeed, the comeliness of many lives, yet keeping likewise some visible memory of all that may have been gracious in this thy friend?

THE EYES OF THE PANTHER[7]

By Ambrose Bierce

I

ONE DOES NOT ALWAYS MARRY WHEN INSANE

A man and a woman—nature had done the grouping—sat on a rustic seat, in the late afternoon. The man was middle-aged, slender, swarthy, with the expression of a poet and the complexion of a pirate—a man at whom one would look again. The woman was young, blonde, graceful, with something in her figure and movements suggesting the word "lithe." She was habited in a gray gown with odd brown markings in the texture. She may have been beautiful; one could not readily say, for her eyes denied attention to all else. They were gray-green, long and narrow, with an expression defying analysis. One could only know that they were disquieting. Cleopatra may have had such eyes.

The man and the woman talked.

"Yes," said the woman, "I love you, God knows! But marry you, no. I cannot, will not."

"Irene, you have said that many times, yet always have denied me a reason. I've a right to know, to understand, to feel and prove my fortitude if I have it. Give me a reason."

"For loving you?"

The woman was smiling through her tears and her pallor. That did not stir any sense of humor in the man.

"No; there is no reason for that. A reason for not marrying me. I've a right to know. I must know. I will know!"

He had risen and was standing before her with clenched hands, on his face a frown—it might have been called a scowl. He looked as if he might attempt to learn by strangling her. She smiled no more—merely sat looking up into his face with a fixed, set regard that was utterly without emotion or sentiment. Yet it had something in it that tamed his resentment and made him shiver.

"You are determined to have my reason?" she asked in a tone that was entirely mechanical—a tone that might have been her look made audible.

"If you please—if I'm not asking too much."

---

7 From "In the Midst of Life" (Boni & Liveright).

Apparently this lord of creation was yielding some part of his dominion over his co-creature.

"Very well, you shall know: I am insane."

The man started, then looked incredulous and was conscious that he ought to be amused. But, again, the sense of humor failed him in his need and despite his disbelief he was profoundly disturbed by that which he did not believe. Between our convictions and our feelings there is no good understanding.

"That is what the physicians would say," the woman continued, "if they knew. I might myself prefer to call it a case of 'possession.' Sit down and hear what I have to say."

The man silently resumed his seat beside her on the rustic bench by the wayside. Over against them on the eastern side of the valley the hills were already sunset-flushed and the stillness all about was of that peculiar quality that foretells the twilight. Something of its mysterious and significant solemnity had imparted itself to the man's mood. In the spiritual, as in the material world, are signs and presages of night. Rarely meeting her look, and whenever he did so conscious of the indefinable dread with which, despite their feline beauty, her eyes always affected him, Jenner Brading listened in silence to the story told by Irene Marlowe. In deference to the reader's possible prejudice against the artless method of an unpracticed historian the author ventures to substitute his own version for hers.

II

A ROOM MAY BE TOO NARROW FOR THREE, THOUGH ONE IS OUTSIDE

In a little log house containing a single room sparely and rudely furnished, crouching on the floor against one of the walls, was a woman, clasping to her breast a child. Outside, a dense unbroken forest extended for many miles in every direction. This was at night and the room was black dark; no human eye could have discerned the woman and the child. Yet they were observed, narrowly, vigilantly, with never even a momentary slackening of attention; and that is the pivotal fact upon which this narrative turns.

Charles Marlowe was of the class, now extinct in this country, of woodmen pioneers—men who found their most acceptable surroundings in sylvan solitudes that stretched along the eastern slope of the Mississippi Valley, from the Great Lakes to the Gulf of Mexico. For more than a hundred years these men pushed ever westward, generation after generation, with rifle and ax, reclaiming from Nature and her savage children here and there an isolated acreage for the plow, no sooner reclaimed than surrendered to their less venturesome but more thrifty successors. At last they burst through the edge of the forest into the open country and vanished as if they had fallen over a cliff. The woodman pioneer is no more; the pioneer of the plains—he whose easy task it was to subdue for occupancy two-thirds of the country in a single generation—is another and inferior creation. With Charles Marlowe in the wilderness, sharing the dangers, hardships and privations of that strange unprofitable life, were his wife and child, to whom, in the manner of his class in which the domestic virtues were a religion, he was passionately attached. The woman was still young enough to be comely, new enough to the awful isolation of her lot to be cheerful. By withholding the large capacity for happiness which the simple satisfactions of the forest life could not have filled, Heaven had dealt honorably with her. In her light household tasks, her child, her husband and her few foolish books, she found abundant provision for her needs.

One morning in midsummer Marlowe took down his rifle from the wooden hooks on the wall and signified his intention of getting game.

"We've meat enough," said the wife; "please don't go out to-day. I dreamed last night, O, such a dreadful thing! I cannot recollect it, but I'm almost sure that it will come to pass if you go out."

It is painful to confess that Marlowe received this solemn statement with less of gravity than was due to the mysterious nature of the calamity foreshadowed. In truth, he laughed.

"Try to remember," he said. "Maybe you dreamed that Baby had lost the power of speech."

The conjecture was obviously suggested by the fact that Baby, clinging to the fringe of his hunting-coat with all her ten pudgy thumbs, was at that moment uttering her sense of the situation in a series of exultant goo-goos inspired by sight of her father's raccoon-skin cap.

The woman yielded: lacking the gift of humor she could not hold out against his kindly badinage. So, with a kiss for the mother and a kiss for the child, he left the house and closed the door upon his happiness forever.

At nightfall he had not returned. The woman prepared supper and waited. Then she put Baby to bed and sang softly to her until she slept. By this time the fire on the hearth, at which she had cooked supper, had burned out and the room was lighted by a single candle. This she afterward placed in the open window as a sign and welcome to the hunter if he should approach from that side. She had thoughtfully closed and barred the door against such wild animals as might prefer it to an open window—of the habits of beasts of prey in entering a house uninvited she was not advised, though with true female prevision she may have considered the possibility of their entrance by way of the chimney. As the night wore on she became not less anxious, but more drowsy, and at last rested her arms upon the bed by the child and her head upon the arms. The candle in the window burned down to the socket, sputtered and flared a moment and went out unobserved; for the woman slept and dreamed.

In her dreams she sat beside the cradle of a second child. The first one was dead. The father was dead. The home in the forest was lost and the dwelling in which she lived was unfamiliar. There were heavy oaken doors, always closed, and outside the windows, fastened into the thick stone walls, were iron bars, obviously (so she thought) a provision against Indians. All this she noted with an infinite self-pity, but without surprise—an emotion unknown in dreams. The child in the cradle was invisible under its coverlet which something impelled her to remove. She did so, disclosing the face of a wild animal! In the shock of this dreadful revelation the dreamer awoke, trembling in the darkness of her cabin in the wood.

As a sense of her actual surroundings came slowly back to her she felt for the child that was not a dream, and assured herself by its breathing that all was well with it; nor could she forbear to pass a hand lightly across its face. Then, moved by some impulse for which she probably could not have accounted, she rose and took the sleeping babe in her arms, holding it close against her breast. The head of the child's cot was against the wall to which the woman now turned her back as she stood. Lifting her eyes she saw two bright objects starring the darkness with a reddish-green glow. She took them to be two coals on the hearth, but with her returning sense of direction came the disquieting consciousness that they were not in that quarter of the room, moreover were too high, being nearly at the level of the eyes—of her own eyes. For these were the eyes of a panther.

The beast was at the open window directly opposite and not five paces away. Nothing but those terrible eyes was visible, but in the dreadful tumult of her feelings as the situation disclosed itself to her understanding she somehow knew that the animal was standing on its hinder feet, supporting itself with its paws on the window-ledge. That signified a malign interest—not the mere gratification of an indolent curiosity. The consciousness of the attitude was an added horror, accentuating the menace of those awful eyes, in whose steadfast fire her strength and courage were alike consumed. Under their silent questioning she shuddered and turned sick. Her knees failed her, and by degrees, instinctively striving to avoid a sudden movement that might bring the beast upon her, she sank to the floor, crouched against the wall and tried to shield the babe with her trembling body without withdrawing her gaze from the luminous orbs that were killing her. No thought of her husband came to her in her agony—no hope nor suggestion of rescue or escape. Her capacity for thought and feeling had narrowed to the dimensions of a single emotion—fear of the animal's spring, of the impact of its body, the buffeting of its great arms, the feel of its teeth in her throat, the mangling of her babe. Motionless now and in absolute silence, she awaited her doom, the moments growing to hours, to years, to ages; and still those devilish eyes maintained their watch.

Returning to his cabin late at night with a deer on his shoulders Charles Marlowe tried the door. It did not yield. He knocked; there was no answer. He laid down his deer and went around to the window. As he turned the angle of the building he fancied he heard a sound as of stealthy footfalls and a rustling in the undergrowth of the forest, but they were too slight for certainty, even to his practiced ear. Approaching the window, and to his surprise finding it open, he threw his leg over the sill and entered. All was darkness and silence. He groped his way to the fire-place, struck a match and lit a candle. Then he looked about. Cowering on the floor against a wall was his wife, clasping his child. As he sprang toward her she rose and broke into laughter, long, loud, and mechanical, devoid of gladness and devoid of sense—the laughter that is not out of keeping with the clanking of a chain. Hardly knowing what he did he extended his arms. She laid the babe in them. It was dead—pressed to death in its mother's embrace.

III

THE THEORY OF THE DEFENSE

That is what occurred during a night in a forest, but not all of it did Irene Marlowe relate to Jenner Brading; not all of it was known to her. When she had concluded the sun was below the horizon and the long summer twilight had begun to deepen in the hollows of the land. For some moments Brading was silent, expecting the narrative to be carried forward to some definite connection with the conversation introducing it; but the narrator was as silent as he, her face averted, her hands clasping and unclasping themselves as they lay in her lap, with a singular suggestion of an activity independent of her will.

"It is a sad, a terrible story," said Brading at last, "but I do not understand. You call Charles Marlowe father; that I know. That he is old before his time, broken by some great sorrow, I have seen, or thought I saw. But, pardon me, you said that you—that you—"

"That I am insane," said the girl, without a movement of head or body.

"But, Irene, you say—please, dear, do not look away from me—you say that the child was dead, not demented."

"Yes, that one—I am the second. I was born three months after that night, my mother being mercifully permitted to lay down her life in giving me mine."

Brading was again silent; he was a trifle dazed and could not at once think of the right thing to say. Her face was still turned away. In his embarrassment he reached impulsively toward the hands that lay closing and unclosing in her lap, but something—he could not have said what—restrained him. He then remembered, vaguely, that he had never altogether cared to take her hand.

"Is it likely," she resumed, "that a person born under such circumstances is like others—is what you call sane?"

Brading did not reply; he was preoccupied with a new thought that was taking shape in his mind—what a scientist would have called an hypothesis; a detective, a theory. It might throw an added light, albeit a lurid one, upon such doubt of her sanity as her own assertion had not dispelled.

The country was still new and, outside the villages, sparsely populated. The professional hunter was still a familiar figure, and among his trophies were heads and pelts of the larger kinds of game. Tales variously credible of nocturnal meetings with savage animals in lonely roads were sometimes current, passed through the customary stages of growth and decay, and were forgotten. A recent addition to these popular apocrypha, originating, apparently, by spontaneous generation in several households, was of a panther which had frightened some of their members by looking in at windows by night. The yarn had caused its little ripple of excitement—had even attained to the distinction of a place in the local newspaper; but Brading had given it no attention. Its likeness to the story to which he had just listened now impressed him as perhaps more than accidental. Was it not possible that the one story had suggested the other—that finding congenial conditions in a morbid mind and a fertile fancy, it had grown to the tragic tale that he had heard?

Brading recalled certain circumstances of the girl's history and disposition of which, with love's incuriosity, he had hitherto been heedless—such as her solitary life with her father, at whose house no one apparently was an acceptable visitor, and her strange fear of the night by which those who knew her best accounted for her never being seen after dark. Surely in such a mind imagination once kindled might burn with a lawless flame, penetrating and enveloping the entire structure. That she was mad, though the conviction gave him the acutest pain, he could no longer doubt; she had only mistaken an effect of her mental disorder for its cause, bringing into imaginary relation with her own personality the vagaries of the local myth-makers. With some vague intention of testing his new "theory," and no very definite notion of how to set about it he said gravely, but with hesitation:

"Irene, dear, tell me—I beg you will not take offense, but tell me—"

"I have told you," she interrupted, speaking with a passionate earnestness that he had not known her to show, "I have already told you that we cannot marry; is anything else worth saying?"

Before he could stop her she had sprung from her seat and without another word or look was gliding away among the trees toward her father's house. Brading had risen to detain her; he stood watching her in silence until she had vanished in the gloom. Suddenly he started as if he had been shot, his face took on an expression of amazement and alarm: in one of the black shadows into which she had disappeared he had caught a quick, brief glimpse of shining eyes! For an instant he was dazed and irresolute; then he dashed into the wood after her, shouting, "Irene, Irene, look out! The panther! The panther!"

In a moment he had passed through the fringe of forest into open ground and saw the girl's gray skirt vanishing into her father's door. No panther was visible.

IV

AN APPEAL TO THE CONSCIENCE OF GOD

Jenner Brading, attorney-at-law, lived in a cottage at the edge of the town. Directly behind the dwelling was the forest. Being a bachelor, and therefore by the Draconian moral code of the time and place denied the services of the only species of domestic servant known thereabout, the "hired girl," he boarded at the village hotel where also was his office. The woodside cottage was merely a lodging maintained—at no great cost, to be sure—as an evidence of prosperity and respectability. It would hardly do for one to whom the local newspaper had pointed with pride as "the foremost jurist of his time" to be "homeless," albeit he may sometimes have suspected that the words "home" and "house" were not strictly synonymous. Indeed, his consciousness of the disparity and his will to harmonize it were matters of logical inference, for it was generally reported that soon after the cottage was built its owner had made a futile venture in the direction of marriage—had, in truth, gone so far as to be rejected by the beautiful but eccentric daughter of Old Man Marlowe, the recluse. This was publicly believed because he had told it himself and she had not—a reversal of the usual order of things which could hardly fail to carry conviction.

Brading's bedroom was at the rear of the house, with a single window facing the forest. One night he was awakened by a noise at that window—he could hardly have said what it was like. With a little thrill of the nerves he sat up in bed and laid hold of the revolver which, with a forethought most commendable in one addicted to the habit of sleeping on the ground floor with an open window, he had put under his pillow. The room was in absolute darkness, but being unterrified he knew where to direct his eyes, and there he held them, awaiting in silence what further might occur. He could now dimly discern the aperture—a square of lighter black. Presently there appeared at its lower edge two gleaming eyes that burned with a malignant luster inexpressibly terrible! Brading's heart gave a great jump, then seemed to stand still. A chill passed along his spine and through his hair; he felt the blood forsake his cheeks. He could not have cried out—not to save his life; but being a man of courage he would not, to save his life, have done so if he had been able. Some trepidation his coward body might feel, but his spirit was of sterner stuff. Slowly the shining eyes rose with a steady motion that seemed an approach, and slowly rose Brading's right hand, holding the pistol. He fired!

Blinded by the flash and stunned by the report, Brading nevertheless heard, or fancied that he heard, the wild high scream of the panther, so human in sound, so devilish in suggestion. Leaping from the bed he hastily clothed himself and pistol in hand, sprang from the door, meeting two or three men who came running up from the road. A brief explanation was followed by a cautious search of the house. The grass was wet with dew; beneath the window it had been trodden and partly leveled for a wide space, from which a devious trail, visible in the light of a lantern, led away into the bushes. One of the men stumbled and fell upon his hands, which as he rose and rubbed them together were slippery. On examination they were seen to be red with blood.

An encounter, unarmed, with a wounded panther was not agreeable to their taste; all but Brading turned back. He, with lantern and pistol, pushed courageously forward into the wood. Passing through a difficult undergrowth he came into a small opening, and there his courage had its reward, for there he found the body of his victim. But it was no panther. What it was is told, even to this day, upon a weather-worn headstone in the village churchyard, and for many years was attested daily at the graveside by the bent figure and sorrow-seamed face of Old Man Marlowe, to whose soul, and to the soul of his strange, unhappy child, peace—peace and reparation.

PHOTOGRAPHING INVISIBLE BEINGS

By Wm. T. Stead

"Millions of Spiritual creatures walk the earth
Unseen, both when we wake and when we sleep."

—Milton

It was during the South African War that my father obtained one of his best authenticated spirit photographs, so I think that it is well to give here his own account of his experiments in that direction. He writes:

"While recording the results at which I have arrived, I wish to repudiate any desire to dogmatize as to their significance or their origin. I merely record the facts, and although I may indicate conclusions and inferences which I have drawn from them, I attach no importance to anything but the facts themselves.

"There is living in London at the present moment an old man of seventy-one years of age, a man of no education; he can write, but he cannot spell, and he has for many years earned his living as a photographer. He was always in a small way of business, a quiet, inoffensive man who brought up his family respectably, and lived in peace with his neighbors, attracting no particular remark....

"When he started in business as a photographer it was in the days when the wet process was almost universal, and he was much annoyed by finding that when he exposed plates other forms than that of the sitter would appear in the background. So many plates were spoiled by these unwelcome intruders that his partner became very angry, and insisted that the plates had not been washed before they were used. He protested this was not so, and asked his partner to bring a packet of completely new plates with which he would take a photograph and see what was the result. His partner accepted the challenge, and produced a plate which had never previously been used; but when the portrait of the next sitter was taken, there appeared a shadow form in the background. Angry and frightened at this unwelcome appearance he flung the plate to the ground with an oath, and from that time for very many years he was never again troubled by an occurrence of similar phenomena.

"About ten years ago he became interested in spiritualism, and to his surprise, and also to his regret, the shadow figures began to re-appear on the background of the photographs. He repeatedly had to destroy negatives and ask his customer to give him another sitting. It did his business harm, and in order to avoid this annoyance he left most of the photographing to his son.

"I happened to hear of these curious experiences of his and sought him out. I found him very reluctant to speak about the matter. He said frankly he did not know how the figures came; it had been a great annoyance to him, and it gave his shop a bad name. He did not wish anything to be said about the matter. In deference, however, to repeated pressing on my part, he consented to make experiments with me, and I had at various times a considerable number of sittings.

"At first I brought my own plates (half plate size). He allowed me to place them in his slide in the dark room, to put them in the camera, which I was allowed to turn inside-out, and after they were exposed I was permitted to go into the dark room and develop them in his presence. Under these conditions I repeatedly obtained pictures of persons who were certainly not visible to me in the studio. I was allowed to do almost anything that I pleased, to alter the background, to change the position of the camera, to sit at any angle that I chose—in short to act as if the studio and all belonging to it was my own. And I repeatedly obtained what the old photographer called 'shadow pictures,' but none of them bore any resemblance to any person whom I had known.

"In all these earlier experiments the photographer, whom I will call Mr. B——, made no charge, and the only request that he made was that I should not publish his name, or do anything to let his neighbors know of the curious shadow pictures which were obtainable in his studio.

"After a time I was so thoroughly satisfied that the shadow photographs, or spirit forms, were not produced by any fraud on the part of the photographer, that I did not trouble to bring my own marked plates—I allowed him to use his own, and to do all the work of loading the slide and of developing the plate without my assistance or supervision. What I wanted was to see whether it would be possible for me to obtain a photograph of any person known to me in life who has passed over to the other side. The production of one such picture, if the person was unknown to the photographer, and he had no means of obtaining the photograph of the original while on earth, seemed to me so much better a test of the genuineness of the phenomena than could be secured by any amount of personal supervision of the process of photography, that I left him to operate without interference. The results he obtained when left to himself were precisely the same as those when the slides passed only through my own hands. But, although I obtained a great variety of portraits of unknown persons, I got none whom I could recognize.

"In a conversation with Mr. B— as to how these shadow pictures, as he called them, came on the plate, I found him almost as much at sea as myself. He said that he did not know how they came, but that he had noticed that they came more frequently and with greater distinctness at some times than at others. He could never say beforehand whether they would come or not. He frequently informed me when my sitting began that he could guarantee nothing. And often the set of plates would bear no trace of any portrait save mine.

"He was very reluctant to continue the experiments, and used to complain that after exposing four plates with a view to obtaining such pictures he felt quite exhausted. And sometimes he complained that his 'innards seemed to be turned upside-down,' to use his own phrase. I usually sat with him between two and three in the afternoon, and on the days which I came he always abstained from the usual glass of beer which he took with his midday meal. If I came unexpectedly, and he had had a single glass of beer, which formed his usual beverage, he would always assure me that I need not expect any good results. I, however, never found any particular difference in the results.

"We often discussed the matter together. And he was evidently working out a theory of his own, as any one might under such circumstances. He knew that when he was excited or irritated he got bad results. Hence he often used to keep a music-box going, for the music, in his opinion, tended to set up good and tranquil conditions. He said he thought something must come out of him—what, he did not know, but something was taken out of him, and with this something he thought the entities, whoever they were, built themselves up and acquired sufficient substance to reflect the rays of light so as to impress the sensitive plate in his camera. He also thought that his old camera had become what he called magnetized, and although it was an old-fashioned piece of furniture, which I not only examined myself, but have had examined by expert photographers, nothing could be discovered within or without it which would account for the results obtained. He also was of the opinion that even although he did not touch the photographic plate, it was necessary for him to touch or to hold his hand over the photographic slide, and also to hold his hand over the plate when it was in the developing bath. His theory was that in some way or other this process magnetized the plate and brought out a shadow portrait.

"One peculiarity of almost all the shadow pictures obtained in all these series of experiments is that they have around them the same kind of white drapery which is so familiar to those who have taken part in a materializing séance. Sometimes this drapery is more voluminous than at others; often, when the conditions are good, the form which at first appears with its head encompassed with drapery will appear on the second plate without any drapery. On asking Mr. B— what explanation he could give for this, he said he did not know, but he believed that the bodily appearance assumed by the spirit was very sensitive and needed to be shielded from currents, which might harm it. But when harmony prevailed they could venture to remove the drapery, and be photographed without it. Whatever may be the value of Mr. B—'s theory, there is little doubt that something is given off from his body which can be photographed. The white mist that appears to emanate from him forms into cloudy folds out of which there protrudes a more or less clearly defined face with human features. Sometimes this white and misty cloud obscures the sitter, at other times it seems to be condensed as if it were in the process of being worked up into a definite form for the completion of which either time or some other conditions were lacking. It was also noticeable that the entity—whoever it may be—which builds up the form, who is giving off sufficient solidity to impress its image upon the plate in the camera, having once created a form, will use it repeatedly without any change of position or expression. This will no doubt seem a great stumbling-block to many. But the fact is as I have stated it, and our first business is to ascertain facts, whether they tell for or against any particular hypothesis. It may be that the disembodied spirit, in order to establish its identity, constructs, out of the 'aura' given off by the photographer or other medium, a mask or cast bearing the unmistakable resemblance to the body which it wore in its sojourn on earth. Having once built it up for use in the studio, it may be easier to employ the same cast again and again instead of building up a new one at each fresh sitting. Upon this point, however, I shall have something to say further on.

"I was very much interested in the results I obtained, although as none of the photographs were identified I did not deem the experiment completely successful. I was very anxious to induce Mr. B— to devote some months to an uninterrupted series of experiments, and asked him on what terms I could secure his services. But he absolutely refused; he said he did not like it, it made him unwell, made people speak ill of him, and it did not matter what terms were offered, he would not consent. He was an old man, he said, and he could not find out how these things came; and, in short, neither scientific curiosity nor financial consideration would induce him to consent to more than an occasional sitting. I therefore dropped the matter, and for some years I discontinued my experiments.

"I had a friend who often accompanied me to Mr. B—'s studio, where she had been photographed both with and without shadow pictures appearing on the background. We often promised each other that if either of us passed over we would come back and be photographed by Mr. B— if possible, in order to prove the reality of spirit return. Shortly after this my friend died. But it was not until nearly four years after her death, at the request of a friend who was very anxious to know whether she could communicate with those on the other side, that I went back to Mr. B—'s studio.

"He had always been slightly clairvoyant and clairaudient. He told me that a few days before I had written asking for the appointment, my deceased friend had appeared in the studio and told him that I was coming. This reminded me of her promise, and I said at once that I hoped he would be able to photograph her. He said he didn't know; he was rather frightened of her, for reasons into which I need not enter, but if she came he would see what he could do. My friend and I sat together. The first plate was exposed, nothing appeared in the background. When the second plate was placed in the camera Mr. B— nodded with a quick look of recognition. We saw nothing. After he had exposed the second plate and before he developed it he asked us to change seats. We did this, and as he was exposing the third plate he said, 'I am told to ask you to do this,' and then when he closed the shutter he said, 'it is Mrs. M—.' On the fourth plate there appeared a picture of a woman whom I had never seen before, and whom my friend had never seen, neither had Mr. B—. When the plates came to be developed I found the second and third plates contained unmistakable likenesses of my friend Mrs. M—. These portraits were immediately recognized by my friend as unmistakable likenesses of the deceased Mrs. M—. It will be objected that she had frequently been photographed by the same photographer, and that he had simply faked a photograph from one of his old negatives. I don't believe that this is possible, for these portraits, although recognized immediately by every one who knew her, including her nearest relative, are quite different from any photograph she ever had taken in life. She certainly never was photographed enveloped in white drapery, nor do I believe that Mr. B— had any negative of any of her portraits in his possession. But I fully admit that from the point of view of one who wishes to exclude every possibility of error, the fact that Mrs. M— had been frequently photographed in her lifetime by the same photographer renders it impossible to regard these photographs as conclusive testimony as to their authenticity as a photograph of a form assumed by a disembodied spirit. I have mentioned that on the fourth plate there appeared a portrait of an unknown female. On my return I was showing the print of this shadow picture to a friend when she startled me by declaring that the shrouded form which appeared behind me in the photograph was a portrait of her mother who had died some months before in Dublin. I had never seen her mother, my friend did not know of her existence, neither did the photographer, nor does he to this day. It was only many months afterwards that I was able to obtain a photograph of my friend's mother, but it was taken when she was a comparatively young woman and bore no manner of resemblance to the portrait of the lady who appeared behind me. Her daughter, however, had not the slightest hesitation in asserting that it was her mother, that she had recognized her instantly, and that it was a very good portrait of her as she appeared in the later years of her life. This startled me not a little, and convinced me that I had a good prospect of attaining some definite results as an outcome of my experiments.

"Mr. B—, encouraged by this success, was willing to continue his experiments, and this time I insisted upon paying him for his work.

"From this time onward the occurrence of photographs that were recognizable on the background of the photographs taken by Mr. B— became frequent. Sometimes the plates were marked; but not invariably. For my part I attach comparatively no importance to the marking of plates and the close supervision of the operator. The test of the genuineness of a photograph that is obtained when the unknown relative of an unknown sitter appears in the background of the photograph, is immeasurably superior to precautions any expert conjurer or trick photographer might evade. Again and again I sent friends to Mr. B—, giving him no information as to who they were, nor telling him anything as to the identity of the persons' deceased friend or relative whose portrait they wished to secure; and time and again when the negative was developed the portrait would appear in the background, or sometimes in front of the sitter. This occurred so frequently that I am quite convinced of the impossibility of any fraud. One time it was a French editor, who finding the portrait of his deceased wife appear on the negative when developed, was so transported with delight that he insisted on kissing the photographer, Mr. B—, much to the old man's embarrassment. On another occasion it was a Lancashire engineer, himself a photographer, who took marked plates and all possible precautions. He obtained portraits of two of his relatives and another of an eminent personage with whom he had been in close relations. Or again, it was a near neighbor, who, going as a total stranger to the studio, obtained the portrait of her deceased daughter.

"I attach no importance whatever to the appearance of portraits of well-known personages, which might easily be copied from existing pictures, but I attach immense importance to the production of the spirit photographs of unknown relatives of sitters who are unknown to the photographer, who receives them solely as a lady or gentleman who is one of my friends.

"Although, as I have said, I do not attach much importance to photographs appearing of well-known men, I confess that I was rather impressed by one of my most recent experiments. I received a message from a medium in Sheffield, who is unknown to me, saying that Cecil Rhodes, who had then been dead about nine months, had spoken to her clairaudiently, and had told her to ask me to go to the photographer's, and that he would come and be photographed. The medium was a stranger to me, and I confess that I received the message with considerable skepticism. However, when she came up to town I accompanied her to the studio. She declared that she saw Cecil Rhodes, and that he spoke to her, and that he was standing behind me when the plate was exposed. When the plate came to be developed, although there was one well-defined figure standing behind me and several other faces half visible in the background, there was no portrait of Cecil Rhodes. I was not surprised, and went away. A month afterwards I went to have another sitting with the photographer. I chatted with him for a short time, and then he left the room for a moment. When he came back he said to me: 'There is a round-faced well set-up man here with a short moustache and a dimple in his chin. Do you know him?' 'No,' I said, 'I don't know any such man.' 'Well, he seems to be very busy about you.' 'Well,' I said, 'if he comes upstairs, we shall see what we can get.' 'I don't know,' said he. When I was sitting, he said, 'There he is, and I see the letter R. Is it Robert or Richard, do you think?' 'I don't know any Robert or Richard,' I said. He took the picture. He then proceeded with the second plate, and said, 'That man is still here, and I see behind him a country road. I wonder what that means.' He went into the dark room, and presently came out and said, 'I see "road or roads." Do you know any one of that name?' 'Of course,' I said, 'Cecil Rhodes.' 'Do you mean him as died in the Transvaal lately?' said he. I said 'Yes.' 'Well,' he said, 'was he a man like that?' 'Well, he had a moustache,' I said. And sure enough, when the plate was developed, there was Cecil Rhodes looking fifteen years younger than when he died.

"Some other plates were exposed. One was entirely blank, on

two others the mist was formed into a kind of clot of light, but no figure was visible, the fifth had a portrait of an unknown man, and on the sixth, when it came to be developed, there was the same portrait of Cecil Rhodes that had appeared on the first, but without the white drapery round the head.

"Of course it may be said that it was well known that I was connected with Cecil Rhodes and that the photographer therefore would have no difficulty in faking a portrait. I admit all that, and therefore I would not have introduced this if it had stood alone, as any evidence showing that it was a bona fide photograph of an invisible being. But it does not stand alone, and I have almost every reason to believe in the almost stupid honesty, if I may use such a phrase, of the photographer. I am naturally much interested in these latest portraits of the African Colossus. They are, at any rate, entirely new, no such portraits, to the best of my knowledge—and I have made a collection of all I can lay my hands on—exactly resembling those portraits which I obtained at Mr. B—'s studio.

"I will conclude the account of my experiments by telling how I secured a portrait under circumstances which preclude any possibility of fake or fraud. One day when I entered the studio, Mr. B— said to me, 'There is a man come with you who has been here before; he came here some days ago when I was by myself; he looked very wild, and he had a gun in his hand, and I did not like the look of him. I don't like guns, so I asked him to go away, for I was frightened of the gun, and he went. But now he has come with you, and he has not got his gun any more, so we will let him stop.' I was rather amused at the old man's story and said, 'Well, see if you can photograph him.' 'I don't know as I can,' he said, 'I never know what I can get,'—which is quite true, for often the photographs which he says he sees clairvoyantly do not come out on the plate. While he was photographing me, I said to him, 'If you can tell this man to go away, you can ask him his name.' 'Yes,' said he. 'Will you do so?' I said. 'Yes,' he said. After seeming to ask the question mentally, he said, 'He says his name is Piet Botha.' 'Piet Botha,' I said, 'I know no such name. There are Louis and Philip, and Chris Botha. I have never heard of Piet; still they are a numerous family and there are plenty of Bothas in South Africa, and it will be interesting to ask General Botha, when he arrives, whether he knows of any Piet Botha.' When the negative was developed, sure enough there appeared behind me a photograph of a stalwart bearded person, who might have been a Boer or a Russian moujik, but who was certainly unknown to me. I had never seen a portrait of any one which bore any resemblance to the photograph.

"When General Botha arrived I did not get an opportunity of

asking him about the photograph, but some time afterwards I asked Mr. Fischer, one of the delegation from the South African Republics, to look at the photograph, and if he got an opportunity to ask General Botha if he knew of such a man as Piet Botha. Mr. Fischer said he thought he had seen the face before, but he could not be certain. He departed with the photograph. Some days afterwards Mr. Wessels, a member of the delegation with Mr. Fischer, came down to my office. He said, 'I want to know about that photograph that you gave Mr. Fischer.' 'Yes,' I said, 'what about it?' 'I want to know where you got it.' I told him. He replied disdainfully, 'I don't believe in such things; it is superstition; besides, that man didn't know Mr. B—; he has never been in London; how could he come there?' 'What,' I said, 'do you know him?' 'Know him!' said Mr. Wessels. 'He is my brother-in-law.' 'Really!' I said. 'What did they call him?' 'Pietrus Johannes Botha, but we always called him Piet for short.' 'Is he dead, then?' I said. 'Yes,' said Mr. Wessels, 'he was the first Boer officer who was killed in the siege of Kimberley; but there is a mystery about this; you didn't know him?' 'No,' I said. 'And never heard of him?' 'No,' I said. 'But,' he said, 'I have the man's portrait in my house in South Africa, how could you get it?' 'But,' I said, 'I never have had it.' 'I don't understand,' he said, moodily, and so departed. I afterwards showed the photograph to another Free-State Boer who knew Piet Botha very well, and he had not the slightest hesitation in declaring that it was an unmistakable likeness of his dead friend.[8]

"This is a plain, straightforward narrative of my experiences; they are still going on. But if I continue them forever I don't see how I am going to obtain better results than those which I have already secured. At the same time I must admit that when I have taken my own kodak to the studio and taken a photograph immediately before Mr. B— had exposed his plate, I got no results. The same failure occurred with another photographer whom I took, who took

---

[8] Referring to this photo elsewhere, he wrote:—"This at least is not a case which telepathy can explain. Nor can the hypothesis of fraud hold water. It was by the merest accident that I asked the photographer to see if the spirit would give his name. No one in England, so far as I have been able to ascertain, knew that any Piet Botha ever existed.

"As if to render all explanation of fraud or contrivance still more incredible, it may be mentioned that the Daily Graphic of October, 1889, which announced that a Commandant Botha had been killed in the siege of Kimberley, published a portrait alleged to be that of the dead commandant, which not only does not bear the remotest resemblance to the Piet Botha of my photograph, but which was described as Commandant Hans Botha!"

his own camera and his own plates, and took a photograph immediately before and immediately after Mr. B— had exposed his plate, and secured no result. Mr. B—'s explanation of this is that he thinks he does in some way or other magnetize, as he terms it, the plate, and that there is some effluence from his hand which is as necessary for the development of the psychic figure as the developing liquid is for the development of an ordinary photograph. This explanation would no doubt be derided as, I presume, wiseacres would have derided the first photographers when they insisted upon the necessity of darkness whilst developing their plates. What I hold to be established is that in the presence of this particular individual, Mr. B—, who at present is the only person known to me who is able to produce these photographs, it is possible to obtain under test conditions photographs that are unmistakably portraits of deceased persons; the said deceased persons being entirely unknown to him, and in some cases equally unknown to the sitter. Neither was any portrait of such person accessible either to the sitter or the photographer; neither was either the sitter or the photographer conscious of the very existence of these persons, whose identity was subsequently recognized by their friends.[9]

"I am willing to admit that no conceivable conditions in the way of marking plates and supervising the actions or the operations of the photographer are of the least use, in so much as an expert conjurer can easily deceive the eye of the unskilled observer. But what I do maintain is that it is impossible for the cleverest trick photographer and the ablest conjurer in the world to produce a photograph, at a moment's notice, of an unknown relative of an unknown sitter, this portrait to be unmistakably recognizable by all survivors who knew the original in life. This Mr. B— has done again and again. And it seems to me that a great step has been made towards establishing the possibility of verifying by photography the reality of the existence of other intelligences than our own."

The photographer alluded to in this article is Mr. Boursnell. He died shortly after it was written, and although father experimented with others, he never obtained such convincing and satisfactory results.

---

9 Miss Katharine Bates was present when the Piet Botha photograph was taken under the exact conditions specified by my father.

THE SIN-EATER

By Fiona Macleod

Sin.

Taste this bread, this substance: tell me
Is it bread or flesh?

[The Senses approach.]

The Smell.

Its smell Is the smell of bread.
Sin.

Touch, come. Why tremble? Say what's this thou touchest?
The Touch.

Bread.

Sin.
Sight, declare what thou discernest In this object.

The Sight.

Bread alone.

—Calderon,
Los Encantos de la Culpa

A wet wind out of the south mazed and mooned through the sea-mist that hung over the Ross. In all the bays and creeks was a continuous weary lapping of water. There was no other sound anywhere.

Thus was it at daybreak; it was thus at noon; thus was it now in the darkening of the day. A confused thrusting and falling of sounds through the silence betokened the hour of the setting. Curlews wailed in the mist; on the seething limpet-covered rocks the skuas and terns screamed, or uttered hoarse, rasping cries. Ever and again the prolonged note of the oyster-catcher shrilled against the air, as an echo flying blindly along a blank wall of cliff. Out of weedy places, wherein the tide sobbed with long, gurgling moans, came at intervals the barking of a seal.

Inland, by the hamlet of Contullich, there is a reedy tarn called the Loch-a-chaoruinn.[10] By the shores of this mournful water a man moved. It was a slow, weary walk that of the man Neil Ross. He had come from Duninch, thirty miles to the eastward, and had not rested foot, nor eaten, nor had word of man or woman, since his going west an hour after dawn.

At the bend of the loch nearest the clachan he came upon an old woman carrying peat. To his reiterated question as to where he was, and if the tarn were Feur-Lochan above Fionnaphort that is on the strait of Iona on the west side of the Ross of Mull, she did not at first make any answer. The rain trickled down her withered brown face, over which the thin gray locks hung limply. It was only in the deep-set eyes that the flame of life still glimmered, though that dimly.

The man had used the English when first he spoke, but as though mechanically. Supposing that he had not been understood, he repeated his question in the Gaelic.

After a minute's silence the old woman answered him in the native tongue, but only to put a question in return.

"I am thinking it is a long time since you have been in Iona?"

The man stirred uneasily.

"And why is that, mother?" he asked, in a weak voice hoarse with damp and fatigue; "how is it you will be knowing that I have been in Iona at all?"

"Because I knew your kith and kin there, Neil Ross."

"I have not been hearing that name, mother, for many a long year. And as for the old face o' you, it is unbeknown to me."

"I was at the naming of you, for all that. Well do I remember the day that Silis Macallum gave you birth; and I was at the house on the croft of Ballyrona when Murtagh Ross—that was your father—laughed. It was an ill laughing that."

"I am knowing it. The curse of God on him!"

"'Tis not the first, nor the last, though the grass is on his head three years agone now."

"You that know who I am will be knowing that I have no kith or kin now on Iona?"

"Ay; they are all under gray stone or running wave. Donald your brother, and Murtagh your next brother, and little Silis, and your mother Silis herself, and your two brothers of your father,

---

10 Contullich: i.e. Ceann-nan-tulaich, "the end of the hillocks." Loch a chaoruinn means the loch of the rowan-trees.

Angus and Ian Macallum, and your father Murtagh Ross, and his lawful childless wife, Dionaid, and his sister Anna—one and all, they lie beneath the green wave or in the brown mould. It is said there is a curse upon all who live at Ballyrona. The owl builds now in the rafters, and it is the big sea-rat that runs across the fireless hearth."

"It is there I am going."

"The foolishness is on you, Neil Ross."

"Now it is that I am knowing who you are. It is old Sheen Macarthur I am speaking to."

"Tha mise ... it is I."

"And you will be alone now, too, I am thinking, Sheen?"

"I am alone. God took my three boys at the one fishing ten years ago; and before there was moonrise in the blackness of my heart my man went. It was after the drowning of Anndra that my croft was taken from me. Then I crossed the Sound, and shared with my widow sister Elsie McVurie till she went; and then the two cows had to go; and I had no rent, and was old."

In the silence that followed, the rain dribbled from the sodden bracken and dripping loneroid. Big tears rolled slowly down the deep lines on the face of Sheen. Once there was a sob in her throat, but she put her shaking hand to it, and it was still.

Neil Ross shifted from foot to foot. The ooze in that marshy place squelched with each restless movement he made. Beyond them a plover wheeled, a blurred splatch in the mist, crying its mournful cry over and over and over.

It was a pitiful thing to hear—ah, bitter loneliness, bitter patience of poor old women. That he knew well. But he was too weary, and his heart was nigh full of its own burthen. The words could not come to his lips. But at last he spoke.

"Tha mo chridhe goirt," he said, with tears in his voice, as he put his hand on her bent shoulder; "my heart is sore."

She put up her old face against his.

"'S tha e ruidhinn mo chridhe," she whispered; "it is touching my heart you are."

After that they walked on slowly through the dripping mist, each dumb and brooding deep.

"Where will you be staying this night?" asked Sheen suddenly, when they had traversed a wide boggy stretch of land; adding, as by an afterthought—"Ah, it is asking you were if the tarn there were Feur-Lochan. No; it is Loch-a-chaoruinn, and the clachan that is near is Contullich."

"Which way?"

"Yonder, to the right."

"And you are not going there?"

"No. I am going to the steading of Andrew Blair. Maybe you are for knowing it? It is called the Baile-na-Chlais-nambuidheag."[11]

"I do not remember. But it is remembering a Blair I am. He was Adam, the son of Adam, the son of Robert. He and my father did many an ill deed together."

"Ay, to the stones be it said. Sure, now, there was, even till this weary day, no man or woman who had a good word for Adam Blair."

"And why that ... why till this day?"

"It is not yet the third hour since he went into the silence."

Neil Ross uttered a sound like a stifled curse. For a time he trudged wearily on.

"Then I am too late," he said at last, but as though speaking to himself. "I had hoped to see him face to face again, and curse him between the eyes. It was he who made Murtagh Ross break his troth to my mother, and marry that other woman, barren at that, God be praised! And they say ill of him, do they?"

"Ay, it is evil that is upon him. This crime and that, God knows; and the shadow of murder on his brow and in his eyes. Well, well, 'tis ill to be speaking of a man in corpse, and that near by. 'Tis Himself only that knows, Neil Ross."

"Maybe ay and maybe no. But where is it that I can be sleeping this night, Sheen Macarthur?"

"They will not be taking a stranger at the farm this night of the nights, I am thinking. There is no place else for seven miles yet, when there is the clachan, before you will be coming to Fionnaphort. There is the warm byre, Neil, my man; or, if you can bide by my peats, you may rest, and welcome, though there is no bed for you, and no food either save some of the porridge that is over."

"And that will do well enough for me, Sheen; and Himself bless you for it."

And so it was.

After old Sheen Macarthur had given the wayfarer food—poor food at that, but welcome to one nigh starved, and for the heartsome way it was given, and because of the thanks to God that was upon it before even spoon was lifted—she told him a lie. It was the good lie of tender love.

"Sure now, after all, Neil, my man," she said, "it is sleeping at the farm I ought to be, for Maisie Macdonald, the wise woman, will be sitting by the corpse, and there will be none to keep her company. It is there I must be going; and if I am weary, there is a good bed for me just beyond the dead-board, which I am not

---

[11] "The farm in the hollow of the yellow flowers."

minding at all. So, if it is tired you are sitting by the peats, lie down on my bed there, and have the sleep; and God be with you."

With that she went, and soundlessly, for Neil Ross was already asleep, where he sat on an upturned claar, with his elbows on his knees, and his flame-lit face in his hands.

The rain had ceased; but the mist still hung over the land, though in thin veils now, and these slowly drifting seaward. Sheen stepped wearily along the stony path that led from her bothy to the farm-house. She stood still once, the fear upon her, for she saw three or four blurred yellow gleams moving beyond her, eastward, along the dyke. She knew what they were—the corpse-lights that on the night of death go between the bier and the place of burial. More than once she had seen them before the last hour, and by that token had known the end to be near.

Good Catholic that she was, she crossed herself, and took heart. Then muttering

"Crois nan naoi aingeal leam
'O mhullach mo chinn Gu craican mo bhonn."

(The cross of the nine angels be about me,
From the top of my head
To the soles of my feet),

she went on her way fearlessly.

When she came to the White House, she entered by the milk-shed that was between the byre and the kitchen. At the end of it was a paved place, with washing-tubs. At one of these stood a girl that served in the house—an ignorant lass called Jessie McFall, out of Oban. She was ignorant, indeed, not to know that to wash clothes with a newly dead body near by was an ill thing to do. Was it not a matter for the knowing that the corpse could hear, and might rise up in the night and clothe itself in a clean white shroud?

She was still speaking to the lassie when Maisie Macdonald, the deid-watcher, opened the door of the room behind the kitchen to see who it was that was come. The two old women nodded silently. It was not till Sheen was in the closed room, midway in which something covered with a sheet lay on a board, that any word was spoken.

"Duit sìth mòr, Beann Macdonald."

"And deep peace to you, too, Sheen; and to him that is there."

"Och, ochone, mise 'n diugh; 'tis a dark hour this."

"Ay; it is bad. Will you have been hearing or seeing anything?"

"Well, as for that, I am thinking I saw lights moving betwixt here and the green place over there."

"The corpse-lights?"

"Well, it is calling them that they are."

"I thought they would be out. And I have been hearing the noise of the planks—the cracking of the boards, you know, that will be used for the coffin to-morrow."

A long silence followed. The old women had seated themselves by the corpse, their cloaks over their heads. The room was fireless, and was lit only by a tall wax death-candle, kept against the hour of the going.

At last Sheen began swaying slowly to and fro, crooning low the while. "I would not be for doing that, Sheen Macarthur," said the deid-watcher in a low voice, but meaningly; adding, after a moment's pause, "The mice have all left the house."

Sheen sat upright, a look half of terror, half of awe in her eyes.

"God save the sinful soul that is hiding," she whispered.

Well she knew what Maisie meant. If the soul of the dead be a lost soul it knows its doom. The house of death is the house of sanctuary; but before the dawn that follows the death-night the soul must go forth, whosoever or whatsoever wait for it in the homeless, shelterless plains of air around and beyond. If it be well with the soul, it need have no fear; if it be not ill with the soul, it may fare forth with surety; but if it be ill with the soul, ill will the going be. Thus is it that the spirit of an evil man cannot stay, and yet dare not go; and so it strives to hide itself in secret places anywhere, in dark channels and blind walls; and the wise creatures that live near man smell the terror, and flee. Maisie repeated the saying of Sheen, then, after a silence, added:

"Adam Blair will not lie in his grave for a year and a day because of the sins that are upon him; and it is knowing that, they are here. He will be the Watcher of the Dead for a year and a day."

"Ay, sure, there will be dark prints in the dawn-dew over yonder."

Once more the old women relapsed into silence. Through the night there was a sighing sound. It was not the sea, which was too far off to be heard save in a day of storm. The wind it was, that was dragging itself across the sodden moors like a wounded thing, moaning and sighing.

Out of sheer weariness, Sheen twice rocked forward from her stool, heavy with sleep. At last Maisie led her over to the niche-bed opposite, and laid her down there, and waited till the deep furrows in the face relaxed somewhat, and the thin breath labored slow across the fallen jaw.

"Poor old woman," she muttered, heedless of her own gray

hairs and grayer years; "a bitter, bad thing it is to be old, old and weary. 'Tis the sorrow, that. God keep the pain of it!"

As for herself, she did not sleep at all that night, but sat between the living and the dead, with her plaid shrouding her. Once, when Sheen gave a low, terrified scream in her sleep, she rose, and in a loud voice cried, "Sheeach-ad! Away with you!" And with that she lifted the shroud from the dead man, and took the pennies off the eyelids, and lifted each lid; then, staring into these filmed wells, muttered an ancient incantation that would compel the soul of Adam Blair to leave the spirit of Sheen alone, and return to the cold corpse that was its coffin till the wood was ready.

The dawn came at last. Sheen slept, and Adam Blair slept a deeper sleep, and Maisie stared out of her wan, weary eyes against the red and stormy flares of light that came into the sky.

When, an hour after sunrise, Sheen Macarthur reached her bothy, she found Neil Ross, heavy with slumber, upon her bed. The fire was not out, though no flame or spark was visible; but she stooped and blew at the heart of the peats till the redness came, and once it came it grew. Having done this, she kneeled and said a rune of the morning, and after that a prayer, and then a prayer for the poor man Neil. She could pray no more because of the tears. She rose and put the meal and water into the pot for the porridge to be ready against his awaking. One of the hens that was there came and pecked at her ragged skirt. "Poor beastie," she said. "Sure, that will just be the way I am pulling at the white robe of the Mother o' God. 'Tis a bit meal for you, cluckie, and for me a healing hand upon my tears. O, och, ochone, the tears, the tears!"

It was not till the third hour after sunrise of that bleak day in that winter of the winters, that Neil Ross stirred and arose. He ate in silence. Once he said that he smelt the snow coming out of the north. Sheen said no word at all.

After the porridge, he took his pipe, but there was no tobacco. All that Sheen had was the pipeful she kept against the gloom of the Sabbath. It was her one solace in the long weary week. She gave him this, and held a burning peat to his mouth, and hungered over the thin, rank smoke that curled upward.

It was within half-an-hour of noon that, after an absence, she returned.

"Not between you and me, Neil Ross," she began abruptly, "but just for the asking, and what is beyond. Is it any money you are having upon you?"

"No."

"Nothing?"

"Nothing."

"Then how will you be getting across to Iona? It is seven long miles to Fionnaphort, and bitter cold at that, and you will be needing food, and then the ferry, the ferry across the Sound, you know."

"Ay, I know."

"What would you do for a silver piece, Neil, my man?"

"You have none to give me, Sheen Macarthur; and, if you had, it would not be taking it I would."

"Would you kiss a dead man for a crown-piece—a crown-piece of five good shillings?"

Neil Ross stared. Then he sprang to his feet.

"It is Adam Blair you are meaning, woman! God curse him in death now that he is no longer in life!"

Then, shaking and trembling, he sat down again, and brooded against the dull red glow of the peats.

But, when he rose, in the last quarter before noon, his face was white.

"The dead are dead, Sheen Macarthur. They can know or do nothing. I will do it. It is willed. Yes, I am going up to the house there. And now I am going from here. God Himself has my thanks to you, and my blessing too. They will come back to you. It is not forgetting you I will be. Good-bye."

"Good-bye, Neil, son of the woman that was my friend. A south wind to you! Go up by the farm. In the front of the house you will see what you will be seeing. Maisie Macdonald will be there. She will tell you what's for the telling. There is no harm in it, sure; sure, the dead are dead. It is praying for you I will be, Neil Ross. Peace to you!"

"And to you, Sheen."

And with that the man went.

When Neil Ross reached the byres of the farm in the wide hollow, he saw two figures standing as though awaiting him, but separate, and unseen of the other. In front of the house was a man he knew to be Andrew Blair; behind the milk-shed was a woman he guessed to be Maisie Macdonald.

It was the woman he came upon first.

"Are you the friend of Sheen Macarthur?" she asked in a whisper, as she beckoned him to the doorway.

"I am."

"I am knowing no names or anything. And no one here will know you, I am thinking. So do the thing and begone."

"There is no harm to it?"

"None."

"It will be a thing often done, is it not?"

"Ay, sure."

"And the evil does not abide?"

"No. The ... the ... person ... the person takes them away, and...."

"Them?"

"For sure, man! Them ... the sins of the corpse. He takes them away; and are you for thinking God would let the innocent suffer for the guilty? No ... the person ... the Sin-Eater, you know ... takes them away on himself, and one by one the air of heaven washes them away till he, the Sin-Eater, is clean and whole as before."

"But if it is a man you hate ... if it is a corpse that is the corpse of one who has been a curse and a foe ... if...."

"Sst! Be still now with your foolishness. It is only an idle saying, I am thinking. Do it, and take the money and go. It will be hell enough for Adam Blair, miser as he was, if he is for knowing that five good shillings of his money are to go to a passing tramp because of an old, ancient silly tale."

Neil Ross laughed low at that. It was for pleasure to him.

"Hush wi' ye! Andrew Blair is waiting round there. Say that I have sent you round, as I have neither bite nor bit to give."

Turning on his heel, Neil walked slowly round to the front of the house. A tall man was there, gaunt and brown, with hairless face and lank brown hair, but with eyes cold and gray as the sea.

"Good day to you, an' good faring. Will you be passing this way to anywhere?"

"Health to you. I am a stranger here. It is on my way to Iona I am. But I have the hunger upon me. There is not a brown bit in my pocket. I asked at the door there, near the byres. The woman told me she could give me nothing—not a penny even, worse luck—nor, for that, a drink of warm milk. 'Tis a sore land this."

"You have the Gaelic of the Isles. Is it from Iona you are?"

"It is from the Isles of the West I come."

"From Tiree ... from Coll?"

"No."

"From the Long Island ... or from Uist ... or maybe from Benbecula?"

"No."

"Oh well, sure it is no matter to me. But may I be asking your name?"

"Macallum."

"Do you know there is a death here, Macallum?"

"If I didn't I would know it now, because of what lies yonder."

Mechanically Andrew Blair looked round. As he knew, a rough bier was there, that was made of a dead-board laid upon three milking-stools. Beside it was a claar, a small tub to hold potatoes. On the bier was a corpse, covered with a canvas sheeting that looked like a sail.

"He was a worthy man, my father," began the son of the dead man, slowly; "but he had his faults, like all of us. I might even be saying that he had his sins, to the Stones be it said. You will be knowing, Macallum, what is thought among the folk ... that a stranger, passing by, may take away the sins of the dead, and that, too, without any hurt whatever ... any hurt whatever."

"Ay, sure."

"And you will be knowing what is done?"

"Ay."

"With the bread ... and the water...?"

"Ay."

"It is a small thing to do. It is a Christian thing. I would be doing it myself, and that gladly, but the ... the ... passer-by who...."

"It is talking of the Sin-Eater you are?"

"Yes, yes, for sure. The Sin-Eater as he is called—and a good Christian act it is, for all that the ministers and the priests make a frowning at it—the Sin-Eater must be a stranger. He must be a stranger, and should know nothing of the dead man—above all, bear him no grudge."

At that Neil Ross's eyes lightened for a moment.

"And why that?"

"Who knows? I have heard this, and I have heard that. If the Sin-Eater was hating the dead man he could take the sins and fling them into the sea, and they would be changed into demons of the air that would harry the flying soul till Judgment-Day."

"And how would that thing be done?"

The man spoke with flashing eyes and parted lips, the breath coming swift. Andrew Blair looked at him suspiciously; and hesitated, before, in a cold voice, he spoke again.

"That is all folly, I am thinking, Macallum. Maybe it is all folly, the whole of it. But, see here, I have no time to be talking with you. If you will take the bread and the water you shall have a good meal if you want it, and ... and ... yes, look you, my man, I will be giving you a shilling too, for luck."

"I will have no meal in this house, Anndramhic-Adam; nor will I do this thing unless you will be giving me two silver half-crowns. That is the sum I must have, or no other."

"Two half-crowns! Why, man, for one half-crown...."

"Then be eating the sins o' your father yourself, Andrew Blair! It is going I am."

"Stop, man! Stop, Macallum. See here—I will be giving you what you ask."

"So be it. Is the.... Are you ready?"

"Ay, come this way."

With that the two men turned and moved slowly towards the bier.

In the doorway of the house stood a man and two women; farther in, a woman; and at the window to the left, the serving-wench, Jessie McFall, and two men of the farm. Of those in the doorway, the man was Peter, the half-witted youngest brother of Andrew Blair; the taller and older woman was Catreen, the widow of Adam, the second brother; and the thin, slight woman, with staring eyes and drooping mouth, was Muireall, the wife of Andrew. The old woman behind these was Maisie Macdonald.

Andrew Blair stooped and took a saucer out of the claar. This he put upon the covered breast of the corpse. He stooped again, and brought forth a thick square piece of new-made bread. That also he placed upon the breast of the corpse. Then he stooped again, and with that he emptied a spoonful of salt alongside the bread.

"I must see the corpse," said Neil Ross simply.

"It is not needful, Macallum."

"I must be seeing the corpse, I tell you—and for that, too, the bread and the water should be on the naked breast."

"No, no, man; it...."

But here a voice, that of Maisie the wise woman, came upon them, saying that the man was right, and that the eating of the sins should be done in that way and no other.

With an ill grace the son of the dead man drew back the sheeting. Beneath it, the corpse was in a clean white shirt, a death-gown long ago prepared, that covered him from his neck to his feet, and left only the dusky yellowish face exposed.

While Andrew Blair unfastened the shirt and placed the saucer and the bread and the salt on the breast, the man beside him stood staring fixedly on the frozen features of the corpse. The new laird had to speak to him twice before he heard.

"I am ready. And you, now? What is it you are muttering over against the lips of the dead?"

"It is giving him a message I am. There is no harm in that, sure?"

"Keep to your own folk, Macallum. You are from the West you say, and we are from the North. There can be no messages between you and a Blair of Strathmore, no messages for you to be giving."

"He that lies here knows well the man to whom I am sending a message"—and at this response Andrew Blair scowled darkly. He would fain have sent the man about his business, but he feared he might get no other.

"It is thinking I am that you are not a Macallum at all. I know all of that name in Mull, Iona, Skye, and the near isles. What will the name of your naming be, and of your father, and of his place?"

Whether he really wanted an answer, or whether he sought only to divert the man from his procrastination, his question had a satisfactory result.

"Well, now, it's ready I am, Anndra-mhic-Adam."

With that, Andrew Blair stooped once more and from the claar brought a small jug of water. From this he filled the saucer.

"You know what to say and what to do, Macallum."

There was not one there who did not have a shortened breath because of the mystery that was now before them, and the fearfulness of it. Neil Ross drew himself up, erect, stiff, with white, drawn face. All who waited, save Andrew Blair, thought that the moving of his lips was because of the prayer that was slipping upon them, like the last lapsing of the ebb-tide. But Blair was watching him closely, and knew that it was no prayer which stole out against the blank air that was around the dead.

Slowly Neil Ross extended his right arm. He took a pinch of the salt and put it in the saucer, then took another pinch and sprinkled it upon the bread. His hand shook for a moment as he touched the saucer. But there was no shaking as he raised it towards his lips, or when he held it before him when he spoke.

"With this water that has salt in it, and has lain on thy corpse, O Adam mhic Anndra mhic Adam Mòr, I drink away all the evil that is upon thee...."

There was throbbing silence while he paused.

"... And may it be upon me and not upon thee, if with this water it cannot flow away."

Thereupon, he raised the saucer and passed it thrice round the head of the corpse sunways; and, having done this, lifted it to his lips and drank as much as his mouth would hold. Thereafter he poured the remnant over his left hand, and let it trickle to the ground. Then he took the piece of bread. Thrice, too, he passed it round the head of the corpse sunways.

He turned and looked at the man by his side, then at the others, who watched him with beating hearts.

With a loud clear voice he took the sins.

"Thoir dhomh do ciontachd, O Adam mhic Anndra mhic Adam Mòr! Give me thy sins to take away from thee! Lo, now, as I stand here, I break this bread that has lain on thee in corpse, and I am eating it, I am, and in that eating I take upon me the sins of thee, O man that was alive and is now white with the stillness!"

Thereupon Neil Ross broke the bread and ate of it, and took

upon himself the sins of Adam Blair that was dead. It was a bitter swallowing, that. The remainder of the bread he crumbled in his hand, and threw it on the ground, and trod upon it. Andrew Blair gave a sigh of relief. His cold eyes lightened with malice.

"Be off with you, now, Macallum. We are wanting no tramps at the farm here, and perhaps you had better not be trying to get work this side Iona; for it is known as the Sin-Eater you will be, and that won't be for the helping, I am thinking! There—there are the two half-crowns for you ... and may they bring you no harm, you that are Scapegoat now!"

The Sin-Eater turned at that, and stared like a hill-bull. Scapegoat! Ay, that's what he was. Sin-Eater, Scapegoat! Was he not, too, another Judas, to have sold for silver that which was not for the selling? No, no, for sure Maisie Macdonald could tell him the rune that would serve for the easing of this burden. He would soon be quit of it.

Slowly he took the money, turned it over, and put it in his pocket.

"I am going, Andrew Blair," he said quietly, "I am going now. I will not say to him that is there in the silence, A chuid do Pharas da!—nor will I say to you, Gu'n gleidheadh Dia thu,—nor will I say to this dwelling that is the home of thee and thine, Gu'n beannaic-headh Dia an tigh!"[12]

Here there was a pause. All listened. Andrew Blair shifted uneasily, the furtive eyes of him going this way and that, like a ferret in the grass.

"But, Andrew Blair, I will say this: when you fare abroad, Droch caoidh ort! and when you go upon the water, Gaoth gun direadh ort! Ay, ay, Anndra-mhic-Adam, Dia ad aghaidh 's ad aodann ... agus bas dunach ort! Dhonas 's dholas ort, agus leat-sa!"[13]

The bitterness of these words was like snow in June upon all there. They stood amazed. None spoke. No one moved.

Neil Ross turned upon his heel, and, with a bright light in his eyes, walked away from the dead and the living. He went by the byres, whence he had come. Andrew Blair remained where he was,

---

[12] A chuid do Pharas da! "His share of heaven be his." Gu'n gleidheadh Dia thu, "May God preserve you." Gu'n beannaic-headh Dia an tigh! "God's blessing on this house."

[13] Droch caoidh ort! "May a fatal accident happen to you" (lit. "bad moan on you"). Gaoth gun direadh ort! "May you drift to your drowning" (lit. "wind without direction on you"). Dia ad aghaidh, etc., "God against thee and in thy face ... and may a death of woe be yours.... Evil and sorrow to thee and thine!"

now glooming at the corpse, now biting his nails and staring at the damp sods at his feet.

When Neil reached the end of the milk-shed he saw Maisie Macdonald there, waiting.

"These were ill sayings of yours, Neil Ross," she said in a low voice, so that she might not be overheard from the house.

"So, it is knowing me you are."

"Sheen Macarthur told me."

"I have good cause."

"That is a true word. I know it."

"Tell me this thing. What is the rune that is said for the throwing into the sea of the sins of the dead? See here, Maisie Macdonald. There is no money of that man that I would carry a mile with me. Here it is. It is yours, if you will tell me that rune."

Maisie took the money hesitatingly. Then, stooping, she said slowly the few lines of the old, old rune.

"Will you be remembering that?"

"It is not forgetting it I will be, Maisie."

"Wait a moment. There is some warm milk here."

With that she went, and then, from within, beckoned to him to enter.

"There is no one here, Neil Ross. Drink the milk."

He drank; and while he did so she drew a leather pouch from some hidden place in her dress.

"And now I have this to give you."

She counted out ten pennies and two farthings.

"It is all the coppers I have. You are welcome to them. Take them, friend of my friend. They will give you the food you need, and the ferry across the Sound."

"I will do that, Maisie Macdonald, and thanks to you. It is not forgetting it I will be, nor you, good woman. And now, tell me, is it safe that I am? He called me a 'scapegoat', he, Andrew Blair! Can evil touch me between this and the sea?"

"You must go to the place where the evil was done to you and yours—and that, I know, is on the west side of Iona. Go, and God preserve you. But here, too, is a sian that will be for the safety."

Thereupon, with swift mutterings she said this charm: an old, familiar Sian against Sudden Harm:

"Sian a chuir Moire air Mac ort,
Sian ro' marbhadh, sian ro' lot ort,
Sian eadar a' chlioch 's a' ghlun,
Sian nan Tri ann an aon ort,
O mhullach do chinn gu bonn do chois ort:

Sian seachd eadar a h-aon ort,
Sian seachd eadar a dha ort,
Sian seachd eadar a tri ort,
Sian seachd eadar a ceithir ort,
Sian seachd eadar a coig ort,
Sian seachd eadar a sia ort,
Sian seachd paidir nan seach paidir dol deiseil ri diugh narach ort,
ga do ghleidheadh bho bheud 's bho mhi-thapadh!"

Scarcely had she finished before she heard heavy steps approaching.

"Away with you," she whispered, repeating in a loud, angry tone, "Away with you! Seachad! Seachad!"

And with that Neil Ross slipped from the milk-shed and crossed the yard, and was behind the byres before Andrew Blair, with sullen mien and swift, wild eyes, strode from the house.

It was with a grim smile on his face that Neil tramped down the wet heather till he reached the high road, and fared thence as through a marsh because of the rains there had been.

For the first mile he thought of the angry mind of the dead man, bitter at paying of the silver. For the second mile he thought of the evil that had been wrought for him and his. For the third mile he pondered over all that he had heard and done and taken upon him that day.

Then he sat down upon a broken granite heap by the way, and brooded deep till one hour went, and then another, and the third was upon him.

A man driving two calves came towards him out of the west. He did not hear or see. The man stopped; spoke again. Neil gave no answer. The drover shrugged his shoulders, hesitated, and walked slowly on, often looking back.

An hour later a shepherd came by the way he himself had tramped. He was a tall, gaunt man with a squint. The small, pale-blue eyes glittered out of a mass of red hair that almost covered his face. He stood still, opposite Neil, and leaned on his cromak.

"Latha math leat," he said at last; "I wish you good day."

Neil glanced at him, but did not speak.

"What is your name, for I seem to know you?"

But Neil had already forgotten him. The shepherd took out his snuff-mull, helped himself, and handed the mull to the lonely wayfarer. Neil mechanically helped himself.

"Am bheil thu 'dol do Fhionphort?" tried the shepherd again: "Are you going to Fionnaphort?"

"Tha mise 'dol a dh' I-challum-chille," Neil answered, in a low, weary voice, and as a man adream: "I am on my way to Iona."

"I am thinking I know now who you are. You are the man Macallum."

Neil looked, but did not speak. His eyes dreamed against what the other could not see or know. The shepherd called angrily to his dogs to keep the sheep from straying; then, with a resentful air, turned to his victim.

"You are a silent man for sure, you are. I'm hoping it is not the curse upon you already."

"What curse?"

"Ah, that has brought the wind against the mist! I was thinking so!"

"What curse?"

"You are the man that was the Sin-Eater over there?"

"Ay."

"The man Macallum?"

"Ay."

"Strange it is, but three days ago I saw you in Tobermory, and heard you give your name as Neil Ross to an Iona man that was there."

"Well?"

"Oh, sure, it is nothing to me. But they say the Sin-Eater should not be a man with a hidden lump in his pack."[14]

"Why?"

"For the dead know, and are content. There is no shaking off any sins, then—for that man."

"It is a lie."

"Maybe ay and maybe no."

"Well, have you more to be saying to me? I am obliged to you for your company, but it is not needing it I am, though no offense."

"Och, man, there's no offense between you and me. Sure, there's Iona in me, too; for the father of my father married a woman that was the granddaughter of Tomais Macdonald, who was a fisherman there. No, no; it is rather warning you I would be."

"And for what?"

"Well, well, just because of that laugh I heard about."

"What laugh?"

"The laugh of Adam Blair that is dead."

Neil Ross stared, his eyes large and wild. He leaned a little forward. No word came from him. The look that was on his face was the question.

---

[14] i.e. With a criminal secret, or an undiscovered crime.

"Yes, it was this way. Sure, the telling of it is just as I heard it. After you ate the sins of Adam Blair, the people there brought out the coffin. When they were putting him into it, he was as stiff as a sheep dead in the snow—and just like that, too, with his eyes wide open. Well, someone saw you trampling the heather down the slope that is in front of the house, and said, 'It is the Sin-Eater!' With that, Andrew Blair sneered, and said—'Ay, 'tis the scapegoat he is!' Then, after a while, he went on, 'The Sin-Eater they call him; ay, just so; and a bitter good bargain it is, too, if all's true that's thought true!' And with that he laughed, and then his wife that was behind him laughed, and then...."

"Well, what then?"

"Well, 'tis Himself that hears and knows if it is true! But this is the thing I was told: After that laughing there was a stillness and a dread. For all there saw that the corpse had turned its head and was looking after you as you went down the heather. Then, Neil Ross, if that be your true name, Adam Blair that was dead put up his white face against the sky, and laughed."

At this, Ross sprang to his feet with a gasping sob.

"It is a lie, that thing!" he cried, shaking his fist at the shepherd. "It is a lie."

"It is no lie. And by the same token, Andrew Blair shrank back white and shaking, and his woman had the swoon upon her, and who knows but the corpse might have come to life again had it not been for Maisie Macdonald, the deid-watcher, who clapped a handful of salt on his eyes, and tilted the coffin so that the bottom of it slid forward, and so let the whole fall flat on the ground, with Adam Blair in it sideways, and as likely as not cursing and groaning, as his wont was, for the hurt both to his old bones and his old ancient dignity."

Ross glared at the man as though the madness was upon him. Fear and horror and fierce rage swung him now this way and now that.

"What will the name of you be, shepherd?" he stuttered huskily.

"It is Eachainn Gilleasbuig I am to ourselves; and the English of that for those who have no Gaelic is Hector Gillespie; and I am Eachainn mac Ian mac Alasdair of Strathsheean that is where Sutherland lies against Ross."

"Then take this thing—and that is, the curse of the Sin-Eater! And a bitter bad thing may it be upon you and yours."

And with that Neil the Sin-Eater flung his hand up into the air, and then leaped past the shepherd, and a minute later was running through the frightened sheep, with his head low, and a white foam on his lips, and his eyes red with blood as a seal's that has the death-wound on it.

On the third day of the seventh month from that day, Aulay Macneill, coming into Balliemore of Iona from the west side of the island, said to old Ronald MacCormick, that was the father of his wife, that he had seen Neil Ross again, and that he was "absent"—for though he had spoken to him, Neil would not answer, but only gloomed at him from the wet weedy rock where he sat.

The going back of the man had loosed every tongue that was in Iona. When, too, it was known that he was wrought in some terrible way, if not actually mad, the islanders whispered that it was because of the sins of Adam Blair. Seldom or never now did they speak of him by his name, but simply as "The Sin-Eater." The thing was not so rare as to cause this strangeness, nor did many (and perhaps none did) think that the sins of the dead ever might or could abide with the living who had merely done a good Christian charitable thing. But there was a reason.

Not long after Neil Ross had come again to Iona, and had settled down in the ruined roofless house on the croft of Ballyrona, just like a fox or a wild-cat, as the saying was, he was given fishing-work to do by Aulay Macneill, who lived at Ard-an-teine, at the rocky north end of the machar or plain that is on the west Atlantic coast of the island.

One moonlit night, either the seventh or the ninth after the earthing of Adam Blair at his own place in the Ross, Aulay Macneill saw Neil Ross steal out of the shadow of Ballyrona and make for the sea. Macneill was there by the rocks, mending a lobster-creel. He had gone there because of the sadness. Well, when he saw the Sin-Eater, he watched.

Neil crept from rock to rock till he reached the last fang that churns the sea into yeast when the tide sucks the land just opposite.

Then he called out something that Aulay Macneill could not catch. With that he springs up, and throws his arms above him.

"Then," says Aulay when he tells the tale, "it was like a ghost he was. The moonshine was on his face like the curl o' a wave. White! there is no whiteness like that of the human face. It was whiter than the foam about the skerry it was; whiter than the moon shining; whiter than ... well, as white as the painted letters on the black boards of the fishing-cobles. There he stood, for all that the sea was about him, the slip-slop waves leapin' wild, and the tide making, too, at that. He was shaking like a sail two points off the wind. It was then that, all of a sudden, he called in a womany, screamin' voice—

"'I am throwing the sins of Adam Blair into the midst of ye, white dogs o' the sea! Drown them, tear them, drag them away out into the black deeps! Ay, ay, ay, ye dancin' wild waves, this is the third time I am doing it, and now there is none left; no, not a sin, not a sin!

"'O-hi O-ri, dark tide o' the sea,
I am giving the sins of a dead man to thee!
By the Stones, by the Wind, by the Fire, by the Tree,
From the dead man's sins set me free, set me free!
Adam mhic Anndra mhic Adam and me,
Set us free! Set us free!'

"Ay, sure, the Sin-Eater sang that over and over; and after the third singing he swung his arms and screamed:

"'And listen to me, black waters an' running tide,
That rune is the good rune told me by Maisie the wise,
And I am Neil the son of Silis Macallum
By the black-hearted evil man Murtagh Ross,
That was the friend of Adam mac Anndra, God against him!'

"And with that he scrambled and fell into the sea. But, as I am Aulay mac Luais and no other, he was up in a moment, an' swimmin' like a seal, and then over the rocks again, an' away back to that lonely roofless place once more, laughing wild at times, an' muttering an' whispering."

It was this tale of Aulay Macneill's that stood between Neil Ross and the isle-folk. There was something behind all that, they whispered one to another.

So it was always the Sin-Eater he was called at last. None sought him. The few children who came upon him now and again fled at his approach, or at the very sight of him. Only Aulay Macneill saw him at times, and had word of him.

After a month had gone by, all knew that the Sin-Eater was wrought to madness because of this awful thing: the burden of Adam Blair's sins would not go from him! Night and day he could hear them laughing low, it was said.

But it was the quiet madness. He went to and fro like a shadow in the grass, and almost as soundless as that, and as voiceless. More and more the name of him grew as a terror. There were few folk on that wild west coast of Iona, and these few avoided him when the word ran that he had knowledge of strange things, and converse, too, with the secrets of the sea.

One day Aulay Macneill, in his boat, but dumb with amaze

and terror for him, saw him at high tide swimming on a long rolling wave right into the hollow of the Spouting Cave. In the memory of man, no one had done this and escaped one of three things: a snatching away into oblivion, a strangled death, or madness. The islanders know that there swims into the cave, at full tide, a Mar-Tarbh, a dreadful creature of the sea that some call a kelpie; only it is not a kelpie, which is like a woman, but rather is a sea-bull, offspring of the cattle that are never seen. Ill indeed for any sheep or goat, ay, or even dog or child, if any happens to be leaning over the edge of the Spouting Cave when the Mar-tarv roars; for, of a surety, it will fall in and straightway be devoured.

With awe and trembling Aulay listened for the screaming of the doomed man. It was full tide, and the sea-beast would be there.

The minutes passed, and no sign. Only the hollow booming of the sea, as it moved like a baffled blind giant round the cavern-bases; only the rush and spray of the water flung up the narrow shaft high into the windy air above the cliff it penetrates.

At last he saw what looked like a mass of seaweed swirled out on the surge. It was the Sin-Eater. With a leap, Aulay was at his oars. The boat swung through the sea. Just before Neil Ross was about to sink for the second time, he caught him and dragged him into the boat.

But then, as ever after, nothing was to be got out of the Sin-Eater save a single saying: Tha e lamhan fuar! Tha e lamhan fuar!—"It has a cold, cold hand!"

The telling of this and other tales left none free upon the island to look upon the "scapegoat" save as one accursed.

It was in the third month that a new phase of his madness came upon Neil Ross.

The horror of the sea and the passion for the sea came over him at the same happening. Oftentimes he would race along the shore, screaming wild names to it, now hot with hate and loathing, now as the pleading of a man with the woman of his love. And strange chants to it, too, were upon his lips. Old, old lines of forgotten runes were overheard by Aulay Macneill, and not Aulay only; lines wherein the ancient sea-name of the island, Ioua, that was given to it long before it was called Iona, or any other of the nine names that are said to belong to it, occurred again and again.

The flowing tide it was that wrought him thus. At the ebb he would wander across the weedy slabs or among the rocks, silent, and more like a lost duinshee than a man.

Then again after three months a change in his madness came. None knew what it was, though Aulay said that the man moaned and moaned because of the awful burden he bore. No drowning seas for the sins that could not be washed away, no grave for the live sins that would be quick till the day of the Judgment!

For weeks thereafter he disappeared. As to where he was, it is not for the knowing.

Then at last came that third day of the seventh month when, as I have said, Aulay Macneill told old Ronald MacCormick that he had seen the Sin-Eater again.

It was only a half-truth that he told, though. For, after he had seen Neil Ross upon the rock, he had followed him when he rose, and wandered back to the roofless place which he haunted now as of yore. Less wretched a shelter now it was, because of the summer that was come, though a cold, wet summer at that.

"Is that you, Neil Ross?" he had asked, as he peered into the shadows among the ruins of the house.

"That's not my name," said the Sin-Eater; and he seemed as strange then and there, as though he were a castaway from a foreign ship.

"And what will it be, then, you that are my friend, and sure knowing me as Aulay mac Luais—Aulay Macneill that never grudges you bit or sup?"

"I am Judas."

"And at that word," says Aulay Macneill, when he tells the tale, "at that word the pulse in my heart was like a bat in a shut room. But after a bit I took up the talk.

"'Indeed,' I said; 'and I was not for knowing that. May I be so bold as to ask whose son, and of what place?'

"But all he said to me was, 'I am Judas.'

"Well, I said, to comfort him, 'Sure, it's not such a bad name in itself, though I am knowing some which have a more home-like sound.' But no, it was no good.

"'I am Judas. And because I sold the Son of God for five pieces of silver....'

"But here I interrupted him and said, 'Sure, now, Neil—I mean, Judas—it was eight times five.' Yet the simpleness of his sorrow prevailed, and I listened with the wet in my eyes.

"'I am Judas. And because I sold the Son of God for five silver shillings, He laid upon me all the nameless black sins of the world. And that is why I am bearing them till the Day of Days.'"

And this was the end of the Sin-Eater; for I will not tell the long story of Aulay Macneill, that gets longer and longer every winter; but only the unchanging close of it.

I will tell it in the words of Aulay.

"A bitter, wild day it was, that day I saw him to see him no more. It was late. The sea was red with the flamin' light that burned up the air betwixt Iona and all that is west of West. I was on the shore, looking at the sea. The big green waves came in like the chariots in the Holy Book. Well, it was on the black shoulder of one of them, just short of the ton o' foam that swept above it, that I saw a spar surgin' by.

"'What is that?' I said to myself. And the reason of my wondering was this: I saw that a smaller spar was swung across it. And while I was watching that thing another great billow came in with a roar, and hurled the double spar back, and not so far from me but I might have gripped it. But who would have gripped that thing if he were for seeing what I saw?

"It is Himself knows that what I say is a true thing.

"On that spar was Neil Ross, the Sin-Eater. Naked he was as the day he was born. And he was lashed, too—ay, sure, he was lashed to it by ropes round and round his legs and his waist and his left arm. It was the Cross he was on. I saw that thing with the fear upon me. Ah, poor drifting wreck that he was! Judas on the Cross! It was his eric!

"But even as I watched, shaking in my limbs, I saw that there was life in him still. The lips were moving, and his right arm was ever for swinging this way and that. 'Twas like an oar, working him off a lee shore; ay, that was what I thought.

"Then, all at once, he caught sight of me. Well he knew me, poor man, that has his share of heaven now, I am thinking!

"He waved, and called, but the hearing could not be, because of a big surge o' water that came tumbling down upon him. In the stroke of an oar he was swept close by the rocks where I was standing. In that flounderin', seethin' whirlpool I saw the white face of him for a moment, an' as he went out on the re-surge like a hauled net, I heard these words fallin' against my ears:

"'An eirig m'anama.... In ransom for my soul!'

"And with that I saw the double-spar turn over and slide down the back-sweep of a drowning big wave. Ay, sure, it went out to the deep sea swift enough then. It was in the big eddy that rushes between Skerry-Mòr and Skerry-Beag. I did not see it again—no, not for the quarter of an hour, I am thinking. Then I saw just the whirling top of it rising out of the flying yeast of a great, black-blustering wave, that was rushing northward before the current that is called the Black-Eddy.

"With that you have the end of Neil Ross; ay, sure, him that was called the Sin-Eater. And that is a true thing; and may God save us the sorrow of sorrows.

"And that is all."

GHOSTS IN SOLID FORM

By Gambier Bolton

Ex-Pres. The Psychological Society, London, F.R.G.S., F.Z.S., etc.

CHAPTER I

"A single grain of solid fact is worth ten tons of theory."

"The more I think of it, the more I find this conclusion impressed upon me, that the greatest thing a human soul ever does in this world is to SEE something and tell what it saw in a plain way. Hundreds of people can talk for one who can think, but thousands can think for one who can see. To SEE clearly is poetry, prophecy, and religion all in one."—John Ruskin.

Working Hypothesis

That under certain known and reasonable conditions of temperature, light, etc., entities, existing in a sphere outside our own, have been demonstrated again and again to manifest themselves on earth in temporary bodies materialized from an, at present, undiscovered source, through the agency of certain persons of both sexes, termed "sensitives," and can be so demonstrated to any person who will provide the conditions proved to be necessary for such a demonstration.

Conditions

Looking back to the seven years of my life which I devoted to a careful and critical investigation of the claim made, not only by both Occidental and Oriental mystics but by well-known men of science like Sir William Crookes, Professor Alfred Russel Wallace, and others—that it was possible under certain clearly defined conditions to produce, apparently out of nothing, fully formed bodies, inhabited by (presumably) human entities from another sphere—the wonder of it still enthralls me; the apparent impossibility of so great an upheaval of such laws of Nature as we are at present acquainted with being proved clearly to be possible, will remain to the end as "the wonder of wonders" in a by no means uneventful life.

For, as compared with this, that greatest of Nature's mysteries—the procreation of a human infant by either the normal or mechanical impregnation of an ovum, its months of foetal growth and development in the uterus, and its birth into the world in a helpless and enfeebled condition, amazing as they are to all physiological students—sinks into comparative insignificance when compared with the nearly instantaneous production of a fully developed human body, with all its organs functioning properly; a body inhabited temporarily by a thinking, reasoning entity, who can see, hear, taste, smell and touch: a body which can be handled, weighed, measured, and photographed.

When these claims were first brought to my notice I realized at once that I was face to face with a problem which would require the very closest investigation; and I then and there decided to give up work of all kinds and to devote years, if necessary, to a critical examination of these claims, to investigate the matter calmly and dispassionately, and, in Sir John Herschel's memorable words, "to stand or fall by the result of a direct appeal to facts in the first instance, and of strict logical deduction from them afterwards."

And, as I have said, the result has been that the apparently impossible has been proved to be possible—the facts have beaten me, and I accept them whole-heartedly, admitting that our working hypothesis has been proved beyond any possibility of doubt, and that these materialized entities can manifest themselves to-day to any person who will provide the conditions necessary for such a demonstration.

Who they are, what they are, whence they come, and whither they go, each investigator must determine for himself, but of their actual existence in a sphere just outside our own there can no longer be any room for doubt. As a busy man, theories have little or no attraction for me. What I demand, and what other busy men and women demand in an investigation of this kind is that there should be a reasonable possibility of getting hold of facts, good solid facts which can be demonstrated as such to any open-minded inquirer, otherwise it would be useless to commence such an investigation. And we have now got these facts, and can prove them on purely scientific lines.

The meaning of the word materialization, so far at least as it concerns our investigation, I understand to be this: the taking on by an entity from a sphere outside our own, an entity representing a man, woman, or child (or even a beast or bird), of a temporary body built up from material drawn partially from the inhabitants of earth, consolidated through the agency of certain persons of both sexes, termed sensitives, and moulded by the entity into a semblance of the body which (it alleges) it inhabited during its existence on earth. In other words, a materialization is the appearance of an entity in bodily, tangible form, i.e., one which we can touch, thus differing from an astralization, etherealization, or apparition, which is, of course, one which cannot be touched, although it may be clearly visible to any one possessing only normal sight.

Let me, then, endeavor to describe to the best of my ability, and in very simple language, how I believe these materializations to be produced, and the conditions which I have proved to be necessary in order that the finest results may be obtained.

I will deal first with the question of the conditions, as without conditions of some kind no materialization can be produced, any more than a scientific experiment—such as mixing various chemicals together, in order to produce a certain result—can be carried out successfully without proper conditions being provided by the experimenter. What, then, do we mean by this word "conditions"?

Take a homely example. The baker mixes exactly the right quantities of flour, salt, and yeast with water, and then places the dough which he has made in an oven heated to just the right temperature, and produces a loaf of bread. Why? Because the conditions were good ones. Had he omitted the flour, the yeast, or the water, or had he used an oven over or under-heated, he could not have produced an eatable loaf of bread, because the conditions made it impossible.

This is what is meant by the terms "good conditions," "bad conditions," "breaking conditions."

The conditions, then, under which I have been able to prove to many hundreds of inquirers that it is possible for materialized entities to appear on earth, in solid tangible form, are these:

First, light, of suitable wave-length, i.e. suitable color, and let me say here, once and for all, that I have proved conclusively for myself that darkness is not necessary, provided that one is experimenting with a sensitive who has been trained to sit always in the light.

On two occasions I have witnessed materializations in daylight; and neither of Sir William Crookes's sensitives—D. D. Home or Florrie Cook (Mrs. Corner)—would ever sit in darkness, the latter—with whom I carried out a long series of experiments—invariably stipulating that a good light should be used during the whole time that the experiment lasted, as she was terrified at the mere thought of darkness.

I find that sunlight, electric light, gas, colza oil, and paraffine are all apt to check the production of the phenomena unless filtered through canary-yellow, orange, red linen or paper—just as they are filtered for photographic purposes—owing to the violent action of the actinic (blue) rays which they contain (the rays from the violet end of the spectrum), which are said to work at about six hundred billions of vibrations per second. But if the light is filtered in the way that I have described, the production of the phenomena will commence at once, the vibrations of the interfering rays being reduced, it is said, to about four hundred billions per second or less.

In dealing with materializations we are apt to overlook the fact that we are investigating forces or modes of energy far more delicate than electricity, for instance. Heat, electricity, and light, as Sir William Crookes tells us, are all closely related; we know the awful power of heat and electricity, but are only too apt to forget—especially if it suits our purpose to do so—that light too has enormous dynamic potency; its vibrations being said to travel in space at the incredible speed of twelve million miles a minute;[15] and it is therefore only reasonable to assume that the power of these vibrations may be sufficient to interfere seriously with the more subtle forces, such as those which we are now investigating.

Secondly, we require suitable heat vibrations, and I find that those given off in a room either warmed or chilled to sixty-three degrees are the very best possible; anything either much above this, or more especially, much below this, tending to weaken the results and to cheek the phenomena.

Thirdly, we require suitable musical vibrations, and, after carrying out a long series of experiments with musical instruments of all kinds, I find that the vibrations given off by the reed organ—termed "harmonium" or "American organ"—or by the concertina, are the most suitable, the peculiar quality of the vibrations given off by the reeds in these instruments proving to be the most suitable ones for use during the production of the phenomena; although on one or two occasions I have obtained good results without musical vibrations of any kind, but this is rare.

Fourthly, we require the presence of a specially organized man or woman, termed the sensitive, one from whom it is alleged a portion of the matter used by the entity in the building up of its temporary body can be drawn, with but little chance of injury to their health. This point is one of vital importance, we are told, for it has been proved by means of a self-registering weighing-machine on which he was seated, and to which he was securely fastened with an electrical apparatus secretly hidden beneath the seat, which would at once ring a bell in an anteroom if he endeavored to rise

[15] 186,900 miles a second (J. Wallace Stewart, B.Sc.).

from his seat during the experiment, that the actual loss in weight to the sensitive, when a fully materialized entity was standing in our midst, was no less than sixty-five pounds!

Before employing any person, then, as a sensitive for these delicate, not to say dangerous, experiments, he or she should be medically examined, in the interests of both the investigator and the sensitive, and should their health prove to be in any way below par, they should not be permitted to take part in the experiment until their health is fully restored.

I have been permitted to examine the sensitive at the moment when an entity, clad in a fully-formed temporary body, was walking amongst the experimenters; and the distorted features, the shrivelled-up limbs and contorted trunk of the sensitive at that moment proclaimed the danger connected with the production of this special form of phenomena far louder than any words of mine could do.

Needless to say, sensitives for materializations are extremely rare, not more than two or three being found to-day amidst the teeming millions who inhabit the British Islands; although a few are to be found on the European continent, and several in North America, where the climatic conditions are said to be more favorable for the development of such persons.

Now, what constitutes a sensitive, and why are they necessary?

Sensitives through whom physical phenomena (including materializations) can be produced have been described, firstly, as persons in whom certain forces are stored up, either far in excess of the amount possessed by the normal man or woman, or else differing in quality from the forces stored up by the normal man or woman; and secondly, as persons who are able to attract from those in close proximity to them—provided that the conditions are favorable—still more of the force, which thus becomes centered in them for the time being. In other words, a sensitive for physical phenomena is said to be a storage battery for the force which is used in the production of physical phenomena—including materializations—although it is by no means improbable that such highly developed sensitives as those required for this special purpose may be found to possess extra nerve-centers as compared with those possessed by normal human beings. But whether this hypothesis be eventually proved or not, there seems to be but very little doubt that "whatever the force may be which constitutes the difference between a sensitive and a non-sensitive, it is certainly of a mental or magnetic character, i.e., a combination of the subtle elements of mind and magnetism, and therefore of a psychological, and not of a purely physical character."

But why is a sensitive necessary? you ask. Think of a telephone for a moment. You wish to communicate with a person who is holding only the end of the wire in his hand, the result being that he cannot hear a single word. Why is this? Because he has forgotten to fit a receiver at his end of the wire, a receiver in which the vibrations set up by your voice may be centralized, focussed, a receiver which he can place to his ear, and in doing so will at once hear your voice distinctly—but without this your message to him is lost.

And it is said that this is exactly the use of the sensitives during our experiments, for they act as "receivers" in which the forces employed in the production of the phenomena may be centralized, focussed, their varying degrees of sensitiveness enabling them to be used by the entities in other spheres for the successful production of such phenomena, we are told.

And lastly, we require about twelve to sixteen earnest and really sympathetic men and women—persons trained on scientific lines for choice—all in the best of health; men and women who, whilst strictly on their guard against anything in the shape of fraud, are still so much in sympathy with the person who is acting as the sensitive that they are all the time sending out kindly thoughts towards him; for if, as has been said, "thoughts are things," it is possible that hostile thoughts would be sufficient not only to enfeeble, but actually to check demonstrations of physical phenomena of all kinds in the presence of such specially organized, highly developed individuals as the sensitives through whom materializations can be produced.

I shall refer to these men and women as the sitters. We generally select an equal number so far as sex is concerned; and, in addition, we endeavor to obtain an equal number of persons possessing either positive or negative temperaments. In this way we form the sitters into a powerful human battery, the combined force given off by them (if the battery is properly arranged, and the individual members of that battery are in good health) proving of enormous assistance during our experiments. If in ill-health, we find that a man or woman is useless to us, for we can no more expect to obtain the necessary power from such an individual than we can expect to produce an electric spark from a discharged accumulator, or pick up needles with a demagnetized piece of steel.

We are told to remember always that "all manifestations of natural laws are the results of natural conditions."

Minor details too, we find, must be thought out most carefully if we are to provide what we may term ideal conditions.

The chairs should be made of wood throughout, those known as Austrian bentwood chairs, having perforated seats, being proved to be the best for the purpose.

The sitters should bathe and then change their clothing—the ladies into white dresses, and the men into dark suits—two hours before the time fixed for the experiment, and should then at once partake of a light meal—meat and alcohol being strictly forbidden—so that the strain upon their constitutions during the experiment may not interfere with their health.

Trivial as such matters must appear to the man in the street, we are told they must all be carried out most carefully, in order that the finest conditions possible may be obtained, the one great object of the sitters being to give off all the power—and the best kind of power—that they are capable of producing, in order that sufficient suitable material may be gathered together from the sensitive and themselves, with which a temporary body may be formed for the use of any entity wishing to materialize in their presence.

Precautions Against Fraud

We are now ready to see what happens at a typical experimental meeting for these materializations, at hundreds of which I have assisted, having the services of no less than six sensitives placed at my disposal for this purpose. I will endeavor to describe what I should consider to be an ideal one, held under ideal (test) conditions.

Our imaginary test meeting is to be carried out—as it was on one occasion in London—in an entirely empty house, which none of us has ever entered before, a house which we will hire for this special event. By doing this we may feel sure that all possibility of fraud, so far as the use of secret trap-doors, large mirrors, and other undesirable things of that description are concerned, can be successfully thwarted.

We are now ready to start our experiment; the general feeling of all those in the room being that every possible precaution against trickery has been taken, and that if any results of any kind whatever should follow they will undoubtedly be genuine.

The sitters having been allotted their seats, so that a person of a positive and a person of a negative temperament are seated together, we now join hands, and form ourselves into what we are told is a powerful human battery; the two persons sitting at the two ends of the half-circle having of course each one hand free, and from the free hands of these two persons, it is said, the power developed and given off by this human battery passes into the sensitive at each of his sides.

Sitting quietly in our chairs and talking gently amongst ourselves, we soon feel a cool breeze blowing across our hands. In another two minutes this will have so increased in volume that it may with truth be described as a strong wind.

On looking at the sensitive now, we see that he is rapidly passing into a state of trance—his head is drooping on one side, his arms and hands hang downwards loosely, his body being in a limp real trance condition, and just in the right state for use by any entity desiring to work through him, we are told.

I have only experimented with one sensitive who did not pass into trance, who, seated amongst the sitters, remained in a perfectly normal condition during the whole of the experiment; watching the materialized forms building up beside him, and talking to and with them during the process. I shall refer to him shortly.

We now set our clairvoyants to work, and the statements made by one must be confirmed in every detail by the statements of the other as to what is occurring at the moment, or no notice is taken of their remarks.

Both now report that they see a thin white mist or vapor[16] coming from the left side of the sensitive, if a man (or from the pelvis, if a woman), which passes into the sitter at the end of the half-circle nearest to the sensitive's left side. It then passes, they state, from Sitter No. 1 to Sitter No. 2, and so on, until it has gone through the whole of the sixteen sitters, passing finally from the last one—No. 16—at the end of the half-circle nearest to the sensitive's right side, and disappears into his right side.

We assume from this that the nerve force, magnetic power—call it what you will—necessary for the formation of one of these temporary bodies starts from the sensitive, passes through each sitter, drawing from each as much more force or power as he or she is capable of giving off at the moment, returning to the sensitive greatly increased in its amount and ready for use in the next process. This, then, we will term the first of the three stages in the evolution of an entity clad in a temporary body.

The Vapor Stage

In a few moments our clairvoyants both report that the force or power is issuing from the side of the sensitive, if a man (or from

[16] Termed teleplasma.

the pelvis, if a woman), in the form of a white, soft, dough-like substance, which on one occasion I was permitted to touch. I could perceive no smell given off by it; it felt cold and clammy, and appeared to have the consistency of heavy dough at the moment that I touched it.

This mass of dough-like substance is said to be the material used by the entities—one by one as a rule—who wish to build up a temporary body. It seems to rest on the floor, somewhere near the right side of the sensitive, until required for use: its bulk depending apparently upon the amount of power given off by the sitters from time to time during the experiment.

This we will term the second of the three stages of the evolution of an entity clad in a temporary body.

The Solid, but Shapeless Stage

We are told that the entity wishing to show himself to us passes into this shapeless mass of dough-like substance, which at once increases in bulk, and commences to pulsate and move up and down, swaying from side to side as it grows in height, the motive power being evidently underneath.

The entity then quickly sets to work to mould the mass into something resembling a human body, commencing with the head. The rest of the upper portion of the body soon follows, and the heart and pulse can now be felt to be beating quite regularly and normally, differing in this respect from those of the sensitive, who, if tested at this time, will be found with both heart and pulse-beats considerably above the normal. The legs and feet come last, and then the entity is able to leave the near neighborhood of the sensitive and to walk amongst the sitters, the third and last stage of its evolution being now complete.

Although occasionally the entity will appear clad in an exact copy of the clothing which he states that he wore when on earth—especially if it should happen to be something a little out of the common, such as a military or naval uniform—they are draped as a rule in flowing white garments of a wonderfully soft texture, and this, too, I have been permitted to handle.

Our clairvoyants both affirm that at all times during the materialization a thin band of, presumably, the dough-like substance can be plainly seen issuing from the side of the sensitive, if a man, (or from the pelvis, if a woman), and joined onto the center of the body inhabited by the entity—just like the umbilical cord attached to a human infant at birth—and we are instructed that this band cannot be stretched beyond a certain radius, say ten to fifteen feet, without doing harm to the sensitive and to the entity; although cases are on record where materializations have been seen at a distance of nearly sixty feet from the sensitive, on occasions when the conditions were unusually favorable.

On handling different portions of the materialized body now, the flesh is found to be both warm and firm. The bodies are well proportioned, those of the females—for they take on sex conditions during the process—having beautiful figures; the hands, arms, legs, and feet are quite perfect in their modelling, but in my opinion the body, head, and limbs of every materialization of either sex or any age which I have scrutinized at close quarters carefully, or have been permitted to handle, have appeared to be at least one-third smaller in size (except as regards actual height) than those possessed by beings on earth of the same sex and age.

Not only have we witnessed materializations of aged entities of both sexes, showing all the characteristics of old age—for the purpose of identification by the sitters, as they tell us—but we have seen materialized infants also; and on one occasion two still-born children appeared in our midst simultaneously, one of them showing distinct traces on its little face of a hideous deformity which it possessed at the time of its premature birth—a deformity known only to the mother, who happened to be present that evening as one of the sitters.

We are told that, for the purpose of identification, the entity will return to earth in an exact counterpart of the body which he alleges that he occupied at the time of his death, in order that he may be recognized by his relatives and friends who happen to be present. Thus, the one who left the earth as an infant will appear in his materialized body as an infant, although he may have been dead for twenty or thirty years. The aged man or woman will appear with bent body, wrinkled face, and snow-white hair, walking amongst us with difficulty, and just as they allege they did before their death, although that may have occurred twenty years before. The one who had lost a limb during his earth-life will return minus that limb; the one who was disfigured by accident or disease will return bearing distinct traces of that disfigurement, for the purpose of identification only.

But as soon as the identification has been established successfully, all this changes instantly; the disfigurement disappears; the four limbs will be seen, and both the infant and the aged will from henceforth show themselves to us in the very prime of life—the young growing upwards and the aged downwards, as we say, and, as they one and all state emphatically, just as they really look and feel in the sphere in which they now exist.

While inhabiting these temporary bodies, they state that they take on, not only sex conditions, but earth conditions temporarily too; for they appear to feel pain if their bodies are injured in any way; complain of the cold if the temperature of the room is allowed to fall much below sixty degrees, or of the heat if the temperature is allowed to rise above seventy degrees; seem to be depressed during a thunderstorm, when our atmosphere is overcharged with electricity; and appear bright and happy in a warm room when the world outside is in the grip of a hard frost, and also on bright, starry nights.

And not only this, but they take on strongly marked characteristics of the numerous races on earth temporarily too; the materialized entities of the white races differing quite as markedly from those of the yellow or brown races, as do these from the black races; and in speaking to us each one will communicate in the particular language only which is characteristic of his race on earth.

Five, six and even seven totally different languages have been employed during a single experimental meeting through a sensitive who had never in his life been out of England, and who was proved conclusively to know no other language than English; the latter number, we were told, being in honor of a ship's doctor who was present on one occasion, and who—although the fact was quite unknown to any of us at the time—proved to be an expert linguist, for he conversed that evening with different entities in English, French, German, Russian, Chinese, Japanese, and in the language of one of the hill-tribes of India.

On another occasion, when I was the only European present at an afternoon experimental meeting held in London by eight Parsees of both sexes from Bombay, during the whole of the time which the meeting lasted—two and a quarter hours—the entities and the Parsee sitters carried on their conversation in Hindustani; two entities and one of the Parsee men simultaneously engaging in a heated controversy, which lasted for nearly three minutes, over the disposal of the bodies of their dead, the entities insisting on cremation only, as opposed to allowing the bodies to be eaten by vultures—the noise which they made during this discussion being almost deafening. The sensitive, it was proved conclusively, knew no other language than English, and had only once been out of the British Islands, when he paid a short visit to France.

CHAPTER II

"Sit down before a fact as a little child: be prepared to give up every preconceived notion: follow humbly wherever and to whatever abysses Nature leads, or you shall learn nothing."—Thomas Huxley.

Tests

The tests given to me and to my fellow-investigators through the six sensitives who so ably assisted us during our seven years of experimental work in this little-known field of research—the tests have been so numerous, and were of such a varied character, that I find it somewhat difficult to know which to select out of the hundreds which were recorded in our books officially and elsewhere, the ones which will prove of the greatest interest to inquirers; but I have made extracts from ten of these records, and these, with a few taken from Sir William Crookes's reports on the experiments conducted in his presence, will, in my opinion, be sufficient to prove that we who have witnessed these marvels are neither hallucinated, insane, nor liars when we solemnly affirm that we have both seen and handled the materialized bodies built up for temporary use by entities from another sphere; all the statements made here being true in every detail, to the best of my knowledge and belief.

Experiment No. 1

Place—Lyndhurst, New Forest, Hampshire.
Sensitive A, male, aged about 46.

As an example of a simple but exceedingly severe test, I would first record one given to me and a fellow-investigator on the outskirts of the New Forest, one for which no special preparation of any kind whatever had been made.

The sensitive, a nearly blind man, was taken by us on a dark night to a spot totally unknown to him, as he had only just arrived from London by train, and was led into a large travelling caravan, one which he had never been near before, as it had only recently left the builder's hands.

During the day I had made a critical examination of the interior of the caravan, and had satisfied myself that no one was or could possibly be concealed in it. I then locked the door, and kept the key in my pocket until the moment when, on the arrival of the sensitive, I unlocked the door and we all passed into the caravan together. I then locked and bolted the door behind us.

As I have already said, no preparation of any kind had been made for the experiment. It was merely the result of a desire to see if anything could be produced through this sensitive, under extremely difficult conditions—conditions which we considered as so utterly bad as to make failure a certainty.

We did not even possess a chair of any kind for the sensitive or ourselves to sit upon, so we placed for his use a board on top of the iron cooking-range which was fixed in the kitchen-portion of the caravan, whilst we sat upon the two couches which were used as beds in the living-portion of the caravan. There was no music, no powerful "human battery" in the shape of a number of picked sitters; in fact, the conditions were just about as bad as they could possibly be, and yet, within ten minutes of my locking the door behind us, the figure of a tall man stood before us, a man so tall that he was compelled to bow his head as he passed under the six-foot high partition which separated the two sections of the caravan.

He said, "I am Colonel — who was 'killed,' as you say, at the battle of — in Egypt. For many years during my earth-life I was deeply interested in materializations, and spent the last night of my life in England experimenting with this very sensitive; and it is a great pleasure to me to be able to return to you—strangers though you both are to me—through him. To prove to you that I am not the sensitive masquerading before you, will you please come here and stand close to me, and so settle the matter for yourself?"

I at once rose and stood beside him, almost touching him. I then discovered that not only were his features and his coloring totally different from those of the sensitive, but that he towered above me, standing, as nearly as I could judge, six foot two or three inches, and was certainly four inches taller than either the sensitive or myself.

Whilst thus standing beside him, and at a distance of about eight feet from the sensitive, we could both hear the unfortunate man moving uneasily on his hard seat on the kitchen-range, sighing and moaning as if in pain.

The entity remained with us for about three minutes, and his place was then taken by a slightly built young man, standing about five feet nine inches, one claiming to be a recently deceased member of the royal family. He talked with us in a soft and pleasing voice, finally whispering a private message to my companion, asking him to deliver it to his mother, Queen —.

Experiment No. 2

Place—Peckham Rye, London, S.E. Sensitive A, male, aged about 46.

An almost equally hopeless task was set this sensitive by the owner of the caravan and myself when we experimented with him at midday on a brilliant morning in July, with sunlight streaming into the room round the edges of the drawn down window-blinds, and round the top, sides, and bottom of the heavy window-curtains, which we had pinned together in a vain attempt to keep out the sunlight during the experiment.

And yet once again, and in spite of the conditions which we regarded as utterly hopeless, the figure of a man appeared in less than ten minutes, materialized from head to foot, as he proved to us by showing us his lower limbs. He left the side of the sensitive, walked out into the room and stood between us, talking to us in a deep rich voice for nearly three minutes. As he stood beside us we could hear the sensitive, twelve feet away, moving uneasily on his chair and groaning slightly.

Five minutes after he disappeared the same (alleged) recently deceased member of the royal family walked out to us and held a short private conversation with my companion, and sent another message to his mother, Queen —.

Experiment No. 3

Place—West Hampstead, London, N. W. Sensitive B, female, aged about 49.

Persons of middle age or older who happened to be in England a few years ago at the time that two lawsuits were brought against a celebrated conjurer by the clever young man who had succeeded in exposing one of his most mystifying tricks, will well remember the sensation caused by the giving of both verdicts against the conjurer; and the young man—to whom I shall refer as Mr. X—at once became famous as the man who had beaten one of the cleverest conjurers of the day.

A friend of mine, who had been present on several occasions when Sir William Crookes's sensitive—Florrie Cook (Mrs. Corner), referred to above as Sensitive B—had produced materializations in gaslight at my house in London, asked her to visit his house at West Hampstead one evening to meet several friends of his, and to see if it were possible for any entity to materialize in my friend's own drawing-room.

She at once accepted his invitation to sit there under strict test conditions; and, talking the matter over with some of his friends a day or two before the one chosen for the experiment, he told me that they had arranged to have the sensitive securely tied to her chair, to have strong iron rings fastened to the floor-boards, through which ropes would be passed, these ropes to be securely fastened to the sensitive's legs; all knots of every size and kind to be sealed, so as to prevent any attempt on her part to leave her chair and to masquerade as a materialized entity.

One of his friends happened to know the celebrated Mr. X—, and, as he had so recently succeeded in beating so notable a conjurer, he was invited to be present and to take entire charge of the tying up, the binding and sealing arrangements, in order to render the escape of the sensitive from her chair an impossibility.

When I joined the party in the drawing-room, Mr. X—, to whom I was introduced, was busily engaged in tying the sensitive up with his own ropes and tapes, sealing every knot with special sealing-wax and with a seal provided by our host. The room was a large one, and a portion at one end had been cleared of all furniture, and in the center of this space only the sensitive seated upon her chair, and Mr. X— busily at work, were to be seen; and the latter, after another fifteen minutes of real hard labor, was asked by our host if he was thoroughly satisfied that the sensitive was fastened to her chair securely. He replied that so securely was she fastened, that if she could produce phenomena of any kind whatever under such conditions, he would at once admit their genuineness.

The sensitive was all this time in a perfectly normal state, and not flurried in any way, her one anxiety being lest we should lower the lights, as she was so terrified at the thought of darkness.

Mr. X—, after stepping backwards to have a final look at the result of his labors, then walked close to the spot where the sensitive was sitting in gaslight, and put one hand up towards the top of the curtain, and was in the act of drawing this round her to keep the direct rays of the gaslight from falling upon her, when a large brown arm and hand suddenly appeared, the hand being clapped heavily upon Mr. X—'s shoulder, whilst a gruff masculine voice asked him in loud tones, "Are you really satisfied?"

I have witnessed some strange happenings in connection with my investigation of occult matters, but to my dying day I shall never forget the look of blank astonishment on Mr. X—'s face at that moment.

Quickly recovering himself, however, he at once examined the sensitive—a little woman, far below the average height, having small hands and feet, as we could all see quite clearly—and declared that every seal and every knot was unbroken, and just as he had left them not sixty seconds before.

Amongst other entities who materialized that evening was a young girl of about eighteen years of age who stated that when she left her earth-body she had been a dancer at a café in Algiers.

She came from the spot where the sensitive was seated, laughing heartily, stating that the hand and arm belonged to an old English sailor, whom she spoke of as "the Captain." She said, further, that he had been standing with her watching the tying-up process from their sphere, and laughing at Mr. X—'s vain attempt to prevent the production of the phenomena. The Captain had very much wished to materialize fully, so as to surprise Mr. X— as he stepped back from the sensitive; but, finding that he could only get sufficient "power" to produce a hand and arm, he was in a bad temper. And this was evidently the case, for during the ten minutes that the girl remained talking to us we could now and then hear the gruff voice of the Captain rolling out language which can only be described as "forcible and free."

The experiment lasted for nearly an hour, and at its conclusion Mr. X— examined the sensitive, and once again reported that every seal and knot were just as he had left them at the commencement of the experiment.

Experiment No. 4

Place—My House in London. Sensitive D, male, aged about 34.

On numerous occasions this sensitive has been seen by all present, in gaslight shaded by red paper, seated on his chair in a state of deep trance, and was heard to be breathing heavily, whilst two materialized entities stood beside him; or with one beside him, and the other standing five to eight feet away from him and close to the sitters.

Again, two female entities were seen simultaneously when this male sensitive was experimenting with us, one of them inside the half-circle formed by the sixteen sitters, and talking to them in a low sweet voice, at a distance of about eight feet from the sensitive; whilst the other female entity passed through or over the sitters, and, walking about the room outside the half-circle formed by the sitters, came up behind two of them, and not only spoke audibly to them, but also held a short conversation with the entity inside the ring, both speaking almost instantaneously.

THE PHANTOM ARMIES SEEN IN FRANCE[17]

By Hereward Carrington

History abounds in cases showing the apparent intrusion of spiritual help in time of trouble, and in the annals of military history these accounts are not lacking. On several occasions the Crusaders thought that they saw angelic hosts fighting for them—phantom horsemen charging the enemy, when their own utter destruction seemed imminent. In the wars between the English and the Scotch, several such cases were cited, and the Napoleonic wars also furnished examples. But the most striking evidence of this character—because the newest—and supported, apparently, by a good deal of first-hand and sincere testimony, is that afforded by the Phantom Armies seen in France during the retreat of the British army from Mons—the field of Agincourt. Cut off by overwhelming numbers, and all but annihilated, the British army fought desperately, but the 80,000 were opposed by 300,000 Germans, backed by a terrific fire of artillery, and were indeed in a critical position. They were only saved, as we know, by the heroism of a small force of men—a rear-guard—who were practically wiped out in consequence. At the most critical moment came what appeared to be angelic assistance. The tide of battle seemed to be stemmed by supernatural means. In a letter written by a soldier who actually witnessed these startling events, quoted by the Hon. Mrs. St. John Mildmay (North American Review, August, 1915), the following graphic account is given. Our soldier writes:

"The men joked at the shells and found many funny names for them, and had bets about them, and greeted them with music-hall songs, as they screamed in this terrific cannonade. The climax seemed to have been reached, but 'a seven-times heated hell' of the enemy's onslaught fell upon them, rending brother from brother. At that very moment, they saw from their trenches a tremendous host moving against their lines. Five hundred of the thousand (who had been detailed to fight the rear-guard action) remained, and as far as they could see the German infantry was pressing on against them, column by column, a gray world of men—10,000 of them, as it appeared afterwards. There was no hope at all. Some of them shook hands. One man improvised a new version of the battle song

[17] By permission of the author.

Tipperary, ending 'and we shan't get there!' And all went on firing steadily. The enemy dropped line after line, while the few machine guns did their best. Every one knew it was of no use. The dead gray bodies lay in companies and battalions, but others came on and on, swarming and advancing from beyond and beyond.

"'World without end. Amen!' said one of the British soldiers, with some irreverence, as he took aim and fired. Then he remembered a vegetarian restaurant in London, where he had once or twice eaten queer dishes of cutlets made of lentils and nuts that pretended to be steaks. On all the plates in this restaurant a figure of St. George was painted in blue with the motto, Adsit Anglis Sanctus Georgius (May St. George be a present help to England). The soldier happened to know 'Latin and other useless things,' so now, as he fired at the gray advancing mass, 300 yards away, he uttered the pious vegetarian motto. He went on firing to the end, till at last Bill on his right had to clout him cheerfully on the head to make him stop, pointing out as he did so that the King's ammunition cost money and was not lightly to be wasted. For, as the Latin scholar uttered his invocation, he felt something between a shudder and an electric shock pass through his body. The roar of the battle died down in his ears to a gentle murmur, and instead of it, he says, he heard a great voice louder than a thunder peal, crying 'Array! Array!' His heart grew hot as a burning coal, then it grew cold as ice within him, for it seemed to him a tumult of voices answered to the summons. He heard or seemed to hear thousands shouting:

"'St. George! St. George!

"'Ha! Messire, Ha! Sweet Saint, grant us good deliverance!

"'St. George for Merrie England!

"'Harow! Harow! Monseigneur St. George, succour us, Ha! St. George! A low bow, and a strong bow, Knight of Heaven, aid us!'

"As the soldier heard these voices, he saw before him, beyond the trench, a long line of shapes with a shining about them. They were like men who drew the bow, and with another shout their cloud of arrows flew singing through the air toward the German host. The other men in the trenches were firing all the while. They had no hope, but they aimed just as if they had been shooting at Bisley.

"Suddenly one of these lifted up his voice in plain English. 'Gawd help us!' he bellowed to the man next him, 'but we're bloomin' marvels! Look at those gray gentlemen! Look at them! They 're not going down in dozens or hundreds—it's thousands it is! Look, look! There's a regiment gone while I'm talking to ye!'

"'Shut it,' the other soldier bellowed, taking aim. 'What are ye talkin' about?' But he gulped with astonishment even as he spoke, for indeed the gray men were falling by the thousands. The English could hear the guttural scream of their revolvers as they shot, and line after line crashed to the earth. All the while the Latin-bred soldier heard the cry 'Harow, Harow! Monseigneur! Dear Saint! Quick to our aid! St. George help us!'

"The singing arrows darkened the air, the hordes melted before them. 'More machine guns,' Bill yelled to Tom. 'Don't hear them,' Tom yelled back, 'but thank God, anyway, that they have got it in the neck!'

"In fact, there were ten thousand dead German soldiers left before that salient of the English army, and consequently—no Sedan. In Germany the General Staff decided that the English must have employed turpenite shells, as no wounds were discernible on the bodies of the dead soldiers. But the man who knew what nuts tasted like when they called themselves steak, knew also that St. George had brought his Agincourt Bowmen to help the English."

Such accounts have been confirmed by others. Thus, Miss Phyllis Campbell, writing in The Occult Review (October, 1915), says:

"I tremble, now that it is safely past, to look back on the terrible week that brought the Allies to Vitry-le-François. We had not had our clothes off for the whole of that week, because no sooner had we reached home, too weary to undress, or to eat, and fallen on our beds, than the 'chug-chug' of the commandant's car would sound into the silence of the deserted street, and the horn would imperatively summon us back to duty—because, in addition to our duties as ambulancier auxiliare, we were interpreters to the post, now at this moment diminished to half a dozen.

"Returning at 4:30 in the morning, we stood on the end of the platform, watching the train crawl through the blue-green mist of the forest into the clearing, and draw up with the first wounded from Vitry-le-François. It was packed with dead and dying and badly wounded. For a time we forgot our weariness in a race against time—removing the dead and dying, and attending to those in need. I was bandaging a man's shattered arm with the majeur instructing me, while he stitched a horrible gap in his head, when Madame de A—, the heroic president of the post, came and replaced me. 'There is an English in the fifth wagon,' she said. 'He wants something—I think a holy picture!'

"The idea of an English soldier wanting a holy picture struck me, even in that atmosphere of blood and misery, as something to smile at—but I hurried away. 'The English' was a Lancashire Fusilier. He was propped in a corner, his left arm tied-up in a peasant woman's handkerchief, and his head newly bandaged. He should have been in a state of collapse from loss of blood, for his tattered uniform was soaked and caked in blood, and his face paper-white under the dirt of conflict. He looked at me with bright, courageous eyes and asked for a picture or a medal (he didn't care which) of St. George. I asked him if he was a Catholic. 'No,' he was Wesleyan Methodist, and he wanted a picture or a medal of St. George, because he had seen him on a white horse, leading the British at Vitry-le-François, when the Allies turned.

"There was an F. R. A. man, wounded in the leg, sitting beside him on the floor; he saw my look of amazement, and hastened in: 'It's true, sister,' he said. 'We all saw it. First there was a sort of yellow mist-like, sort of risin' before the Germans as they came on the top of the hill—come on like a solid wall, they did—springing out of the earth just solid—no end to 'em! I just give up. No use fighting the whole German race, thinks I; it's all up with us. The next minute comes this funny cloud of light, and when it clears off, there's a tall man with yellow hair in golden armor, on a white horse, holding his sword up, and his mouth open as if he was saying: "Come on, boys! I'll put the kybosh on the devils!" Sort of "This is my picnic" expression. Then, before you could say "knife," the Germans had turned, and we were after them, fighting like ninety ..."

"Where was this?" I asked. But neither of them could tell. They had marched, fighting a rear-guard action, from Mons, till St. George had appeared through the haze of light, and turned the enemy. They both knew it was St. George. Hadn't they seen him with a sword on every 'quid' they'd ever seen? The Frenchies had seen him too—ask them; but they said it was St. Michael...."

Much additional testimony of a like nature might be given—and has been collected by students of psychical research. If the spiritual world ever intervenes in matters mundane, it assuredly did so on this occasion. And it could hardly have chosen a more opportune time. Could the aspiring thoughts of the dead and dying, and those still living and fighting for their country, have drawn "St. George" to earth, to aid in again redeeming his country from a foreign foe? Could a simple "hallucination" have been so widespread and so prevalent? Or might there not have been some spiritual energy behind the visions thus seen—stimulating them, and inspiring and encouraging the stricken soldiers? We cannot say. We only know what the soldiers themselves say; and we also know the undoubted effects upon the enemy. For on both occasions were the Germans repulsed with terrible slaughter. Perhaps the vision of St. George led our soldiers into closer touch and rapport with the consciousness of some high intelligence—or the veil separating the two worlds was rent—as so often appears to be the case in apparitions and visions of this character.

THE PORTAL OF THE UNKNOWN

By Andrew Jackson Davis, "The Seer"

When the hour of her death arrived, I was fortunately in a proper state of mind and body to produce the superior (clairvoyant) condition; but, previous to throwing my spirit into that condition, I sought the most convenient and favorable position, that I might be allowed to make the observations entirely unnoticed and undisturbed. Thus situated and conditioned, I proceeded to observe and investigate the mysterious processes of dying, and to learn what it is for an individual human spirit to undergo the changes consequent upon physical death or external dissolution. They were these:

I saw that the physical organization could no longer subserve the diversified purposes or requirements of the spiritual principle. But the various internal organs of the body appeared to resist the withdrawal of the animating soul. The body and the soul, like two friends, strongly resisted the various circumstances which rendered their eternal separation imperative and absolute. These internal conflicts gave rise to manifestations of what seemed to be, to the material senses, the most thrilling and painful sensations; but I was unspeakably thankful and delighted when I perceived and realized the fact that those physical manifestations were indications, not of pain or unhappiness, but simply that the spirit was eternally dissolving its co-partnership with the material organism.

Now the head of the body became suddenly enveloped in a fine, soft, mellow, luminous atmosphere; and, as instantly, I saw the cerebrum and the cerebellum expand their most interior portions; I saw them discontinue their appropriate galvanic functions; and then I saw that they became highly charged with the vital electricity and vital magnetism which permeate subordinate systems and structures. That is to say, the brain, as a whole, suddenly declared itself to be tenfold more positive, over the lesser proportions of the body, than it ever was during the period of health. This phenomenon invariably precedes physical dissolution.

Now the process of dying, or the spirit's departure from the body, was fully commenced. The brain began to attract the elements of electricity, of magnetism, of motion, of life, and of sensation, into its various and numerous departments. The head became intensely brilliant; and I particularly remarked that just in the same proportion as the extremities of the organism grow dark and cold, the brain appears light and glowing.

Now I saw, in the mellow, spiritual atmosphere which emanated from and encircled her head, the indistinct outlines of the formation of another head. This new head unfolded more and more distinctly, and so indescribably compact and intensely brilliant did it become, that I could neither see through it, nor gaze upon it as steadily as I desired. While this spiritual head was being eliminated and organized from out of and above the material head, I saw that the surrounding aromal atmosphere which had emanated from the material head was in great commotion; but, as the new head became more distinct and perfect, this brilliant atmosphere gradually disappeared. This taught me that those aromal elements, which were, in the beginning of the metamorphosis, attracted from the system into the brain, and thence eliminated in the form of an atmosphere, were indissolubly united in accordance with the divine principle of affinity in the universe, which pervades and destinates every particle of matter, and developed the spiritual head which I beheld.

In the identical manner in which the spiritual head was eliminated and unchangeably organized, I saw, unfolding in their natural progressive order, the harmonious development of the neck, the shoulders, the breast and the entire spiritual organization. It appeared from this, even to an unequivocal demonstration, that the innumerable particles of what might be termed unparticled matter which constitute the man's spiritual principle, are constitutionally endowed with certain elective affinities, analogous to an immortal friendship. The innate tendencies which the elements and essences of her soul manifested by uniting and organizing themselves, were the efficient and imminent causes which unfolded and perfected her spiritual organization. The defects and deformities of her physical body were, in the spiritual body which I saw thus developed, almost completely removed. In other words, it seemed that those hereditary obstructions and influences were now removed, which originally arrested the full and proper development of her physical constitution; and, therefore, that her spiritual constitution, being elevated above those obstructions, was enabled to unfold and perfect itself, in accordance with the universal tendencies of all created things.

While this spiritual formation was going on, which was perfectly visible to my spiritual perceptions, the material body manifested, to the outer vision of observing individuals in the room, many symptoms of uneasiness and pain; but the indications were totally deceptive; they were wholly caused by the departure of the vital or spiritual forces from the extremities and viscera into the brain, and thence into the ascending organism.

The spirit arose at right angles over the head or brain of the deserted body. But immediately previous to the final dissolution of the relationship which had for so many years subsisted between the two, the spiritual and material bodies, I saw—playing energetically between the feet of the elevated spiritual body and the head of the prostrate physical body—a bright stream or current of vital electricity. And here I perceived what I had never before obtained a knowledge of, that a small portion of this vital electrical element returned to the deserted body immediately subsequent to the separation of the umbilical thread; and that that portion of this element which passed back into the earthly organism instantly diffused itself through the entire structure, and thus prevented immediate decomposition.

As soon as the spirit, whose departing hour I thus watched, was wholly disengaged from the tenacious physical body, I directed my attention to the movements and emotions of the former; and I saw her begin to breathe the most interior or spiritual portions of the surrounding terrestrial atmosphere. At first it seemed with difficulty that she could breathe the new medium; but in a few seconds she inhaled and exhaled the spiritual elements of nature with the greatest possible ease and delight. And now I saw that she was in possession of exterior and physical proportions, which were identical, in every possible particular—improved and beautified—with those proportions which characterized her earthly organization. Indeed, so much like her former self was she that, had her friends beheld her as I did, they certainly would have exclaimed—as we often do upon the sudden return of a long-absent friend, who leaves us and returns in health—'Why, how well you look! How improved you are!' Such was the nature—most beautifying in their extent—of the improvements that were wrought upon her.

I saw her continue to conform and accustom herself to the new elements and elevating sensations which belong to the inner life. I did not particularly notice the workings and emotions of her newly-awakening and fast-unfolding spirit, except that I was careful to remark her philosophical tranquillity throughout the entire process, and her non-participation with the different members of her family in their unrestrained bewailing of her departure from the earth, to unfold in Love and Wisdom throughout eternal spheres. She understood at a glance that they could only gaze upon the cold and lifeless form, which she had but just deserted; and she readily comprehended the fact that it was owing to a want of true knowledge upon their parts that they thus vehemently regretted her merely physical death.

The period required to accomplish the entire change which I saw was not far from two hours and a half; but this furnished no rule as to the time required for every spirit to elevate and reorganize itself above the head of the outer form. Without changing my position or spiritual perceptions I continued to observe the movements of her new-born spirit. As soon as she became accustomed to her new elements which surrounded her, she descended from her elevated position, which was immediately over the body, by an effort of the will-power, and directly passed out of the door of the bedroom in which she had lain, in the material form, prostrated with disease for several weeks. It being in a summer month, the doors were all open, and her egress from the house was attended with no obstruction. I saw her pass through the adjoining room, out of the door, and step from the house into the atmosphere! I was overwhelmed with delight and astonishment when, for the first time, I realized the universal truth that the spiritual organization can tread the atmosphere, which is impossible while in the coarser earthly form—so much more refined is man's spiritual constitution. She walked in the atmosphere as easily, and in the same manner, as we tread the earth and ascend an eminence. Immediately upon her emergement from the house, she was joined by two friendly spirits from the spiritual country, and after tenderly recognizing and communing with each other, the three, in the most graceful manner, began ascending obliquely through the ethereal envelopment of her globe. They walked so naturally and fraternally together that I could scarcely realize the fact that they trod the air—they seemed to be walking upon the side of a glorious but familiar mountain. I continued to gaze upon them until the distance shut them from my view,—whereupon I returned to my external and ordinary condition.

This account of the facts—of what actually happened at death—is confirmed by numerous other witnesses, who agree as to the main details.

THE SUPERNORMAL: EXPERIENCES

By St. John B. Seymour

When Mrs. Seymour was a little girl she resided in Dublin; amongst the members of the family was her paternal grandmother. This old lady was not as kind as she might have been to her granddaughter, and consequently the latter was somewhat afraid of her. In process of time the grandmother died. Mrs. Seymour, who was then about eight years of age, had to pass the door of the room where the death occurred in order to reach her own bedroom, which was a flight higher up. Past this door the child used to fly in terror with all possible speed. On one occasion, however, as she was preparing to make the usual rush past, she distinctly felt a hand placed on her shoulder, and became conscious of a voice saying, "Don't be afraid, Mary!" From that day on the child never had the least feeling of fear, and always walked quietly past the door.

The Rev. D. B. Knox sends a curious personal experience, which was shared by him with three other people. He writes as follows: "Not very long ago my wife and I were preparing to retire for the night. A niece, who was in the house, was in her bedroom and the door was open. The maid had just gone to her room. All four of us distinctly heard the heavy step of a man walking along the corridor, apparently in the direction of the bathroom. We searched the whole house immediately, but no one was discovered. Nothing untoward happened except the death of the maid's mother about a fortnight later. It was a detached house, so that the noise could not have been made by the neighbors."

In the following tale the "double" or "wraith" of a living man was seen by three different people, one of whom, our correspondent, saw it through a telescope. She writes: "In May, 1883, the parish of A— was vacant, so Mr. D—, the Diocesan Curate, used to come out to take service on Sundays. One day there were two funerals to be taken, the one at a graveyard some distance off, the other at A— churchyard. My brother was at both, the far-off one being taken the first. The house we then lived in looked down towards A—churchyard, which was about a quarter of a mile away. From an upper window my sister and I saw two surpliced figures going out to meet the coffin, and said, 'Why, there are two clergy!' having supposed that there would be only Mr. D—. I, being short-sighted, used a telescope, and saw the two surplices showing between the people. But when my brother returned he said: 'A strange thing has happened. Mr. D— and Mr. W— (curate of a neighboring parish) took the far-off funeral. I saw them both again at A—, but when I went into the vestry I only saw Mr. W—. I asked where Mr. D— was, and he replied that he had left immediately after the first funeral, as he had to go to Kilkenny, and that he (Mr. W—) had come on alone to take the funeral at A—.'"

Here is a curious tale from the city of Limerick of a lady's "double" being seen, with no consequent results. It is sent by Mr. Richard Hogan as the personal experience of his sister, Mrs. Mary Murnane. On Saturday, October 25, 1913, at half-past four o'clock in the afternoon, Mr. Hogan left the house in order to purchase some cigarettes. A quarter of an hour afterwards Mrs. Murnane went down the town to do some business. As she was walking down George Street she saw a group of four persons standing on the pavement engaged in conversation. They were her brother, a Mr. O'S—, and two ladies, a Miss P. O'D—, and her sister, Miss M. O'D—. She recognized the latter, as her face was partly turned towards her, and noted that she was dressed in a knitted coat, and light blue hat, while in her left hand she held a bag or purse; the other lady's back was turned towards her. As Mrs. Murnane was in a hurry to get her business done she determined to pass them by without being noticed, but a number of people coming in the opposite direction blocked the way, and compelled her to walk quite close to the group of four, but they were so intent on listening to what one lady was saying that they took no notice of her. The speaker appeared to be Miss M. O'D—, and though Mrs. Murnane did not actually hear her speak as she passed her, yet from their attitudes the other three seemed to be listening to what she was saying, and she heard her laugh when right behind her—not the laugh of her sister P—and the laugh was repeated after she had left the group a little behind.

So far there is nothing out of the common. When Mrs. Murnane returned to her house about an hour later she found her brother Richard there before her. She casually mentioned to him how she had passed him and his three companions on the pavement. To which he replied that she was quite correct except in one point, namely that there were only three in the group, as M. O'D— was not present, as she had not come to Limerick at all that day. She then described to him the exact position each one of the four occupied, and the clothes worn by them, to all of which facts he assented, except as to the presence of Miss M. O'D—. Mrs. Murnane adds, "That is all I can say in the matter, but most certainly the fourth person was in the group, as I both saw and heard her. She wore the same clothes I had seen on her previously, with the exception of the hat; but the following Saturday she had on the same colored hat I had seen on her the previous Saturday. When I told her about it she was as much mystified as I was and am. My brother stated that there was no laugh from any of the three present."

Mrs. G. Kelly sends an experience of a "wraith" which seems in some mysterious way to have been conjured up in her mind by the description she had heard, and then externalized. She writes: "About four years ago a musical friend of ours was staying in the house. He and my husband were playing and singing Dvorak's 'Spectre's Bride,' a work which he had studied with the composer himself. This music appealed very much to both, and they were excited and enthusiastic over it. Our friend was giving many personal reminiscences of Dvorak, and his method of explaining the way he wanted his work done. I was sitting by, an interested listener, for some time. On getting up at last, and going into the drawing-room, I was startled and somewhat frightened to find a man standing there in a shadowy part of the room. I saw him distinctly, and could describe his appearance accurately. I called out, and the two men ran in, but as the apparition only lasted for a second, they were too late. I described the man whom I had seen, whereupon our friend exclaimed, 'Why, that was Dvorak himself!' At that time I had never seen a picture of Dvorak, but when our friend returned to London he sent me one which I recognized as the likeness of the man whom I had seen in our drawing-room."

A curious vision, a case of second sight, in which a quite unimportant event, previously unknown, was revealed, is sent by the percipient, who is a lady well known to both the compilers, and a life-long friend of one of them. She says: "Last summer I sent a cow to the fair of Limerick, a distance of about thirteen miles, and the men who took her there the day before the fair left her in a paddock for the night close to Limerick city. I awoke up very early next morning, and was fully awake when I saw (not with my ordinary eyesight, but apparently inside my head) a light, an intensely brilliant light, and in it I saw the back gate being opened by a red-haired woman and the cow I had supposed in the fair walking through the gate. I then knew that the cow must be home, and going to the yard later on I was met by the wife of the man who was in charge in a great state of excitement. 'Oh law! Miss,' she exclaimed, 'you'll be mad! Didn't Julia [a red-haired woman find the cow outside the lodge gate as she was going out at 4 o'clock to the milking!' That's my tale—perfectly true, and I would give a good deal to be able to control that light, and see more if I could."

Another curious vision was seen by a lady who is also a friend of both the compilers. One night she was kneeling at her bedside saying her prayers (hers was the only bed in the room), when suddenly she felt a distinct touch on her shoulder. She turned round in the direction of the touch and saw at the end of the room a bed, with a pale, indistinguishable figure laid therein, and what appeared to be a clergyman standing over it. About a week later she fell into a long and dangerous illness.

An account of a dream which implied an extraordinary coincidence, if coincidence it be and nothing more, was sent as follows by a correspondent, who requested that no names be published. "That which I am about to relate has a peculiar interest for me, inasmuch as the central figure in it was my own grand-aunt, and moreover the principal witness (if I may use such a term) was my father. At the period during which this strange incident occurred my father was living with his aunt and some other relatives.

"One morning at the breakfast-table, my grand-aunt announced that she had had a most peculiar dream during the previous night. My father, who was always very interested in that kind of thing, took down in his notebook all the particulars concerning it. They were as follows:

"My grand-aunt dreamt that she was in a cemetery, which she recognized as Glasnevin, and as she gazed at the memorials of the dead which lay so thick around, one stood out most conspicuously, and caught her eye, for she saw clearly cut on the cold white stone an inscription bearing her own name:

CLARE·S·D—
Died 14th of March, 1873
Dearly loved and ever mourned
R.I.P.

while, to add to the peculiarity of it, the date on the stone as given above was, from the day of her dream, exactly a year in advance.

"My grand-aunt was not very nervous, and soon the dream faded from her mind. Months rolled by, and one morning at breakfast it was noticed that my grand-aunt had not appeared, but as she was a very religious woman it was thought that she had gone out to church. However, as she did not appear my father sent someone to her room to see if she were there, and as no answer was given to repeated knocking the door was opened, and my grand-aunt was found kneeling at her bedside, dead. The day of her death was March 14, 1873, corresponding exactly with the date seen in her dream a twelvemonth before. My grand-aunt was buried in Glasnevin, and on her tombstone (a white marble slab) was placed the inscription which she had read in her dream." Our correspondent sent us a photograph of the stone and its inscription.

The present Archdeacon of Limerick, Ven. J. A. Haydn, LL.D., sends the following experience: "In the year 1870 I was rector of the little rural parish of Chapel Russell. One autumn day the rain fell with a quiet, steady, and hopeless persistence from morning to night. Wearied at length from the gloom, and tired of reading and writing, I determined to walk to the church about half a mile away, and pass a half-hour playing the harmonium, returning for the lamp-light and tea.

"I wrapped up, put the key of the church in my pocket, and started. Arriving at the church, I walked up the straight avenue, bordered with graves and tombs on either side, while the soft, steady rain quietly pattered on the trees. When I reached the church door, before putting the key in the lock, moved by some indefinable impulse I stood on the doorstep, turned round, and looked back upon the path I had just trodden. My amazement may be imagined when I saw, seated on a low, tabular tombstone close to the avenue, a lady with her back towards me. She was wearing a black velvet jacket or short cape, with a narrow border of vivid white; her head and luxuriant jet-black hair were surmounted by a hat of the shape and make that I think used to be called at that time a 'turban'; it was also of black velvet, with a snow-white wing or feather at the right-hand side of it. It may be seen how deliberately and minutely I observed the appearance, when I can thus recall it after more than forty years.

"Actuated by a desire to attract the attention of the lady, and induce her to look towards me, I noisily inserted the key in the door, and suddenly opened it with a rusty crack. Turning around to see the effect of my policy—the lady was gone!—vanished. Not yet daunted, I hurried to the place, which was not ten paces away, and closely searched the stone and the space all around it, but utterly in vain; there were absolutely no traces of the late presence of a human being! I may add that nothing particular or remarkable followed the singular apparition, and that I never heard anything calculated to throw any light on the mystery."

Here is a story of a ghost who knew what it wanted—and got it! "In the part of County Wicklow from which my people come," writes a Miss D—, "there was a family who were not exactly related, but of course of the clan. Many years ago a young daughter, aged about twenty, died. Before her death she had directed her parents to bury her in a certain graveyard. But for some reason they did not do so, and from that hour she gave them no peace. She appeared to them at all hours, especially when they went to the well for water.

So distracted were they, that at length they got permission to exhume the remains and have them reinterred in the desired graveyard. This they did by torchlight—a weird scene truly! I can vouch for the truth of this latter portion, at all events, as some of my own relatives were present."

Mr. T. J. Westropp contributes a tale of a ghost of an unusual type, i.e. one which actually did communicate matters of importance to his family. "A lady who related many ghost stories to me, also told me how, after her father's death, the family could not find some papers or receipts of value. One night she awoke, and heard a sound which she at once recognized as the footsteps of her father, who was lame. The door creaked, and she prayed that she might be able to see him. Her prayer was granted: she saw him distinctly holding a yellow parchment book tied with tape. 'F—, child,' said he, 'this is the book your mother is looking for. It is in the third drawer of the cabinet near the cross-door; tell your mother to be more careful in future about business papers.' Incontinently he vanished, and she at once awoke her mother, in whose room she was sleeping, who was very angry and ridiculed the story, but the girl's earnestness at length impressed her. She got up, went to the old cabinet, and at once found the missing book in the third drawer."

Here is another tale of an equally useful and obliging ghost. "A gentleman, a relative of my own," writes a lady, "often received warnings from his dead father of things that were about to happen. Besides the farm on which he lived, he had another some miles away which adjoined a large demesne. Once in a great storm a fir-tree was blown down in the demesne, and fell into his field. The woodranger came to him and told him he might as well cut up the tree, and take it away. Accordingly one day he set out for this purpose, taking with him two men and a cart. He got into the fields by a stile, while his men went on to a gate. As he approached a gap between two fields he saw his father standing in it, as plainly as he ever saw him in life, and beckoning him back warningly. Unable to understand this, he still advanced, whereupon his father looked very angry, and his gestures became imperious. This induced him to turn away, so he sent his men home, and left the tree uncut. He subsequently discovered that a plot had been laid by the woodranger, who coveted his farm, and who hoped to have him dispossessed by accusing him of stealing the tree."

A clergyman in the diocese of Clogher gave a personal experience of table-turning to the present Dean of St. Patrick's, who kindly sent the same to the writer. He said: "When I was a young man, I met some friends one evening, and we decided to amuse ourselves with table-turning. The local dispensary was vacant at the time, so we said that if the table would work we should ask who would be appointed as medical officer. As we sat round it touching it with our hands it began to knock. We said:

"'Who are you?'

"The table spelt out the name of a bishop of the Church of Ireland. We asked, thinking that the answer was absurd, as we knew him to be alive and well:

"'Are you dead?'

"The table answered 'Yes.'

"We laughed at this and asked:

"'Who will be appointed to the dispensary!'

"The table spelt out the name of a stranger, who was not one of the candidates, whereupon we left off, thinking that the whole thing was nonsense.

"The next morning I saw in the papers that the bishop in question had died that afternoon about two hours before our meeting, and a few days afterwards I saw the name of the stranger as the new dispensary doctor. I got such a shock that I determined never to have anything to do with table-turning again."

The following extraordinary personal experience is sent by a lady, well-known to the present writer, but who requests that all names be omitted. Whatever explanation we may give of it, the good faith of the tale is beyond doubt.

"Two or three months after my father-in-law's death, my husband, myself, and three small sons lived in the west of Ireland. As my husband was a young barrister, he had to be absent from home a good deal. My three boys slept in my bedroom, the eldest being about four, the youngest some months. A fire was kept up every night, and with a young child to look after, I was naturally awake more than once during the night. For many nights I believed I distinctly saw my father-in-law sitting by the fireside. This happened, not once or twice, but many times. He was passionately fond of his eldest grandson, who lay sleeping calmly in his cot. Being so much alone probably made me restless and uneasy, though I never felt afraid. I mentioned this strange thing to a friend who had known and liked my father-in-law, and she advised me to 'have his soul laid,' as she termed it. Though I was a Protestant and she was a Roman Catholic (as had also been my father-in-law), yet I fell in with her suggestion. She told me to give a coin to the next beggar that came to the house, telling him (or her) to pray for the rest of Mr. So-and-so's soul. A few days later a beggar-woman and her children came to the door, to whom I gave a coin and stated my desire. To my great surprise I learned from her manner that such requests were not unusual. Well, she went down on her knees on the steps, and prayed with apparent earnestness and devotion that his soul might find repose. Once again he appeared, and seemed to say to me, 'Why did you do that, E——? To come and sit here was the only comfort I had.' Never again did he appear, and strange to say, after a lapse of more than thirty years I have felt regret at my selfishness in interfering.

"After his death, as he lay in the house awaiting burial, and I was in a house some ten miles away, I thought that he came and told me that I would have a hard life, which turned out only too truly. I was then young, and full of life, with every hope of a prosperous future."

Of all the strange beliefs to be found in Ireland that in the Black Dog is the most widespread. There is hardly a parish in the country but could contribute some tale relative to this specter, though the majority of these are short, and devoid of interest. There is said to be such a dog just outside the avenue gate of Donohill Rectory, but neither of the compilers have had the good luck to see it. It may be, as some hold, that this animal was originally a cloud or nature-myth; at all events, it has now descended to the level of an ordinary haunting. The most circumstantial story that we have met with relative to the Black Dog is that related as follows by a clergyman of the Church of Ireland, who requests us to refrain from publishing his name.

"In my childhood I lived in the country. My father, in addition to his professional duties, sometimes did a little farming in an amateurish sort of way. He did not keep a regular staff of laborers, and consequently when anything extra had to be done, such as hay-cutting or harvesting, he used to employ day-laborers to help with the work. At such times I used to enjoy being in the fields with the men, listening to their conversation. On one occasion I heard a laborer remark that he had once seen the devil! Of course I was interested and asked him to give me his experience. He said he was walking along a certain road, and when he came to a point where there was an entrance to a private place (the spot was well known to me), he saw a black dog sitting on the roadside. At the time he paid no attention to it, thinking it was an ordinary retriever, but after he had passed on about two or three hundred yards he found the dog was beside him, and then he noticed that its eyes were blood-red. He stooped down, and picked up some stones in order to frighten it away, but though he threw the stones at it they did not injure it, nor indeed did they seem to have any effect. Suddenly, after a few moments, the dog vanished from his sight.

"Such was the laborer's tale. After some years, during which time I had forgotten altogether about the man's story, some friends of my own bought the place at the entrance to which the apparition had been seen. When my friends went to reside there I was a constant visitor at their house. Soon after their arrival they began to be troubled by the appearance of a black dog. Though I never saw it myself, it appeared to many members of the family. The avenue leading to the house was a long one, and it was customary for the dog to appear and accompany people for the greater portion of the way. Such an effect had this on my friends that they soon gave up the house, and went to live elsewhere. This was a curious corroboration of the laborer's tale."

A distinction must be drawn between the so-called Headless Coach, which portends death, and the Phantom Coach, which appears to be a harmless sort of vehicle. With regard to the latter we give two tales below, the first of which was sent by a lady whose father was a clergyman, and a gold medalist of Trinity College, Dublin.

"Some years ago my family lived in County Down. Our house was some way out of a fair-sized manufacturing town, and had a short avenue which ended in a gravel sweep in front of the hall door. One winter's evening, when my father was returning from a sick call, a carriage going at a sharp pace passed him on the avenue. He hurried on, thinking it was some particular friends, but when he reached the door no carriage was to be seen, so he concluded it must have gone round to the stables. The servant who answered his ring said that no visitors had been there, and he, feeling certain that the girl had made some mistake, or that some one else had answered the door, came into the drawing-room to make further inquiries. No visitors had come, however, though those sitting in the drawing-room had also heard the carriage drive up.

"My father was most positive as to what he had seen, viz. a closed carriage with lamps lit; and let me say at once that he was a clergyman who was known throughout the whole of the north of Ireland as a most level-headed man, and yet to the day of his death he would insist that he met that carriage on our avenue.

"One day in July one of our servants was given leave to go home for the day, but was told she must return by a certain train. For some reason she did not come by it, but by a much later one, and rushed into the kitchen in a most penitent frame of mind. 'I am so sorry to be late,' she told the cook, 'especially as there were visitors. I suppose they stayed to supper, as they were so late going away, for I met the carriage on the avenue.' The cook thereupon told her that no one had been at the house, and hinted that she must have seen the ghost-carriage, a statement that alarmed her very much, as the story was well known in the town, and car-drivers used to whip up their horses as they passed our gate, while pedestrians refused to go at all except in numbers. We have often heard the carriage, but these are the only two occasions on which I can positively assert that it was seen."

The following personal experience of the phantom coach was given to the present writer by Mr. Matthias Fitzgerald, coachman to Miss Cooke, of Cappagh House, County Limerick. He stated that one moonlight night he was driving along the road from Askeaton to Limerick when he heard coming up behind him the roll of wheels, the clatter of horses' hoofs, and the jingling of the bits. He drew over to his own side to let this carriage pass, but nothing passed. He then looked back, but could see nothing, the road was perfectly bare and empty, though the sounds were perfectly audible. This continued for about a quarter of an hour or so, until he came to a cross-road, down one arm of which he had to turn. As he turned off he heard the phantom carriage dash by rapidly along the straight road. He stated that other persons had had similar experiences on the same road.

NATURE-SPIRITS OR ELEMENTALS[18]

BY NIZIDA

"Life is one all-pervading principle, and even the thing that seems to die and putrefy but engenders new life and changes to new forms of matter. Reasoning, then, by analogy—if not a leaf, if not a drop of water, but is, no less than yonder star, a habitable and breathing world, common sense would suffice to teach that the circumfluent Infinite, which you call space—the boundless Impalpable which divides the earth from the moon and stars—is filled also with its correspondent and appropriate life."—Zanoni.

Within the last fifty years the human mind has been awakening slowly to the fact that there is a world, invisible to ordinary powers of vision, existing in close juxtaposition to the world cognized by our material senses. This world, or condition of existence for more ethereal beings, has been variously called Spirit-world, Summer-land, Astral-world, Hades, Kama-loca, or Desire-world, etc. Slowly and with difficulty do ideas upon the nature and characteristics of this world dawn upon the modern mind. The imagination, swayed by pictures of sensuous life, revels in the fantastic imagery it attributes to this unknown and dimly conceived state of existence, more often picturing what is false than what is true. Generally speaking, the most crude conceptions are entertained; these embrace but two conditions of life, the embodied and disembodied, for which there are only the earth and heaven, or hell, with that intermediate state accepted by Roman Catholics, called purgatory. There is, therefore, for such minds, only two orders of beings, i.e., mankind, and angels or devils, categorically termed spirits; but what would be the mode of life of those spirits, is a subject upon which ordinary intellects can throw no light at all. Their ideas are walled in by an impenetrable darkness, and not a ray of light glimmers across the unfathomable gulf lying beyond the grave; that portal of death which, for them, opens upon unknown darkness, and closes upon the light, vivacity, and gaiety of the earth.

The idea that the beings we would term disembodied do actually inhabit bodies of an aerial substance, invisible to our grosser senses, in a world exactly suited to their needs, surpasses the comprehension of an ordinary understanding, which can conceive only of gross matter, visible and tangible. Yet science

[18] From Journal of Proceedings of Theosophical Society.

begins to talk of mind-stuff, or soul-substance, in reality that ethereal substance which ranks next to dense matter, and which it wears as an external, more hardened shell. For there is space within space. Once realizing the existence of an inner world, we shall find that all our ideas concerning space, time, and every particular of our existence, and the world we live in must become entirely revolutionized.

The principal source of knowledge which has been opened in modern times concerning the next state of existence has revealed itself in a manner homogeneous to itself. It has come by an interior method—a revelation from within acting upon the without. The inner world, although always acting upon and through its external covering, in a hidden or veiled way, as from an inscrutable cause, has manifested itself in a manner more overt and cognizable by the bodily senses of man. At least that which has usually been termed, with more or less awe, the supernatural, the ghostly, has impinged upon the mental incrassation of sensual man as a thing to be reckoned with in daily life; no longer to be relegated to the region of vague darkness d'outre tombe. Hence the human mind is being awakened to study and dive into the depths of that life within life, wherein dwell the disembodied, the so-called dead, the angels, and, per contra, the devils. Those hidden aerial and ethereal regions, wherein the souls of things, and beings, draw life from the bosom of nature; wherein they find their active habitat; wherein nature keeps a store of objects more wonderful, and infinitely more varied, than serve for her regions of dense matter; wherein man can discern the occult causes and beginnings of all things, even of his own thoughts; and whereupon he learns, at length, that he possesses the power of projecting by thought-creation forms more or less endued with life and intelligence, which compose his mental world, and with which he, as it were, "peoples space." He finds the sphere of his responsibilities immensely enlarged by this new knowledge, of which he is taking the first honeyed sips, delighted with the self-importance which the heretofore unsuspected power of diving into the unseen seems to bestow. If hitherto he has had to hold himself responsible for the consequences of his external actions, that they should not militate against the order of society as regards the laws of morality and virtue, he has at least acted upon the impression that his secret thoughts were his own, and remained with him, affecting no one but himself; were incognizable in their veiled chambers, and of which it was not necessary to take any notice; the transitory, evanescent, spontaneous workings of mind, unknown and inscrutable, which begin and end like the flight of a bird, whence coming and where going it is impossible to know.

By the first faint gleams of the light of hidden wisdom, which are beginning to dawn upon his mind, he now perceives that responsibility does not end upon the plane of earth, but extends into the aerial regions of that inner world where his thoughts are no longer secret, and where they affect the astral currents, acting for the good or detriment of others to almost infinite extent; that he may act upon the ambient atmospheres, not only of the outer but inner planes of life, like a plant of poisonous exhalations, if his thoughts be not pure and good; peopling unseen space with the outcome of a debased mind, in the shape of hideous and maleficent creatures. He becomes responsible, therefore, for the consequences of his mental actions and thought-life, as well as those actions carefully prepared to pass unchallenged before this world's gaze.

Diving into the unseen by the light of the new spiritual knowledge now radiating into all minds, we learn that there are three degrees of life in man, the material, the aerial, and the ethereal, corresponding to body, soul, and spirit; and that there are three corresponding planes of existence inhabited by beings suited to them.

The subject of our paper will limit us at present to the aerial, or soul-plane—the next contiguous, or astral world. The beings that more especially live in this realm of the soul, have by common consent been termed elementals. Nature in illimitable space teems with life in forms ethereal, evanescent as thought itself, or more objectively condensed and solidified, according to the inherent attraction which holds them together; enduring according to the force, energy, or power which gave them birth; intelligent, or non-intelligent, from the same source, which is mental. These spirits of the soul-world are possessed of aerial bodies, and their world has its own firmament, its own atmosphere and conditions of existence, its own objects, scenes, habitations. Yet their world and the world of man intermingle, interpenetrate, and "throw their shadows upon each other," says Paracelsus. Again, he says: "As there are in our world water and fire, harmonies and contrasts, visible bodies and invisible essences, likewise these beings are varied in their constitution, and have their own peculiarities, for which human beings have no comprehension."

Matter, as known to men in bodies, is seen and felt by means of the physical senses; but to beings not provided with such senses, the things of our world are as invisible and intangible as things of more ethereal substance are to our grosser senses. Elementals which find their habitat in the interior of the earth's shell, usually called gnomes, are not conscious of the density of the element of earth as we perceive it; but breathe in a free atmosphere, and behold objects of which we cannot form the remotest conception. In like manner exist the undines in water, sylphs in air, and salamanders in fire. The elementals of the air, sylphs, are said to be friendly towards man; those of the water, undines, are malicious. The salamanders can, but rarely do, associate with man, "on account of the fiery nature of the element they inhabit." The pigmies (gnomes) are friendly; but as they are the guardians of treasure they usually oppose the approach of man, baffling by many mysterious arts the selfish greed of seekers for buried wealth. We, however, read of their alluring miners either by stroke of pick, or hammer, or by floating lights to the best mineral "leads." Paracelsus says of these subterranean elementals that they build houses, vaults, and strange-looking edifices of certain immaterial substances unknown to us. "They have some kind of alabaster, marble, cement, etc., but these substances are as different from ours as the web of a spider is different from our linen."

These inhabitants of the elements, or "nature-spirits," may, or may not be, conscious of the existence of man; oftentimes feeling him merely as a force which propels, or arrests them; for by his will and by his thought, he acts upon the astral currents of the aerial world in which they live; and by the use of his hands he sways the material elements of earth, fire, and water wherein they are established. They perceive the soul-essence of man with its "currents and forms," and they also are capable of reading such thoughts as do not spiritually transcend their powers of discernment. They perceive the states of feeling and emotions of men by the "colors and impressions produced in their auras," and may thus irresistibly be drawn into overt action upon man's plane of life. They are the invisible stone-throwers we hear of so frequently, supposed to be human spirits; the perpetrators of mischief, such as destruction of property in the habitations of men, noises, and mysterious nocturnal annoyances.

Of all writers upon occult subjects to whose works we have as yet gained access, Paracelsus throws the greatest light upon these tricky sprites celebrated in the realm of poesy, and inhabiting that disputed land popularly termed fairydom. From open vision, and that wonderful insight of the master or adept into the secrets of nature, Paracelsus is able to give us the most positive information concerning their bodily formation, the nature of their existence, and other extraordinary particulars, which proves that he has actually seen and observed them, and doubtless also employed them as the obedient servants of his purified will; a power into which the spiritual man ascends by a species of right, when he has thrown off, or conquered, the thraldom of matter in his own body, and stands open-eyed at "the portals of his deep within."

We will quote certain extracts from the pages of this wonderful interpreter of nature. "There are two kinds of flesh. One that comes from Adam, and another that does not come from Adam. The former is gross material, visible and tangible for us; the other one is not tangible and not made from earth. If a man who is a descendant from Adam wants to pass through a wall, he will have first to make a hole through it; but a being who is not descended from Adam needs no hole nor door, but may pass through matter that appears solid to us without causing any damage to it. The beings not descended from Adam, as well as those descended from him, are organized and have substantial bodies; but there is as much difference between the substance composing their bodies as there is between matter and spirit. Yet the elementals are not spirits, because they have flesh, blood, and bones; they live and propagate offspring; they eat and talk, act and sleep, etc., and consequently they cannot be properly called spirits. They are beings occupying a place between man and spirits, resembling men and women in their organization and form, and resembling spirits in the rapidity of their locomotion. They are intermediary beings or composita, formed out of two parts joined into one; just as two colors mixed together will appear as one color, resembling neither one nor the other of the two original ones. The elementals have no higher principles; they are therefore not immortal, and when they die they perish like animals. Neither water nor fire can injure them, and they cannot be locked up in our material prisons. They are, however, subject to diseases. Their costumes, actions, forms, ways of speaking, etc., are not very unlike those of human beings; but there are a great many varieties. They have only animal intellects, and are incapable of spiritual development."

In saying the elementals have "no higher principles," and "When they die they perish like animals," Paracelsus does not stop to explain that the higher principles in them are absolutely latent, as in plants; and that animals in "perishing" are not destroyed, but the psychical or soul-part of the animal passes, by the processes of evolution, into higher forms.

"Each species moves only in the element to which it belongs, and neither of them can go out of its appropriate element, which is to them as the air is to us, or the water to fishes; and none of them can live in the element belonging to another class. To each elemental being the element in which it lives is transparent, invisible, and respirable, as the atmosphere is to ourselves."

"As far as the personalities of the elementals are concerned, it may be said that those belonging to the element of water resemble human beings of either sex; those of the air are greater and stronger; the salamanders are long, lean, and dry; the pigmies (gnomes) are the length of about two spans, but they may extend or elongate their forms until they appear like giants.

"Nymphs (undines, or naiads) have their residences and palaces in the element of water; sylphs and salamanders have no fixed dwellings. Salamanders have been seen in the shape of fiery balls, or tongues of fire running over the fields or appearing in houses;" or at psychical séances as starry lights, darting and dancing about.

"There are certain localities where large numbers of elementals live together, and it has occurred that a man has been admitted into their communities and lived with them for a while, and that they have become visible and tangible to him."

Poets, in their moments of exaltation, have an unconscious soul-vision before which nature's invisible worlds lie like an open volume, and they translate her secrets into language of mystic meanings whose harmonies are re-interpreted by sympathetic minds. The poet Hogg, in his Rapture of Kilmeny, would seem to have had a vision of some such visit as that described above, into the fairyland of pure, peaceful elementals.

"Bonny Kilmeny gaed up the glen"—and is represented as having fallen asleep. During this sleep she is transported to "a far countrye," whose gentle, lovely inhabitants receive her with delight. The following lines reveal the poet's power of inner vision, as will be seen by the words italicized. They are in wonderful accord with the descriptions given by Paracelsus from the actual observation of a conscious seer:

"They lifted Kilmeny, they led her away,
And she walk'd in the light of a sunless day;
The sky was a dome of crystal bright,
The fountain of vision and fountain of light;
The emerald fields were of dazzling glow,
And the flowers of everlasting blow."

It needs but a brushing away of the films of flesh, which occurs in moments of rapt inspiration, for the soul, escaping from its prison-house, to revel in the innocent, peaceful scenes of its own inner world, and give a true description of what it beholds. The inner meanings of things, the symbolical correspondences are revealed in a flash of light, and the poet-soul becomes revelator and prophet all in one. He sets it down to imagination and fancy, when he returns into his normal state, and it is what we call "a flight of genius"—the power of the soul to enter its own appropriate world. Certainly les ames de boue have no such power. It is, however, a proof that world exists, if we will but understand it aright.

There has never existed a poet with a truer conception of "elemental" life than Shakespeare. What more exquisite creation of the poet's fancy, which might be every word of it true, for in no particular does it surpass the truth, than that of Ariel, whom the "foul witch Sycorax," "by help of her more potent ministers, and in her most unmitigable rage," did confine "into a cloven pine;" for Ariel, the good elemental, was "a spirit too delicate to act her earthly and abhorred commands." When Prospero, the Adept and White Magician, arrived upon the scene, by his superior art he liberated the delicate Ariel, who afterwards becomes his ministering servant for good, not for evil.

In the Midsummer Night's Dream, Titania transports a human child into her elemental world, where she keeps him with so jealous a love as to refuse to yield him even to her "fairy lord," as Puck calls him. Puck himself is almost as exquisite a realization of elemental life as Ariel. As Shakespeare unfolds the lovely, innocent tale of the occupations, sports and pranks of this aerial people, he introduces us to the elementals of his own beautiful thought world; and, although indulging in the "sports of fancy," there is so broad a foundation of truth, that, being enlightened by the revelations of Paracelsus, we no longer think we are merely entertained by the poetical inventions of a master of his art, but may well believe we have been witnesses of a charming reality beheld through the "rift in the veil" of the poet's unconscious inner sight. Indeed, one of the tenets of occult science is that there is nothing on earth, nor that the mind of man can conceive, which is not already existent in the unseen world.

We reflect in the translucence, or diaphane of our mental world those concrete images of things which we attract by the irresistible magnetism of desire working through the thought. It is a spontaneous, unconscious mental process with us; but there is no reason why it should not become a perfectly conscious process regulated by a divine wisdom to functions of harmony with nature's laws, and to productions of beauty and beneficence for the good of the whole world. As the world is the concreted emanation of divine thought, so it is by thought that man, the microcosm, creates upon his petty, finite plane. Given the desire—even if it be only as the lightest breath of a summer zephyr upon the sleeping bosom of the ocean, scarcely ruffling its surface—it becomes a center of attraction for suitable molecules of thought-substance floating in space, which immediately "agglomerate round the idea proceeding to reveal itself," by means of clothing itself in substance. By these silent processes in the invisible world wherein our souls draw the breath of life, we form our mental world, our personal character, even our very physical bodies. The perisprit, or astral body, the vehicle for formless spirit, is essentially builded up from the mental life, and grows by the accretion of those atoms or molecules of thought-substance which are assimilable by the mind. Hence a good man, a man of lofty aspirations, forms, as the nearest external clothing of his inner spirit, a beautiful soul-body, which irradiates through and beautifies the physical body. The man of low and groveling mind will, on the contrary, attract the depraved and poisoned substances of the lower astral world; the malarial emanations thrown off by other equally depraved beings, by which his mind becomes embruted, his soul diseased, whilst his physical form presents in a concrete image the ugliness of his inner nature. Such a man never ascends above the dense, mephitic vapors of the sin-laden world, nor takes into his soul the slightest breath of pure, vitalizing air. He is diseased by invisible astral microbes, being most effectually self-inoculated with them by the operation of desires which never transcend the earth. Did we lift the veil which shrouds from mortal sight the elemental world of such a moral pervert, we should behold a world teeming with hideous forms, and as actively working as the bacteria of fermentation revealed by a powerful microscope, elementals of destruction, death, and decay, which must pass out into other forms for the purification of the spiritual atmosphere; creatures produced by the man's own thoughts, living upon and in him, and reflecting, like mirrors, his hideousness back again to himself. It is from the presence of innumerable foci of evil of this kind that the world is befouled, and the moral atmosphere of our planet tainted. They emit poisoned astral currents, from which none are safe but those who are in the positive condition of perfect moral health.

From the fountain of life we draw in the materials of life, and become, upon our lower plane, other living fountains, which from liberty of choice, and freedom of will, have the power of so muddying the pure stream, that in its turbidness and foulness it becomes death instead of life, and produces hell instead of heaven. When we, by self-purification, and that constant mental discipline which trains us upwards, clinging to our highest ideal by the tendrils of faith, and love, and continual aspiration, as the vine would cling to a rock—have eliminated all that is impure in our thought world, we become fountains of life, and make our own heavens, wherein are reflected only images of divine beauty. The whole elemental world on our immediate astral plane becomes gradually transformed during the progress of our evolution into the higher spiritual grades of being. And as humanity en masse advances, throwing off the moral and spiritual deformity of the selfish, ignorant ego, the astral atmospheres belonging to our planet world become filled with elementals of a peaceful, loving character, of beautiful forms, and of beneficent influences. The currents of evil force which now act with a continually jarring effect upon those striving to maintain the equilibrium of harmony with nature upon the side of good, would cease. That depression, agitation, and distress which now, from inscrutable causes, assail minds otherwise rejoicing in an innocent happiness, forewarning them of some impending calamity, or of some evil presence it seems impossible to shake off, would become unknown. The horrible demons of war, with which humanity, in its sinful state of separateness, is continually threatening itself—as if the members of one body were self-opposed, and revolting from that state of agreement that can alone ensure the well-being of the whole—would no longer be held, like ravenous bloodhounds chafing against their leashes, ready to spring, at a word, upon their hellish work; but they will have passed away, like other hideous deformities of evil; and the serene astral atmospheres would no longer reflect ideas of cruel wrongs to fellow-beings, revenge, lust of power, injustice, and ruthless hatred. We are taught that around an "idea" agglomerate the suitable molecules of soul-substance—"Monads," as Leibnitz terms them, until a concrete form stands created, the production of a mind, or minds. All the hideous man-created beings, powers or forces, which now act like ravaging pestilences and storms in the astral atmospheres of our planet will have disappeared like the monstrous phantoms of a frightful dream, when the whole of humanity has progressed into a state of higher spiritual evolution. It is well to reflect that each individual, however humble and apparently insignificant his position in the great human family, can aid by his life, by the silent emanation of his pure and wise thoughts, as well as by his active labors for humanity, in bringing nearer this halcyon period of peace, harmony, and purity—that millennium, in short, we are all looking forward to, as a dream we can never hope to see realized.

In Man: Fragments of Forgotten History, we read: "Violence was the most baneful manifestation of man's spiritual decadence, and it rebounded upon him from the elemental beings, whom it was his duty to develop"—those sub-mundanes, towards whom man is now learning that he incurs responsibilities of which he is at present utterly unconscious, but of which he will indubitably become more and more aware as he ascends the ladder of spiritual evolution.

To continue our extract from Fragments. "When this duty was ignored, and the separation of interests was accentuated, the natural man forcibly realized an antagonism with the elemental spirits. As violence increased in man, these spirits waxed strong in their way, and, true to their natures, which had been outraged by the neglect of those who were in a sense their guardians, they automatically responded with resentment. No longer could man rely upon the power of love or harmony to guide others, because he himself had ceased to be impelled solely by its influence; distrust had marred the symmetry of his inner self, and beings who could not perceive but only receive impressions projected towards them, quickly adapted themselves to the altered conditions." (Elementals as forces, respond to forces, or are swayed by them; man, as a superior force, acts upon them, therefore, injuriously, or beneficially, and they in their turn, poisoned by his baleful influence, when he is depraved, become injurious forces to him by the laws of reaction.) "At once nature itself took on the changed expression; and where all before was gladness and freshness there were now indications of sorrow and decay. Atmospheric influences hitherto unrecognized began to be noted; there was felt a chill in the morning, a dearth of magnetic heat at noon-tide, and a universal deadness at the approach of night, which began to be looked upon with alarm. For a change in the object must accompany every change in the subject. Until this point was reached there was nothing to make man afraid of himself and his surroundings.

"And as he plunged deeper and deeper into matter, he lost his consciousness of the subtler forms of existence, and attributed all the antagonism he experienced to unknown causes. The conflict continued to wax stronger, and, in consequence of his ignorance, man fell a readier victim. There were exceptions among the race then, as there are now, whose finer perceptive faculties outgrew, or kept ahead, of the advancing materialization; and they alone, in course of events, could feel and recognize the influences of these earliest progeny of the earth.

"Time came when an occasional appearance was viewed with alarm, and was thought to be an omen of evil. Recognizing this fear on the part of man, the elementals ultimately came to realize for him the dangers he apprehended, and they banded together to terrify him." (They reflected back to him his own fears in a concrete form, sufficiently intelligent, perhaps, to take some malicious pleasure in it, for man in propelling into space a force of any kind is met by a reactionary force, which seems to give exactly what his mind foreshadowed. In the negative coldness of fear, he lays himself open to infesting molecules or atoms which paralyze life, and he falls a victim to his own lack of faith, cheerful courage and hope.) "They found strong allies in an order of existence which was generated when physical death made its appearance" (i.e., elementaries, or shells); "and their combined forces began to manifest themselves at night, for which man had a dread as being the enemy of his protector, the sun.[19]

"The elementaries galvanized into activity by the elemental beings began to appear to man under as many varieties of shape as his hopes and fears allowed. And as his ignorance of things spiritual became denser, these agencies brought in an influx of error, which accelerated his spiritual degeneration. Thus, it will be seen that man's neglect of his duty to the nature-spirits is the cause which has launched him into a sea of troubles, that has shipwrecked so many generations of his descendants. Famines, plagues, wars, and other catastrophes are not so disconnected with the agency of nature-spirits as it might appear to the sceptical mind."[20]

It is therefore evident that the world of man exercises a controlling power over this invisible world of elementals. Even in the most remote and inaccessible haunts of nature, where we may imagine halcyon days of an innocent bliss elapsing in poetic peace and beauty for the more harmless of these irresponsible, evanescent offspring of nature's teeming bosom, they must inevitably, sooner or later, yield up their peaceful sovereignty to the greater monarch, man, who usually comes with a harsh and discordant influence, like the burning sirocco of the desert, like the overwhelming avalanche from the silent peaks of snow, or the earthquake, convulsing and tearing to atoms the beauty of gardens, palaces, cities. It is said that elementals die; it is presumable that at such times they die by myriads, when the whole surface of the earth becomes changed from the unavoidable passing away of nature's wildernesses, the peaceful homes of bird and beast, as the improving, commercial, money-grasping man—that contradiction of God, that industrious destroyer, who lives at war with beauty, peace, and goodness—appears upon the scene. These may be called poetical rhapsodies; yet poetry is, in a mysterious way, closely allied to that hidden truth which has its birth on the soul-plane, and the imagination of man is, according to Eliphas Lévi, a clairvoyant and magical faculty—"the wand of the magician."

To speak of elementals dying, is to use a word which expresses for us change of condition; the passing from one sphere of life to another, or from one plane of consciousness to another. This to the

---

19 Fragments of Forgotten History.
20 Fragments of Forgotten History.

sensual man is "death." But there is no death—it is merely a passing from one phase of existence to another. Hence the elementals lose the forms they once held, changing their plane of consciousness, and appearing in other forms.

We have shown somewhat of the mysterious way in which man acts upon these invisible denizens of his soul-world, and by which he incurs a certain responsibility. By the dynamic power of thought and will it is done—as everything is done. The elementals pushed by man, as by a superior force, off that equilibrium of harmony with pure, innocent nature, which they originally maintained when our planet was young, have been transformed into powers of evil, which man brings upon himself as retribution—the reaction of that force he ignorantly sets in motion when he breaks the beneficent laws of nature. Originally dependent upon him, and capable of aiding him in a thousand ways when he is wise and good, they have become his enemies, who thwart him at every turn, and guard the secrets of their abodes with none the less implacable sternness because they are probably only semi-conscious of the functions they perform. It is nature acting through them—the great cosmic consciousness, which forbids that desecrating footsteps shall invade the holy precincts of her stupendous life-secrets. But to the spiritual man—the god—these secrets open of themselves, like a hand laden with gifts, readily unclosing to a favorite and deserving child.

Giving forth a current of evil, and sinking therefrom into a state of bestial ignorance, man has enveloped himself in clouds of darkness which assume monstrous shapes threatening to overwhelm him. A wicked man is generally a coward because he lives in a state of perpetual dread of the reactionary effect of the evil forces he has set in motion. These are volumes of elemental forms banded together, and swaying like the thunder-clouds of a gathering storm.

To disperse these, his own spiritual mind must ray forth the light reflected from the source of light—omniscience. In the astral atmospheres of the spiritual man, there are no clouds, and fear is unknown. In the mental world of the innocent and pure, those are only forms of gracious beauty, as lovely as the shapes of nature's innocent embryons, which reveal themselves in the forests, the running streams, the floating breeze, and in company with the birds and flowers, to the clairvoyant sight of those nature-lovers before whom she withdraws her veils, communing with their souls by an intuitional speech which fills them with rapturous admiration. It is not only the learned scientist who may read nature's marvelous revelations; for she whispers them with maternal tenderness into the open ears of babes, where they remain ever safe from desecration, and are cherished as the soul's innocent delights in hours of isolation from the busy, jarring world.

The spiritual soul is ever looking beneath nature's material veils for correspondences. Every natural object means something else to such penetrating vision—a vision which begins to be spontaneously exercised by the soul when it has fairly reached that stage of spiritual evolution; and to this silent exploration many a secret meaning reveals itself by object-pictures, which awaken reflection and inquiry as to the why and wherefore. Thus the spiritual man drinks, as it were, from nature's own hand the pure waters of an inexhaustible spring—that occult knowledge which feeds his soul, and aids in forming for him a beautiful and powerful astral body. And nature becomes invested to his penetrating sight with a beauty she never wore before, and which the clay-blinded eyes of animal man can never behold. Such a man would enter the isolated haunts of the purer nature-spirits with gentle footsteps, and loving thoughts. To him the breeze is wafted wooingly, the streams whisper music, and everything wears an aspect of loving joyousness, and inviting confidence. Beside the rigid material forms, he sees their aromal counter-parts; everything is life; the very stones live, and have a consciousness suited to their state; and he feels as if every atom of his own body vibrated in unison with the living things about him—as if all were one flesh. To injure a single thing would be impossible to him. Such is the soul-condition of the perfect man, to whom evil has become impossible.

An adept has written—"Every thought of man upon being evolved passes into another world and becomes an active entity by associating itself—coalescing, we might term it—with an elemental; that is to say, with one of the semi-intelligent forces of the kingdoms. It survives as an active intelligence—a creature of the mind's begetting—for a longer or shorter period, proportionate with the original intensity of the cerebral action which generated it. Thus, a good thought is perpetuated as an active, beneficent power, an evil one as a maleficent demon. And so man is continually peopling his current in space with the offspring of his fancies, desires, impulses, and passions; a current which re-acts upon any sensitive or nervous organization which comes in contact with it, in proportion to its dynamic intensity. The adept evolves these shapes consciously, other men throw them off unconsciously."

Therefore, man must be held responsible not only for his outward actions, but his secret thoughts, by which he puts into existence irresponsible entities of more or less maleficent power, if his thoughts be of an evil nature. These are revelations of a deep and abstruse character; but would they have come at all if man had not reached that stage of evolution when it is necessary he should step up into his spiritual kingdom, and rule as a master over his lower self, and as a beneficent god over every department of unintelligent nature?

We note the closing words of the adept's letter: "The adept evolves these shapes consciously, other men throw them off unconsciously." In the adept's soul-world then—the man who has ascended, by self-conquest primarily, into his spiritual kingdom, and who has graduated through years of probation and study in spiritual or occult science—i.e., the White Magician, the Son of God, the inheritor by spiritual evolution, of divinity—there would reign peace, happiness, beauty, order, absolute harmony with nature on the side of good. No discordant note, no deformed astral production to embarrass or obstruct the current of divine magnetism he emanates into space—the delicious, soul-purifying, healing, and uplifting aura which radiates from him as from a center of beneficence to the lower world of struggling humanity. The semi-intelligent forces of nature, the innocent nature spirits would in such a soul-world, find an appropriate and harmonious habitat, clustering in waiting obedience upon the behests of a master whose every thought-breath would be as an uplifting life.

To such a state and condition of complete harmony with God and nature must the truly perfect spiritual man ascend by evolution.

The Difference Between Elementals and Elementaries

From the similarity of the terms used to designate two classes of astral beings who are able to communicate with man, a certain confusion has arisen in the public mind, which it would be as well, perhaps, to aid in removing.

Elementals is a term applied to the nature spirits, the living existences which belong peculiarly to the elements they inhabit; "beings of the mysteria specialia," according to Paracelsus, "soul-forms, which will return into their chaos, and who are not capable of manifesting any higher spiritual activity because they do not possess the necessary kind of constitution in which an activity of a spiritual character can manifest itself.... Matter is connected with spirit by an intermediate principle which it receives from this spirit. This intermediate link between matter and spirit belongs to all the three kingdoms of nature. In the mineral kingdom it is called Stannar, or Trughat; in the vegetable kingdom, Jaffas; and it forms in connection with the vital force of the vegetable kingdom, the Primum Ens, which possesses the highest medicinal properties.... In the animal kingdom, this semi-material body is called Evestrum, and in human beings it is called the Sidereal Man. Each living being is connected with the Macrocosmos and Microcosmos by means of this intermediate element of soul, belonging to the Mysterium Magnum from whence it has been received, and whose form and qualities are determined by the quality and quantity of the spiritual and material elements." From this we may infer that the Elementals, properly speaking, are the Soul-forms of the elements they inhabit—the activities and energies of the world-soul differentiated into forms, endowed with more or less consciousness and capacities for feeling, and hours of enjoyment, or pain. But these, never or rarely, entering any more deeply into dense matter than enabled so to do by their aerial invisible bodies, do not appear upon our gross physical plane otherwise than as forces, energies, or influences. Their soul-forms are the intermediate link between matter and spirit, resembling the soul-forms of animals and men, which also form this intermediate link, the difference being that the souls of animals and men have enveloped themselves in a casing of dense matter for the purposes of existence upon the more external planes of life. Consequently, after the death of the external bodies of men and animals, there remain astral remnants which undergo gradual disintegration in the astral atmospheres. These have been termed elementaries; i.e., "the astral corpses of the dead; the ethereal counterpart of the once living person, which will sooner or later be decomposed into its astral elements, as the physical body is dissolved into the elements to which it belongs. The elementaries of good people have little cohesion and evaporate soon; those of wicked people may exist a long time; those of suicides, etc., have a life and consciousness of their own as long as a division of principles has not taken place. These are the most dangerous."

In the introduction to Isis Unveiled, we find the following definition of elemental spirits:

"The creatures evolved in the four kingdoms of earth, air, fire, and water, and called by the Kabalists gnomes, sylphs, salamanders, and undines. They may be termed the forces of nature, and will either operate effects as the servile agents of general law, or may be employed by the disembodied spirits—whether pure or impure—and by living adepts of magic and sorcery, to produce desired phenomenal results. Such beings never become men." (But there are classes of elemental spirits who do become men, as we shall see further on.)

"Under the general designation of fairies and fays, these spirits of the elements appear in the myth, fable, tradition, and poetry of all nations, ancient and modern. Their names are legion—peris, devs, djins, sylvans, satyrs, fawns, elves, dwarfs, trolls, kobolds, brownies, stromkarls, undines, nixies, salamanders, goblins, banshees, kelpies, prixies, moss people, good people, good neighbors, wild women, men of peace, white ladies, and many more. They have been seen, feared, blessed, banned, and invoked in every quarter of the globe and in every age. These elementals are the principal agents of disembodied but never visible spirits at séances, and the producers of all the phenomena except the 'subjective.'"—(Preface xxix, vol. I.)

"In the Jewish Kabala the nature spirits were known under the general name of Shedim, and divided into four classes. The Persians called them devs; the Greeks indistinctly designated them as demons; the Egyptians knew them as afrites. The ancient Mexicans, says Kaiser, believed in numerous spirit-abodes, into one of which the shades of innocent children were placed until final disposal; into another, situated in the sun, ascended the valiant souls of heroes; while the hideous specters of incorrigible sinners were sentenced to wander and despair in subterranean caves, held in the bonds of the earth-atmosphere, unwilling and unable to liberate themselves. They passed their time in communicating with mortals, and frightening those who could see them. Some of the African tribes know them as Yowahoos."—(P. 313, vol. I.)

Of the ideas of Proclus on this subject it is said in Isis Unveiled:

"He held that the four elements are all filled with demons, maintaining with Aristotle that the universe is full, and that there is no void in nature. The demons of earth, air, fire, and water, are of an elastic, ethereal, semi-corporeal essence. It is these classes which officiate as intermediate agents between the gods and men. Although lower in intelligence than the sixth order of the higher demons, these beings preside directly over the elements and organic life. They direct the growth, the inflorescence, the properties, and various changes of plants. They are the personified ideas or virtues shed from the heavenly ule into the inorganic matter; and, as the vegetable kingdom is one remove higher than the mineral, these emanations from the celestial gods take form in the plant, and become its soul. It is that which Aristotle's doctrine terms the form in the three principles of natural bodies, classified by him as privation, matter, and form. His philosophy teaches that besides the original matter, another principle is necessary to complete the triune nature of every particle, and this is form; an invisible, but still, in an ontological sense of the word, a substantial being, really distinct from matter proper. Thus, in an animal or a plant, besides the bones, the flesh, the nerves, the brains, and the blood in the former; and besides the pulpy matter, tissues, fibers, and juice in the latter, which blood and juice by circulating through the veins and fibers nourish all parts of both animal and plant; and besides the animal spirits which are the principles of motion, and the chemical energy which is transformed into vital force in the green leaf, there must be a substantial form, which Aristotle called in the horse, the horse's soul; and Proclus, the demon of every mineral, plant, or animal, and the medieval philosophers, the elementary spirits of the four kingdoms."—(P. 312, vol. I.)

"According to the ancient doctrines, the soulless elemental spirits were evolved by the ceaseless motion inherent in the astral light. Light is force, and the latter is produced by will. As this will proceeds from an intelligence which cannot err, for it has nothing of the material organs of human thought in it, being the super-fine pure emanation of the highest divinity itself—(Plato's Father)—it proceeds from the beginning of time, according to immutable laws, to evolve the elementary fabric requisite for subsequent generations of what we term human races. All of the latter, whether belonging to this planet or to some other of the myriads in space, have their earthly bodies evolved in the matrix out of the bodies of a certain class of these elemental beings which have passed away in the invisible worlds." (P. 285, vol. I.)

Speaking of Pythagoras, Iamblichus, and other Greek philosophers, Isis says:

"The universal ether was not, in their eyes, simply a something stretching, tenantless, throughout the expanse of heaven; it was a boundless ocean peopled, like our familiar seas, with monstrous and minor creatures, and having in its every molecule the germs of life. Like the finny tribes which swarm in our oceans and smaller bodies of water, each kind having its 'habitat' in some spot to which it is curiously adapted; some friendly and some inimical to man; some pleasant and some frightful to behold; some seeking the refuge of quiet nooks and land-locked harbors, and some traversing great areas of water, the various races of the elemental spirits were believed by them to inhabit the different portions of the great ethereal ocean, and to be exactly adapted to their respective conditions." (P. 284, vol. I.)

"Lowest in the scale of being are those invisible creatures called by the Kabalists the elementary. There are three distinct classes of these. The highest, in intelligence and cunning, are the so-called terrestrial spirits, the larvæ, or shadows of those who have lived on earth, have refused all spiritual light, remained and died deeply immersed in the mire of matter, and from whose sinful souls the immortal spirit has gradually separated. The second class is composed of invisible antitypes of men to be born. No form can come into objective existence, from the highest to the lowest, before the abstract idea of this form, or as Aristotle would call it, the privation of this form is called forth.... These models, as yet devoid of immortal spirits, are elementals properly speaking, psychic embryos—which when their time arrives, die out of the invisible world, and are borne into this visible one as human infants, receiving in transitu that divine breath called spirit which completes the perfect man. This class cannot communicate objectively with man.

"The third class of elementals proper never evolve into human beings, but occupy, as it were, a specific step of the ladder of being, and, by comparison with the others, may properly be called nature-spirits, or cosmic agents of nature, each being confined to its own element, and never transgressing the bounds of others. These are what Tertullian called 'the princes of the powers of the air.'

"This class is believed to possess but one of the three attributes of man. They have neither immortal souls nor tangible bodies; only astral forms, which partake, in a distinguishing degree, of the element to which they belong, and also of the ether. They are a combination of sublimated matter and a rudimental mind. Some are changeless, but still have no separate individuality, acting collectively so to say. Others, of certain elements and species, change form under a fixed law which Kabalists explain. The most solid of their bodies is ordinarily just immaterial enough to escape perception by our physical eyesight, but not so unsubstantial but that they can be perfectly recognized by the inner or clairvoyant vision. They not only exist, and can all live in ether, but can handle and direct it for the production of physical effects, as readily as we can compress air or water for the same purpose by pneumatic or hydraulic apparatus; in which occupation they are readily helped by the 'human elementary.' More than this; they can so condense it as to make to themselves tangible bodies, which by their protean powers they can cause to assume such likenesses as they choose, by taking as their models the portraits they find stamped in the memory of the persons present. It is not necessary that the sitter should be thinking at the moment of the one represented. His image may have faded away years before. The mind receives indelible impression even from chance acquaintance, or persons encountered but once." (Pp. 310, 311, vol. I.)

"If spiritualists are anxious to keep strictly dogmatic in their notions of the spirit-world, they must not set scientists to investigate their phenomena in the true experimental spirit. The attempt would most surely result in a partial re-discovery of the magic of old—that of Moses and Paracelsus. Under the deceptive beauty of some of their apparitions, they might find some day the sylphs and fair undines of the Rosicrucians playing in the currents of psychic and odic force.

"Already Mr. Crookes, who fully credits the being, feels that under the fair skin of Katie, covering a simulacrum of heart borrowed partially from the medium and the circle, there is no soul! And the learned authors of the Unseen Universe, abandoning their "electro-biological" theory, begin to perceive in the universal ether the possibility that it is a photographic album of En-Soph the Boundless.—(P. 67, vol. I.)

"We are far from believing that all the spirits that communicate at circles are of the classes called 'elemental' and 'elementary.'" Many, especially among those who control the medium subjectively to speak, write, and otherwise act in various ways, are human, disembodied spirits. Whether the majority of such spirits are good or bad, largely depends on the private morality of the medium, much on the circle present, and a great deal on the intensity and object of their purpose.... But in any case, human spirits can never materialize themselves in propriâ personâ.[21]—(P. 67, vol. I.)

In Art Magic we find the following pertinent remarks, p. 322. "There are some features of mediumship, especially amongst those persons known as physical force mediums, which long since should have awakened the attention of philosophical spiritualists to the fact that there were influences kindred only with animal natures at work somewhere, and unless the agency of certain classes of elemental spirits was admitted into the category of occasional control, humanity has at times assumed darker shades than we should be willing to assign to it. Unfortunately in discussing these subjects, there are many barriers to the attainment of truth on this subject. Courtesy and compassion alike protest against pointing to illustrations in our own time, whilst prejudice and ignorance intervene to stifle inquiry respecting phenomena, which a long lapse of time has left us free to investigate.

"The judges whose ignorance and superstition disgraced the

[21] By which it is doubtless meant that the full individuality is not present; the higher principles, the true spirit, having ascended to its appropriate house, from which there is no attraction to earth. That which materializes would be an elemental, or elementals molding their fluidic forms in the likeness of the departed human being; or, on the other hand, considering and revivifying the atomic remnants of the sidereal encasement, or astral body, still left undissipated in the soul-world.

witchcraft trials of the sixteenth and seventeenth centuries, found a solvent for all occult, or even suspicious circumstances, in the control of 'Satan and his imps.' The modern spiritualists, with few exceptions, are equally stubborn in attributing everything that transpires in spiritualistic circles, even to the wilful cunningly contrived preparations for deception on the part of pretended media, to the influence of disembodied human spirits—good, bad, or indifferent; but the author's own experience, confirmed by the assurances of wise-teaching spirits, impels him to assert that the tendencies to exhibit animal proclivities, whether mental, passional, or phenomenal, are most generally produced by elementals.

"The rapport with this realm of beings is generally due to certain proclivities in the individual; or, when whole communities are affected, the cause proceeds from revolutionary movements in the realms of astral fluid; these continually affect the elementals, who, in combination with low undeveloped spirits of humanity (elementaries), avail themselves of magnetic epidemics to obsess susceptible individuals, and sympathetically affect communities."

In the introduction to Isis Unveiled, we find the following definition of elementary spirits:

"Properly, the disembodied souls of the depraved; these souls, having at some time prior to death, separated from themselves their divine spirits, and so lost their chance of immortality. Eliphas Lévi and some other Kabalists make little distinction between elementary spirits, who have been men, and those beings which people the elements and are the blind forces of nature. Once divorced from their bodies, these souls (also called astral bodies) of purely materialistic persons, are irresistibly attracted to the earth, where they live a temporary and finite life amid elements congenial to their gross natures. From having never, during their natural lives, cultivated this spirituality, but subordinated it to the material and gross, they are now unfitted for the lofty career of the pure, disembodied being, for whom the atmosphere of earth is stifling and mephitic, and whose attractions are all away from it. After a more or less prolonged period of time these material souls will begin to disintegrate, and finally, like a column of mist, be dissolved, atom by atom, in the surrounding elements.—(Preface xxx., vol. I.)

"After the death of the depraved and the wicked, arrives the critical moment. If during life the ultimate and desperate effort of the inner-self to reunite itself with the faintly-glimmering ray of its divine parent is neglected; if this ray is allowed to be more and more shut out by the thickening crust of matter, the soul, once freed from the body, follows its earthly attractions, and is magnetically drawn into and held within the dense fogs of the material atmosphere. Then it begins to sink lower and lower, until it finds itself, when returned to consciousness, in what the ancients termed Hades. The annihilation of such a soul is never instantaneous; it may last centuries perhaps; for nature never proceeds by jumps and starts, and the astral soul, being formed of elements, the law of evolution must bide its time. Then begins the fearful law of compensation, the Yin-Youan of the Buddhists. This class of spirits is called the terrestrial, or earthly elementary, in contradistinction to the other classes." (They frequent séance rooms, &c.)—(P. 319, vol. I.)

Of the danger of meddling in occult matters before understanding the elementals and elementaries, Isis says, in the case of a rash intruder:

"The spirit of harmony and union will depart from the elements, disturbed by the imprudent hand; and the currents of blind forces will become immediately infested by numberless creatures of matter and instinct—the bad demons of the theurgists, the devils of theology; the gnomes, salamanders, sylphs, and undines will assail the rash performer under multifarious aerial forms. Unable to invent anything, they will search your memory to its very depths; hence the nervous exhaustion and mental oppression of certain sensitive natures at spiritual circles. The elementals will bring to light long-forgotten remembrances of the past; forms, images, sweet mementos, and familiar sentences, long since faded from our own remembrance, but vividly preserved in the inscrutable depths of our memory and on the astral tablets of the imperishable 'Book of Life.'"—(P. 343, vol. I.)

Paracelsus speaks of Xeni Nephidei: "Elemental spirits that give men occult powers over visible matter, and then feed on their brains, often causing thereby insanity.

"Man rules potentially over all lower existences than himself," says the author of Art Magic (p. 333), "but woe to him, who by seeking aid, counsel, or assistance, from lower grades of being, binds himself to them; henceforth he may rest assured they will become his parasites and associates, and as their instincts—like those of the animal kingdom—are strong in the particular direction of their nature, they are powerful to disturb, annoy, prompt to evil, and avail themselves of the contact induced by man's invitation to drag him down to their own level. The legendary idea of evil compacts between man and the 'Adversary' is not wholly mythical. Every wrong-doer signs that compact with spirits who have sympathy with his evil actions.

"Except for the purposes of scientific investigation, or with a view to strengthening ourselves against the silent and mysterious promptings to evil that beset us on every side, we warn mere curiosity-seekers, or persons ambitious to attach the legions of an unknown world to their service, against any attempts to seek communion with elemental spirits, or beings of any grade lower than man. Beings below mortality can grant nothing that mortality ought to ask. They can only serve man in some embryonic department of nature, and man must stoop to their state before they can thus reach him.... Knowledge is only good for us when we can apply it judiciously. Those who investigate for the sake of science, or with a view to enlarging the narrow boundaries of man's egotistical opinions, may venture much further into the realms of the unknown than curiosity-seekers, or persons who desire to apply the secrets of being to selfish purposes. It may be as well also for man to remember that he and his planet are not the all of being, and that, besides the revelations included in the stupendous outpouring called 'Modern Spiritualism,' there are many problems yet to be solved in human life and planetary existences, which spiritualism does not cover, nor ignorance and prejudice dream of.... Besides these considerations, we would warn man of the many subtle, though invisible, enemies which surround him, and, rather by the instinct of their embryonic natures than through malice prepense, seek to lay siege to the garrison of the human heart. We would advise him, moreover, that into that sacred entrenchment no power can enter, save by invitation of the soul itself. Angels may solicit, or demons may tempt, but none can compel the spirit within to action, unless it first surrenders the will to the investing power."—(Art Magic, p. 335.)

From the Theosophist of July 1886, we make the following extract, bearing upon the subject of the loss of immortality by soul-death, and the dangers of Black Magic:

"It is necessary to say a few words as regards the real nature of soul-death, and the ultimate fate of a black magician. The soul, as we have explained above, is an isolated drop in the ocean of cosmic life. This current of cosmic life is but the light and the aura of the Logos. Besides the Logos, there are innumerable other existences, both spiritual and astral, partaking of this life and living in it. These beings have special affinities with particular emotions of the human soul, and particular characteristics of the human mind. They have, of course, a definite individual existence of their own, which lasts up to the end of the Manwantara. There are three ways in which a soul may cease to retain its special individuality. Separated from its Logos, which is, as it were, its source, it may not acquire a strong and abiding individuality of its own, and may in course of time be reabsorbed into the current of universal life. This is real soul-death.

It may also place itself en rapport with a spiritual or elemental existence by evoking it, and concentrating its attention and regard upon it for purposes of black magic and Tantric worship. In such a case it transfers its individuality to such existence and is sucked up into it, as it were. In such a case the black magician lives in such a being, and as such a being he continues until the end of Manwantara."

A good deal of highly interesting information on the subject of elementals and elementaries is to be found in numbers of The Path. A few of the points contained in these articles may be mentioned here, but the reader is strongly recommended to study these articles, entitled Conversations on Occultism, for himself. According to the writer:

An elemental is a center of force, without intelligence, as we understand the word, without moral character or tendencies similar to ours, but capable of being directed in its movements by human thoughts, which may, consciously or not, give it any form, and endow it to a certain extent with what we call intelligence. We give them form by a species of thought which the mind does not register—involuntary and unconscious thought—"as, one person might shape an elemental so as to seem like an insect, and not be able to tell whether he had thought of such a thing or not." The elemental world interpenetrates this one, and elementals are constantly being attracted to, or repelled from, human beings, taking the prevailing color of their thoughts. Time and space, as we understand them, do not exist for elementals. They can be seen clairvoyantly in the shapes they assume under different influences, and they do many of the phenomena of the séance room. Light and the concentrated attention of any one make a disturbance in the magnetism of a room, interfering with their work in that respect. At séances elementaries also are present; these are shells, or half-dead human beings. The elementaries are not all bad, however, but the worst are the strongest, because the most attracted to material life. They are all helped and galvanized into action by elementals.

Contact with these beings has a deteriorating effect in all cases. Clairvoyants see in the astral light surrounding a person the images of people or events that have made an impression on that person's mind, and they frequently mistake these echoes and reflections for astral realities; only the trained seer can distinguish. The whole astral world is full of illusions.

Elementals have not got being such as mortals have. There are different classes for the different planes of nature. Each class is confined to its own plane, and many can never be recognized by men. The elemental world is a strong factor in Karma. Formerly, when men were less selfish and more spiritual, the elementals were friendly. They have become unfriendly by reason of man's indifference to, and want of sympathy with the rest of creation. Man has also colored the astral world with his own selfish and brutal thoughts, and produced an atmosphere of evil which he himself breathes. When men shall cultivate feelings of brotherly affection for each other, and of sympathy with nature, the elementals will change their present hostile attitude for one of helpfulness.

Elementals aid in the performance of phenomena produced by adepts. They also enter the sphere of unprotected persons, and especially of those who study occultism, thus precipitating the results of past Karma.

The adepts are reluctant to speak of elementals for two reasons. Because it is useless, as people could not understand the subject in their present state of intellectual and spiritual development; and because, if any knowledge of them were given, some persons might be able to come into contact with them to their own detriment and that of the world. In the present state of universal selfishness and self-seeking, the elementals would be employed to work evil, as they are in themselves colorless, taking their character from those who employ them. The adepts, therefore, keep back or hide the knowledge of these beings from men of science, and from the world in general. By-and-by, however, material science will rediscover black magic, and then will come a war between the good and evil powers, and the evil powers will be overcome, as always happens in such cases. Eventually all about the elementals will be known to men—when they have developed intellectually, morally, and spiritually sufficiently to have that knowledge without danger.

Elementals guard hidden treasures; they obey the adepts, however, who could command the use of untold wealth if they cared to draw upon these hidden deposits.

N. B.—Nizida has quoted from Man: Fragments of Forgotten History. The S. P. S. desires to say that while some of the statements contained in that work are correct, there is also in it a large admixture of error. Therefore, the S. P. S. does not recommend this work to the attention of students who have not yet learned enough to be able to separate the grain from the husk. The same may be said of Art-Magic.

A WITCH'S DEN

By Mme. Helena Blavatsky

Our kind host Sham Rao was very gay during the remaining hours of our visit. He did his best to entertain us, and would not hear of our leaving the neighborhood without having seen its greatest celebrity, its most interesting sight. A jadu wâlâ—sorceress—well known in the district, was just at this time under the influence of seven sister-goddesses, who took possession of her by turns, and spoke their oracles through her lips. Sham Rao said we must not fail to see her, be it only in the interests of science.

The evening closes in, and we once more get ready for an excursion. It is only five miles to the cavern of the Pythia of Hindostan; the road runs through a jungle, but it is level and smooth. Besides, the jungle and its ferocious inhabitants have ceased to frighten us. The timid elephants we had in the "dead city" are sent home, and we are to mount new behemoths belonging to a neighboring Râjâ. The pair that stand before the verandah like two dark hillocks are steady and trustworthy. Many a time these two have hunted the royal tiger, and no wild shrieking or thunderous roaring can frighten them. And so, let us start! The ruddy flames of the torches dazzle our eyes and increase the forest gloom. Our surroundings seem so dark, so mysterious. There is something indescribably fascinating, almost solemn, in these night-journeys in the out-of-the-way corners of India. Everything is silent and deserted around you, everything is dozing on the earth and overhead. Only the heavy, regular tread of the elephants breaks the stillness of the night, like the sound of falling hammers in the underground smithy of Vulcan. From time to time uncanny voices and murmurs are heard in the black forest.

"The wind sings its strange song amongst the ruins," says one of us, "what a wonderful acoustic phenomenon!"

"Bhûta, bhûta!" whisper the awestruck torch-bearers. They brandish their torches and swiftly spin on one leg, and snap their fingers to chase away the aggressive spirits.

The plaintive murmur is lost in the distance. The forest is once more filled with the cadences of its invisible nocturnal life—the metallic whirr of the crickets, the feeble, monotonous croak of the tree-frog, the rustle of the leaves. From time to time all this suddenly stops short and then begins again, gradually increasing and increasing.

Heavens! What teeming life, what stores of vital energy are hidden under the smallest leaf, the most imperceptible blades of grass, in this tropical forest! Myriads of stars shine in the dark blue of the sky, and myriads of fireflies twinkle at us from every bush, moving sparks, like a pale reflection of the far-away stars.

We left the thick forest behind us, and reached a deep glen, on three sides bordered with the thick forest, where even by day the shadows are as dark as by night. We were about two thousand feet above the foot of the Vindhya ridge, judging by the ruined wall of Mandu, straight above our heads.

Suddenly a very chilly wind rose that nearly blew our torches out. Caught in the labyrinth of bushes and rocks, the wind angrily shook the branches of the blossoming syringas, then, shaking itself free, it turned back along the glen and flew down the valley, howling, whistling and shrieking, as if all the fiends of the forest together were joining in a funeral song.

"Here we are," said Sham Rao, dismounting. "Here is the village; the elephants cannot go any further."

"The village? Surely you are mistaken. I don't see anything but trees."

"It is too dark to see the village. Besides, the huts are so small, and so hidden by the bushes, that even by daytime you could hardly find them. And there is no light in the houses, for fear of the spirits."

"And where is your witch? Do you mean we are to watch her performance in complete darkness?"

Sham Rao cast a furtive, timid look round him; and his voice, when he answered our questions, was somewhat tremulous.

"I implore you not to call her a witch! She may hear you.... It is not far off, it is not more than half a mile. Do not allow this short distance to shake your decision. No elephant, and not even a horse, could make its way there. We must walk.... But we shall find plenty of light there...."

This was unexpected, and far from agreeable. To walk in this gloomy Indian night; to scramble through thickets of cactuses; to venture in a dark forest, full of wild animals—this was too much for Miss X—. She declared that she would go no further. She would wait for us in the howdah on the elephant's back, and perhaps would go to sleep.

Narayan was against this parti de plaisir from the very beginning, and now, without explaining his reasons, he said she was the only sensible one among us.

"You won't lose anything," he remarked, "by staying where you are. And I only wish every one would follow your example."

"What ground have you for saying so, I wonder?"

remonstrated Sham Rao, and a slight note of disappointment rang in his voice, when he saw that the excursion, proposed and organized by himself, threatened to come to nothing. "What harm could be done by it? I won't insist any more that the 'incarnation of gods' is a rare sight, and that the Europeans hardly ever have an opportunity of witnessing it; but, besides, the Kangalim in question is no ordinary woman. She leads a holy life; she is a prophetess, and her blessing could not prove harmful to any one. I insisted on this excursion out of pure patriotism."

"Sahib, if your patriotism consists in displaying before foreigners the worst of our plagues, then why did you not order all the lepers of your district to assemble and parade before the eyes of our guests? You are a patèl, you have the power to do it."

How bitterly Narayan's voice sounded to our unaccustomed ears. Usually he was so even-tempered, so indifferent to everything belonging to the exterior world.

Fearing a quarrel between the Hindus, the colonel remarked, in a conciliatory tone, that it was too late for us to reconsider our expedition. Besides, without being a believer in the "incarnation of gods," he was personally firmly convinced that demoniacs existed even in the West. He was eager to study every psychological phenomenon, wherever he met with it, and whatever shape it might assume.

It would have been a striking sight for our European and American friends if they had beheld our procession on that dark night. Our way lay along a narrow winding path up the mountain. Not more than two people could walk together—and we were thirty, including the torch-bearers. Surely some reminiscence of night sallies against the Confederate Southerners had revived in the colonel's breast, judging by the readiness with which he took upon himself the leadership of our small expedition. He ordered all the rifles and revolvers to be loaded, despatched three torch-bearers to march ahead of us, and arranged us in pairs. Under such a skilled chieftain we had nothing to fear from tigers; and so our procession started, and slowly crawled up the winding path.

It cannot be said that the inquisitive travelers, who appeared later on, in the den of the prophetess of Mandu, shone through the freshness and elegance of their costumes. My gown, as well as the traveling suits of the colonel and of Mr. Y— were nearly torn to pieces. The cactuses gathered from us whatever tribute they could, and the Babu's disheveled hair swarmed with a whole colony of grasshoppers and fireflies, which probably, were attracted thither by the smell of cocoanut oil. The stout Sham Rao panted like a steam engine. Narayan alone was like his usual self—that is to say, like a bronze Hercules, armed with a club. At the last abrupt turn of the path, after having surmounted the difficulty of climbing over huge, scattered stones, we suddenly found ourselves on a perfectly smooth place; our eyes, in spite of our many torches, were dazzled with light, and our ears were struck by a medley of unusual sounds.

A new glen opened before us, the entrance of which, from the valley, was well masked by thick trees. We understood how easily we might have wandered round it, without ever suspecting its existence. At the bottom of the glen we discovered the abode of the celebrated Kangalim.

The den, as it turned out, was situated in the ruin of an old Hindu temple in tolerably good preservation. In all probability it was built long before the "Dead City," because during the epoch of the latter, the heathen were not allowed to have their own places of worship; and the temple stood quite close to the wall of the town, in fact, right under it. The cupolas of the two smaller lateral pagodas had fallen long ago, and huge bushes grew out of their altars. This evening their branches were hidden under a mass of bright-colored rags, bits of ribbon, little pots, and various other talismans, because, even in them, popular superstition sees something sacred.

"And are not these poor people right? Did not these bushes grow on sacred ground? Is not their sap impregnated with the incense of offerings, and the exhalations of holy anchorites, who once lived and breathed here?"

The learned but superstitious Sham Rao would only answer our questions by new questions.

But the central temple, built of red granite, stood unharmed by time, and, as we learned afterwards, a deep tunnel opened just behind its closely-shut door. What was beyond it no one knew. Sham Rao assured us that no man of the last three generations had ever stepped over the threshold of this thick iron door; no one had seen the subterranean passage for many years. Kangalim lived there in perfect isolation, and, according to the oldest people in the neighborhood, she had always lived there. Some people said she was three hundred years old; others alleged that a certain old man on his death-bed had revealed to his son that this old woman was no one else than his own uncle. This fabulous uncle had settled in the cave in the times when the "Dead City" still counted several hundreds of inhabitants. The hermit, busy paving his road to Moksha, had no intercourse with the rest of the world, and nobody knew how he lived and what he ate. But a good while ago, in the days when the Bellati (foreigners) had not yet taken possession of this mountain, the old hermit suddenly was transformed into a hermitess. She continues his pursuits and speaks with his voice, and often in his name; but she receives worshippers, which was not the practice of her predecessor.

We had come too early, and the Pythia did not at first appear. But the square before the temple was full of people, and a wild though picturesque scene it was. An enormous bonfire blazed in the center, and round it crowded the naked savages like so many black gnomes, adding whole branches of trees sacred to the seven sister-goddesses. Slowly and evenly they all jumped from one leg to another to a tune of a single monotonous musical phrase, which they repeated in chorus, accompanied by several local drums and tambourines. The hushed trill of the latter mingled with the forest echoes and the hysterical moans of two little girls, who lay under a heap of leaves by the fire. The poor children were brought here by their mothers, in the hope that the goddesses would take pity upon them and banish the two evil spirits under whose obsession they were. Both mothers were quite young, and sat on their heels blankly and sadly staring at the flames. No one paid us the slightest attention when we appeared, and afterwards during all our stay these people acted as if we were invisible. Had we worn a cap of darkness they could not have behaved more strangely.

"They feel the approach of the gods! The atmosphere is full of their sacred emanations!" mysteriously explained Sham Rao, contemplating with reverence the natives, whom his beloved Haeckel might have easily mistaken for his "missing link," the brood of his Bathybius Haeckelii.

"They are simply under the influence of toddy and opium!" retorted the irreverent Babu.

The lookers-on moved as in a dream, as if they all were only half-awakened somnambulists, but the actors were simply victims of St. Vitus's dance. One of them, a tall old man, a mere skeleton with a long white beard, left the ring and begun whirling vertiginously, with his arms spread like wings, and loudly grinding his long, wolf-like teeth. He was painful and disgusting to look at. He soon fell down, and was carelessly, almost mechanically pushed aside by the feet of the others still engaged in their demoniac performance.

All this was frightful enough, but many more horrors were in store for us.

Waiting for the appearance of the prima donna of this forest opera company, we sat down on the trunk of a fallen tree, ready to ask innumerable questions of our condescending host. But I was hardly seated when a feeling of indescribable astonishment and horror made me shrink back.

I beheld the skull of a monstrous animal, the like of which I could not find in my zoölogical reminiscences.

This head was much larger than the head of an elephant skeleton. And still it could not be anything but an elephant, judging by the skilfully restored trunk, which wound down to my feet like a gigantic black leech. But an elephant has no horns, whereas this one had four of them! The front pair stuck from the flat forehead slightly bending forward and then spreading out; and the others had a wide base, like the root of a deer's horn, that gradually decreased almost up to the middle, and bore long branches enough to decorate a dozen ordinary elks. Pieces of the transparent amber-yellow rhinoceros skin were strained over the empty eye-holes of the skull, and small lamps burning behind them only added to the horror, the devilish appearance of this head.

"What can this be?" was our unanimous question. None of us had ever met anything like it, and even the colonel looked aghast.

"It is a Sivatherium," said Narayan. "Is it possible you never came across these fossils in European museums? Their remains are common enough in the Himalayas, though, of course, in fragments. They were called after Shiva."

"If the collector of this district ever hears that this antediluvian relic adorns the den of your—ahem!—witch," remarked the Babu, "it won't adorn it many days longer."

All around the skull and on the floor of the portico there were heaps of white flowers, which, though not quite antediluvian, were totally unknown to us. They were as large as a big rose, and their white petals were covered with a red powder, the inevitable concomitant of every Indian religious ceremony. Further on there were groups of cocoanuts, and large brass dishes filled with rice, each adorned with a red or green taper. In the center of the portico there stood a queer-shaped censer, surrounded with chandeliers. A little boy, dressed from head to foot in white, threw into it handfuls of aromatic powders.

"These people, who assemble here to worship Kangalim," said Sham Rao, "do not actually belong either to her sect or to any other. They are devil-worshippers. They do not believe in Hindu gods; they live in small communities; they belong to one of the many Indian races which usually are called the hill-tribes. Unlike the Shanars of Southern Travancore, they do not use the blood of sacrificial animals; they do not build separate temples to their bhutas. But they are possessed by the strange fancy that the goddess Kâli, the wife of Shiva, from time immemorial has had a grudge against them, and sends her favorite evil spirits to torture them. Save this little difference, they have the same beliefs as the Shanars. God does not exist for them; and even Shiva is considered by them as an ordinary spirit. Their chief worship is offered to the souls of the dead. These souls, however righteous and kind they may be in their lifetime, become after death as wicked as can be; they are happy only when they are torturing living men and cattle. As the opportunities of doing so are the only reward for the virtues they possessed when incarnated, a very wicked man is punished by becoming after his death a very soft-hearted ghost; he loathes his loss of daring, and is altogether miserable. The results of this strange logic are not bad, nevertheless. These savages and devil-worshippers are the kindest and the most truth-loving of all the hill-tribes. They do whatever they can to be worthy of their ultimate reward; because, don't you see, they all long to become the wickedest of devils!"

And put in good humor by his own wittiness, Sham Rao laughed till his hilarity became offensive, considering the sacredness of the place.

"A year ago some business matters sent me to Tinevelli," continued he. "Staying with a friend of mine, who is a Shanar, I was allowed to be present at one of the ceremonies in the honor of devils. No European has as yet witnessed this worship, whatever the missionaries may say; but there are many converts amongst the Shanars, who willingly describe them to the padres. My friend is a wealthy man, which is probably the reason why the devils are especially vicious to him. They poison his cattle, spoil his crops and his coffee plants, and persecute his numerous relations, sending them sunstrokes, madness and epilepsy, over which illnesses they especially preside. These wicked demons have settled in every corner of his spacious landed property—in the woods, the ruins, and even in his stables. To avert all this, my friend covered his land with stucco pyramids, and prayed humbly, asking the demons to draw their portraits on each of them, so that he may recognize them and worship each of them separately, as the rightful owner of this, or that, particular pyramid. And what do you think?... Next morning all the pyramids were found covered with drawings. Each of them bore an incredibly good likeness of the dead of the neighborhood. My friend had known personally almost all of them. He found also a portrait of his own late father amongst the lot."

"Well? And was he satisfied?"

"Oh, he was very glad, very satisfied. It enabled him to choose the right thing to gratify the personal tastes of each demon, don't you see? He was not vexed at finding his father's portrait. His father was somewhat irascible; once he nearly broke both his son's legs, administering to him fatherly punishment with an iron bar, so that he could not possibly be very dangerous after his death. But another portrait, found on the best and the prettiest of the pyramids, amazed my friend a good deal, and put him in a blue funk. The whole district recognized an English officer, a certain Captain Pole, who in his lifetime was as kind a gentleman as ever lived."

"Indeed? But do you mean to say that this strange people worshipped Captain Pole also?"

"Of course they did! Captain Pole was such a worthy man, such an honest officer, that, after his death, he could not help being promoted to the highest rank of Shanar devils. The Pe-Kovil, demon's-house, sacred to his memory, stands side by side with the Pe-Kovil Bhadrakâlî, which was recently conferred on the wife of a certain German missionary, who also was a most charitable lady and so is very dangerous now."

"But what are their ceremonies? Tell us something about their rites."

"Their rites consist chiefly of dancing, singing, and killing sacrificial animals. The Shanars have no castes, and eat all kinds of meat. The crowd assembles about the Pe-Kovil, previously designated by the priest; there is a general beating of drums, and slaughtering of fowls, sheep and goats. When Captain Pole's turn came an ox was killed, as a thoughtful attention to the peculiar tastes of his nation. The priest appeared, covered with bangles, and holding a wand on which tinkled numberless little bells, and wearing garlands of red and white flowers round his neck, and a black mantle, on which were embroidered the ugliest fiends you can imagine. Horns were blown and drums rolled incessantly. And oh, I forgot to tell you there was also a kind of fiddle, the secret of which is known only to the Shanar priesthood. Its bow is ordinary enough, made of bamboo; but it is whispered that the strings are human veins.... When Captain Pole took possession of the priest's body, the priest leaped high in the air, and then rushed on the ox and killed him. He drank off the hot blood, and then began his dance. But what a fright he was when dancing! You know, I am not superstitious.... Am I?..."

Sham Rao looked at us inquiringly, and I, for one, was glad at this moment that Miss X— was half a mile off, asleep in the howdah.

"He turned, and turned, as if possessed by all the demons of Nâraka. The enraged crowd hooted and howled when the priest begun to inflict deep wounds all over his body with the bloody sacrificial knife. To see him, with his hair waving in the wind and his mouth covered with foam; to see him bathing in the blood of the sacrificed animal, mixing it with his own, was more than I could bear. I felt as if hallucinated, I fancied I also was spinning round...."

Sham Rao stopped abruptly, struck dumb. Kangalim stood before us!

Her appearance was so unexpected that we all felt embarrassed. Carried away by Sham Rao's description, we had noticed neither how nor whence she came. Had she appeared from beneath the earth we could not have been more astonished. Narayan stared at her, opening wide his big jet-black eyes; the Babu clicked his tongue in utter confusion.

Imagine a skeleton seven feet high, covered with brown leather, with a dead child's tiny head stuck on its bony shoulders; the eyes set so deep and at the same time flashing such fiendish flames all through your body that you begin to feel your brain stop working, your thoughts become entangled and your blood freeze in your veins.

I describe my personal impressions, and no words of mine can do them justice. My description is too weak. Mr. Y— and the colonel both grew pale under her stare and Mr. Y— made a movement as if about to rise.

Needless to say that such an impression could not last. As soon as the witch had turned her gleaming eyes to the kneeling crowd, it vanished as swiftly as it had come. But still all our attention was fixed on this remarkable creature.

Three hundred years old! Who can tell? Judging by her appearance, we might as well conjecture her to be a thousand. We beheld a genuine living mummy, or rather a mummy endowed with motion. She seemed to have been withering since the creation. Neither time, nor the ills of life, nor the elements could ever affect this living statue of death. The all-destroying hand of time had touched her and stopped short. Time could do no more, and so had left her. And with all this, not a single gray hair. Her long black locks shone with a greenish sheen, and fell in heavy masses down to her knees.

To my great shame, I must confess that a disgusting reminiscence flashed into my memory. I thought about the hair and the nails of corpses growing in the graves, and tried to examine the nails of the old woman.

Meanwhile, she stood motionless as if suddenly transformed into an ugly idol. In one hand she held a dish with a piece of burning camphor, in the other a handful of rice, and she never removed her burning eyes from the crowd. The pale yellow flame of the camphor flickered in the wind, and lit up her death-like head, almost touching her chin; but she paid no heed to it. Her neck, as wrinkled as a mushroom, as thin as a stick, was surrounded by three rows of golden medallions. Her head was adorned with a golden snake. Her grotesque, hardly human body was covered by a piece of saffron-yellow muslin.

The demoniac little girls raised their heads from beneath the leaves, and set up a prolonged animal-like howl. Their example was followed by the old man, who lay exhausted by his frantic dance.

The witch tossed her head convulsively, and began her invocations, rising on tiptoe, as if moved by some external force.

"The goddess, one of the seven sisters, begins to take possession of her," whispered Sham Rao, not even thinking of wiping away the big drops of sweat that streamed from his brow. "Look, look at her!"

This advice was quite superfluous. We were looking at her, and at nothing else.

At first, the movements of the witch were slow, unequal, somewhat convulsive; then, gradually, they became less angular; at last, as if catching the cadence of the drums, leaning all her long body forward, and writhing like an eel, she rushed round and round the blazing bonfire. A dry leaf caught in a hurricane could not fly swifter. Her bare bony feet trod noiselessly on the rocky ground. The long locks of her hair flew round her like snakes, lashing the spectators, who knelt, stretching their trembling arms towards her, and writhing as if they were alive. Whoever was touched by one of this Fury's black curls, fell down on the ground, overcome with happiness, shouting thanks to the goddess, and considering himself blessed forever. It was not human hair that touched the happy elect, it was the goddess herself, one of the seven.

Swifter and swifter fly her decrepit legs; the young, vigorous hands of the drummer can hardly follow her. But she does not think of catching the measure of his music; she rushes, she flies forward. Staring with her expressionless, motionless orbs at something before her, at something that is not visible to our mortal eyes, she hardly glances at her worshippers; then her look becomes full of fire, and whoever she looks at feels burned through to the marrow of his bones. At every glance she throws a few grains of rice. The small handful seems inexhaustible, as if the wrinkled palm contained the bottomless bag of Prince Fortunatus.

Suddenly she stops as if thunderstruck.

The mad race round the bonfire had lasted twelve minutes, but we looked in vain for a trace of fatigue on the death-like face of the witch. She stopped only for a moment, just the necessary time for the goddess to release her. As soon as she felt free, by a single effort she jumped over the fire and plunged into the deep tank by the portico. This time she plunged only once, and whilst she stayed under the water the second sister-goddess entered her body. The little boy in white produced another dish, with a new piece of burning camphor, just in time for the witch to take it up, and to rush again on her headlong way.

The colonel sat with his watch in his hand. During the second obsession the witch ran, leaped, and raced for exactly fourteen minutes. After this, she plunged twice in the tank, in honor of the second sister; and with every new obsession the number of her plunges increased, till it became six.

It was already an hour and a half since the race began. All this time the witch never rested, stopping only for a few seconds, to disappear under the water.

"She is a fiend, she cannot be a woman!" exclaimed the colonel, seeing the head of the witch immersed for the sixth time in the water.

"Hang me if I know!" grumbled Mr. Y—, nervously pulling his beard. "The only thing I know is that a grain of her cursed rice entered my throat, and I can't get it out!"

"Hush, hush! Please, do be quiet!" implored Sham Rao. "By talking you will spoil the whole business!"

I glanced at Narayan and lost myself in conjectures.

His features, which usually were so calm and serene, were quite altered at this moment by a deep shadow of suffering. His lips trembled, and the pupils of his eyes were dilated, as if by a dose of belladonna. His eyes were lifted over the heads of the crowd, as if in his disgust he tried not to see what was before him, and at the same time could not see it, engaged in a deep reverie which carried him away from us and from the whole performance.

"What is the matter with him?" was my thought, but I had no time to ask him, because the witch was again in full swing, chasing her own shadow.

But with the seventh goddess the program was slightly changed. The running of the old woman changed to leaping. Sometimes bending down to the ground, like a black panther, she leaped up to some worshipper, and halting before him touched his forehead with her finger, while her long, thin body shook with inaudible laughter. Then, again, as if shrinking back playfully from her shadow, and chased by it, in some uncanny game, the witch appeared to us like a horrid caricature of Dinorah, dancing her mad dance. Suddenly she straightened herself to her full height, darted to the portico and crouched before the smoking censer, beating her forehead against the granite steps. Another jump, and she was quite close to us, before the head of the monstrous Sivatherium. She knelt down again and bowed her head to the ground several times, with the sound of an empty barrel knocked against something hard.

We had hardly the time to spring to our feet and shrink back when she appeared on the top of the Sivatherium's head, standing there amongst the horns.

Narayan alone did not stir, and fearlessly looked straight in the eyes of the frightful sorceress.

But what was this? Who spoke in those deep manly tones? Her lips were moving, from her breast were issuing those quick, abrupt phrases, but the voice sounded hollow as if coming from beneath the ground.

"Hush, hush!" whispered Sham Rao, his whole body trembling. "She is going to prophesy!..."

"She?" incredulously inquired Mr. Y—. "This a woman's voice? I don't believe it for a moment. Someone's uncle must be stowed away somewhere about the place. Not the fabulous uncle she inherited from, but a real live one!..."

Sham Rao winced under the irony of this supposition, and cast an imploring look at the speaker.

"Woe to you! woe to you!" echoed the voice. "Woe to you, children of the impure Jaya and Vijaya! of the mocking, unbelieving lingerers round great Shiva's door! Ye, who are cursed by eighty thousand sages! Woe to you who believe not in the goddess Kâli, and you who deny us, her seven divine sisters! Flesh-eating, yellow-legged vultures! friends of the oppressors of our land! dogs who are not ashamed to eat from the same trough with the Bellati!" (foreigners).

"It seems to me that your prophetess only foretells the past," said Mr. Y—, philosophically putting his hands in his pockets. "I should say that she is hinting at you, my dear Sham Rao."

"Yes! and at us also," murmured the colonel, who was evidently beginning to feel uneasy.

As to the unlucky Sham Rao, he broke out in a cold sweat, and tried to assure us that we were mistaken, that we did not fully understand her language.

"It is not about you, it is not about you! It is of me she speaks, because I am in Government service. Oh, she is inexorable!"

"Râkshasas! Asuras!" thundered the voice. "How dare you appear before us? how dare you to stand on this holy ground in boots made of a cow's sacred skin? Be cursed for etern——"

But her curse was not destined to be finished. In an instant the Hercules-like Narayan had fallen on the Sivatherium, and upset the whole pile, the skull, the horns and the demoniac Pythia included. A second more, and we thought we saw the witch flying in the air towards the portico. A confused vision of a stout, shaven Brahman, suddenly emerging from under the Sivatherium and instantly disappearing in the hollow beneath it, flashed before my dilated eyes.

But, alas! after the third second had passed, we all came to the embarrassing conclusion that, judging from the loud clang of the door of the cave, the representative of the Seven Sisters had ignominiously fled. The moment she had disappeared from our inquisitive eyes to her subterranean domain, we all realized that the unearthly hollow voice we had heard had nothing supernatural about it and belonged to the Brahman hidden under the Sivatherium—to some one's live uncle, as Mr. Y— had rightly supposed.

Oh, Narayan! how carelessly, how disorderly the worlds rotate around us. I begin to seriously doubt their reality. From this moment I shall earnestly believe that all things in the universe are nothing but illusion, a mere Mâyâ. I am becoming a Vedantin.... I doubt that in the whole universe there may be found anything more objective than a Hindu witch flying up the spout.

Miss X— woke up, and asked what was the meaning of all this noise. The noise of many voices and the sounds of the many retreating footsteps, the general rush of the crowd, had frightened her. She listened to us with a condescending smile, and a few yawns, and went to sleep again.

Next morning, at daybreak, we very reluctantly, it must be owned, bade good-by to the kind-hearted, good-natured Sham Rao. The confoundingly easy victory of Narayan hung heavily on his mind. His faith in the holy hermitess and the seven goddesses was a good deal shaken by the shameful capitulation of the sisters, who had surrendered at the first blow from a mere mortal. But during the dark hours of the night he had had time to think it over, and to shake off the uneasy feeling of having unwillingly misled and disappointed his European friends.

Sham Rao still looked confused when he shook hands with us at parting, and expressed to us the best wishes of his family and himself.

As to the heroes of this truthful narrative, they mounted their elephants once more, and directed their heavy steps towards the high road and Jubbulpore.

REMARKABLE PSYCHIC EXPERIENCES OF FAMOUS PERSONS

By Walter F. Prince, Ph.D.,

Official Investigator American Society for Psychical Research

It does not necessarily give an occult incident more weight that it was experienced or related and credited by a person whose name is prominent for one reason or another. The great are nearly as likely to suffer illusions, pathological hallucinations, and aberrations as the humble remainder of mankind, or, according to Lombroso a good deal more so. Nor have famous persons a monopoly of veracity. Besides, a rare psychological incident is not more or less a problem, nor has it more or less significance in the experience of honest John Jones than in that of William Shakespeare.

And yet it is natural and quite proper to look with somewhat enhanced interest upon the experiences or the testimonies of those whose names are in the cyclopedias and biographical dictionaries. It is legitimate to set these forth and to call attention to them. These persons at least we know something about. William Moggs of Waushegan, Wisconsin, may be a very excellent and trustworthy man but we don't know him, and it is tedious to be told that somebody else whom we may know as little knows and esteems him. How do we know that the avouching unknown could not have been sold a gold brick? But Henry M. Stanley, and General Frémont, and W. P. Frith, and Henry Clews are characters whom we do know something about, or at least whom we can easily look up for ourselves in biographical dictionaries and Who's Whos. They are names which have at the very outset a reputation which has impressed the world, which stand for assured ability, genius, achievement, forcefulness of one kind or another. Even though we have no particular data at hand regarding the veracity of a particular member of the shining circle, it is not easy to see why he, having an assured reputation, should dim it by telling spooky lies. It is easier to conceive of William Moggs, a quite obscure man, calling attention to himself by the device, though as a rule the William Moggs's do nothing of the kind. We spontaneously argue within ourselves, in some inchoate fashion, "That fellow made his mark in the world; he gained a big reputation by his superiority to the rank and file in some particular at least; it will be worth while to hear what he has to say."

We present herewith a group of such testimonies either given out to the world by prominent persons as their own experiences or as the experiences of persons whom they knew and believed, or else as told by friends of the prominent persons whose experiences they were.

It is not owing to any selective process that the material is mostly of the sort which favors supernormal hypotheses. We take what we can get. Whenever an experience is accompanied by a normal explanation, such will be included only a little more willingly than an experience which does not readily suggest a normal explanation. But, let it be noted, the groups which we propose will be composed of human experiences, and not opinions, except as the opinions accompany the experiences. And it cannot be expected that, after certain types of experiences as related by certain men have been given, we shall then proceed to name other men who haven't had any such experiences. True, against Paul du Chaillu's assertion that he had seen gorillas was once urged the fact that nobody else had ever seen gorillas. Nevertheless the sole assertion of the one man who had seen them proved to outweigh in value the lack of experience on the part of all other travelers up to that time.

A Premonition of Sir H. M. Stanley

This incident is related by the famous explorer, Sir Henry M. Stanley, in his autobiography edited by Dorothy Stanley (Houghton Mifflin Co., 1909), on pages 207-208.

Stanley, then a private in the Confederate Army, was captured in the battle of Shiloh and sent to Camp Douglas near Chicago. It was while here that the incident in question occurred.

"On the next day (April 16), after the morning duties had been performed, the rations divided, the cooks had departed contented, and the quarters swept, I proceeded to my nest and reclined alongside of my friend Wilkes in a posture that gave me a command of one half of the building. I made some remarks to him upon the card-playing groups opposite, when suddenly, I felt a gentle stroke on the back of my neck, and in an instant I was unconscious. The next moment I had a vivid view of the village of Tremeirchion and the grassy slopes of the hills of Hirradog, and I seemed to be hovering over the rook woods of Brynbella. I glided to the bed-chamber of my Aunt Mary. My aunt was in bed, and seemed sick unto death. I took a position by the side of the bed, and saw myself, with head bent down, listening to her parting words which sounded regretful, as though conscience smote her for not having been as kind as she might have been, or had wished to be. I heard the boy say, 'I believe you, Aunt. It is neither your fault, nor mine. You were good and kind to me, and I knew you wished to be kinder; but things were so ordered that you had to be what you were. I also dearly wished to love you, but I was afraid to speak of it lest you would check me, or say something that would offend me. I feel our parting was in this spirit. There is no need of regrets. You have done your duty to me, and you had children of your own who required all your care. What has happened to me since, it was decreed should happen. Farewell.'

"I put forth my hand and felt the clasp of the long thin hands of the sore-sick woman. I heard a murmur of farewell, and immediately I awoke.

"It appeared to me that I had but closed my eyes. I was still in the same reclining attitude, the groups opposite me were still engaged in their card games, Wilkes was in the same position. Nothing had changed.

"I asked, 'What has happened?'

"'What could happen?' said he. 'What makes you ask? It is but a moment ago you were speaking to me.'

"'Oh, I thought I had been asleep a long time.'

"On the next day the 17th of April, 1862, my Aunt Mary died at Fynnon Beuno, in Wales!

"I believe that the soul of every human being has its attendant spirit—a nimble, delicate essence, whose method of action is by a subtle suggestion which it contrives to insinuate into the mind, whether asleep or awake. We are too gross to be capable of understanding the signification of the dream, the vision, or the sudden presage, or of divining the source of the premonition or its import. We admit that we are liable to receive a fleeting picture of an act, or a figure at any moment, but, except being struck by certain strange coincidences which happen to most of us, we seldom make an effort to unravel the mystery. The swift, darting messenger stamps an image on the mind, and displays a vision to the sleeper; and if, as sometimes follows, among tricks and twists of the errant mind, by reflex acts of memory, it happens to be a true representation of what is to happen, we are left to grope hopelessly as to the manner and meaning of it, for there is nothing tangible to lay hold of.

"There are many things relating to my existence which are inexplicable to me, and probably it is best so; this death-bed scene, projected on my mind's screen, across four thousand five hundred miles of space, is one of these mysteries."

The precise meaning of the passage wherein Sir Henry speculates on the nature and meaning of such facts, is not entirely clear. Does he by the word spirit mean what is usually meant by that term, or does he mean some part of the mind functioning upon the rest as its object, like Freud's psychic censor though with a different purpose? And the affirmative employment of the terms "presage" and "premonition" do not seem to be consistent with the expression "it happens to be a true representation of what is to happen." It seems plain that the distinguished explorer did believe that the death-bed scene was "projected on" his "mind's screen, across four thousand five hundred miles of space." However, what Stanley thought about the facts is of much less importance than the facts themselves, as reported by one whose life was one long drill in observing, appraising and recording facts.

Coincident Experiences of General Frémont and Relatives

These are related on pages 69-72 of Recollections of Elizabeth Benton Frémont, Daughter of the Pathfinder General John C. Frémont and Jessie Benton Frémont His Wife.

After describing a terrible experience of her father and his men in 1853, while crossing the Wahsatch Mountains, and their rescue from starvation by reaching Parowan, Utah, Miss Benton goes on:

"That night my father sat by his campfire until late in the night, dreaming of home and thinking of the great happiness of my mother. Could she but know that he was safe! Finally he returned to his quarters in the town only a few hundred yards away from the camp. The warm bright room, the white bed with all suggestion of shelter and relief from danger made the picture of home rise up like a real thing before him, and at half-past eleven at night he made an entry in his journal, putting there the thought that had possession of him and that my mother in far away Washington might know that all danger was past and that he was safe and comfortable.

"All this is a prelude to a most uncommon experience which befell my mother in our Washington home on the night in question. We could not possibly hear from father at the earliest until midsummer. Though my mother went into society but little that year, there was no reason for gloomy forebodings. The younger members of the family kept her in close touch with the social side of life, while her father, whose confidant she always was, kept her informed as to the political events of the moment. Her life was busy and filled with her full share of its responsibilities. In midwinter, however, my mother became possessed with the conviction that my father was starving, and no amount of reasoning could calm her fears. The idea haunted her for two weeks or more, and finally began to leave its physical effects upon her. She could neither eat nor sleep; open-air exercise, plenty of company, the management of a household, all combined, could not wean her from the belief that father and his men were starving in the desert.

"The weight of fear was lifted from her as suddenly as it came. Her young sister Susie and a party of relatives returned from a wedding at General Jessup's on the night of February 6, 1854, and came to mother to spend the night, in order not to awaken the older members of my grandmother's family. The girls doffed their party dresses, replaced them with comfortable woolen gowns, and, gathered before the open fire in mother's room, were gaily relating the experiences of the evening. The fire needed replenishing and mother went to an adjoining dressing-room to get more wood. The old-fashioned fire-place required long logs which were too large for her to handle, and as she half knelt, balancing the long sticks of wood on her left arm, she felt a hand rest lightly on her left shoulder, and she heard my father's laughing voice whisper her name, 'Jessie.'

"There was no sound beyond the quick-whispered name, no presence, only the touch, but my mother knew as people know in dreams that my father was there, gay and happy, and intending to startle Susie, who when my mother was married was only a child of eight, and was always a pet playmate of my father's. Her shrill, prolonged scream was his delight, and he never lost an opportunity to startle her.

"Mother came back to the girl's room, but before she could speak, Susie gave a great cry, fell in a heap upon the rug, and screamed again and again, until mother crushed her balldress over her head to keep the sound from the neighbors. Her cousin asked mother what she had seen, and she explained that she had seen nothing, but had heard my father tell her to keep still until he could scare Susie.

"Peace came to my mother instantly, and on retiring she fell into a refreshing sleep from which she did not waken until ten the next morning; all fear for the safety of father had vanished from her mind; with sleep came strength, and she soon was her happy self again.

"When my father returned home, we learned that it was at the time the party was starving that my mother had the premonition of evil having befallen them, and the entry in his journal showed that exactly the moment he had written it in Parowan, my mother had felt his presence, and in the wireless message from heart to heart knew that my father was safe and free from harm. The hour exactly tallied with the entry in his book, allowing for the difference in longitude."

Further details would have been desirable, particularly just what was the immediate occasion of Susie's fright, for she screamed before Mrs. Frémont related what had befallen herself. The only escape from the conclusion that Susie had some separate peculiar experience is to suppose—which we may not unreasonably do—that the elder lady betrayed her own agitation before she spoke, perhaps by dropping the sticks, hurrying back, and looking strangely at Susie. We would have liked a sight of the General's journal, also, and to have been permitted to copy the entry exactly as it stands.

Nevertheless, though we leave Susie and her screams quite out of account, we have a very pretty case remaining, however we explain it. Mrs. Frémont's depression might be explained by the very natural fears of a woman whose husband was engaged in a possibly dangerous expedition, though she picked out for her fears exactly the period of the expedition when there was an actual state of privation and danger. But why did the fear so afflicting to her health and spirits so suddenly leave her, while it was still winter in the mountains? And why did the hour and moment of the cessation of these fears coincide with the hour and moment when the explorer was occupied with thoughts of home and writing his wish that his wife might know that he was safe?

Many a reader will be disposed to answer the question "why?" with the facile answer "telepathy," but that word is a key which does not turn in this lock with perfect ease. There are cases where one person thinks a particular thing under extraordinary circumstances, and precisely that thought, or a hallucination of precisely that nature, occurs to another person at a distance. But in this case General Frémont thinks a wish that his wife knew he was safe, and his wife seems to feel a hand upon her shoulder, seems to hear his voice pronounce her name, and somehow gets the impression that he proposes to play a trick on her sister Susie. If exact coincidence between the thought of the supposed "sender" and that of the supposed "recipient" is a support to the theory of telepathy as applied to one case, then wide discrepancy between the coincident thoughts of two persons in another case should be an argument against the theory of telepathy as applied to that. There should be some limit to the handicap which, by way of courtesy, the spiritistic hypothesis allows to the telepathic.

If there are spirits, and if they have a certain access to human thoughts, and if the limitations of space are little felt by them, then the spiritistic theory would have an easier time than telepathy with the facts in this case. A friendly intermediary might convey the assurance that the Pathfinder wanted conveyed to his wife, and in doing so employ such devices as an intelligent personal agent could think up, and were within its grasp. The touch, the hallucination of a voice resembling that of the absent husband, the sense of gayety, and even the very characteristic trait of liking to startle Susie, might all be the result of the friendly messenger's attempts to implant in Mrs. Frémont's mind a fixed assurance that somebody was safe and happy, and that this somebody was in very truth her husband.

Incidents Related by Dean Hole

The Very Rev. Samuel Reynolds Hole, Dean of Rochester, England, was not only an effective preacher and popular lecturer, but likewise the author of fascinating books, composed of reminiscences and shrewd and witty comments upon men and affairs. He made two lecturing tours in America.

His The Memories of Dean Hole contains a remarkable dream of his own, and one of similar character told him by a trusted friend. They may be found on pages 200-201. After rehearsing the account of a dream and its tragic sequel told him many years before, he goes on:

"Are these dreams coincidences only, imaginations, sudden recollections of events which had been long forgotten? They are marvelous, be this as it may. In a crisis of very severe anxiety, I required information which only one man could give me, and he was in his grave. I saw him distinctly in a vision of the night, and his answer to my question told me all I wanted to know; and when, having obtained the clearest proof that what I had heard was true, I communicated the incident and its results to my solicitor, he told me that he himself had experienced a similar manifestation. A claim was repeated after his father's death which had been resisted in his lifetime and retracted by the claimant, but the son was unable to find the letter in which the retraction was made. He dreamed that his father appeared and told him it was in the left hand drawer of a certain desk. Having business in London, he went up to the offices of his father, an eminent lawyer, but could not discover the desk, until one of the clerks suggested that it might be among some old lumber placed in a room upstairs. There he found the desk and the letter.

"Then, as regards coincidence, are there not events in our lives which come to us with a strange mysterious significance, a prophetic intimation, sometimes of sorrow and sometimes of success? For example, I lived a hundred and fifty miles from

Rochester. I went there for the first time to preach at the invitation of one who was then unknown to me, but is now a dear friend. After the sermon I was his guest in the Precincts. Dean Scott died in the night, almost at the time when he who was to succeed him arrived at the house which adjoins the Deanery. There was no expectation of his immediate decease, and no conjecture as to a future appointment, and yet when I heard the tolling of the cathedral bell, I had a presentiment that Dr. Scott was dead, and that I should be Dean of Rochester."

Again, Dean Hole in his Then and Now, pp. 9-11, together with some opinions of his, sets down a seeming premonition and what he considers answers to prayer.

"There is an immeasurable difference between ghosts and other apparitions—between that which witnesses declare they saw with their own eyes when they were wide awake—as Hamlet saw the ghost of his father, and Macbeth saw Banquo—and that which presents itself to us when we are asleep, or in that condition between waking and sleeping which makes the vision so like reality. I do not believe in the former, and I am fully persuaded in my own mind that the wonderful stories which we hear are to be accounted for either as exaggerations or as the result of natural causes which have been misstated or suppressed; but many of us have had experience of the latter—of those visions of the night which have seemed so real, and which in some instances have brought us information as to occurrences before unknown to us, but subsequently proved to be true.

"George Benfield, a driver on the Midland Railway living at Derby, was standing on the footplate oiling his engine, the train being stationary, when he slipped and fell on the space between the lines. He heard the express coming on, and had only just time to lie full length on the 'six-foot' when it rushed by, and he escaped unhurt. He returned to his home in the middle of the night, and as he was going up the stairs he heard one of his children, a girl about eight years old, crying and sobbing. 'Oh, Father!' she said, 'I thought somebody came and told me that you were going to be killed, and I got out of bed and prayed that God would not let you die.' Was it only a dream, a coincidence?"

Dean Hole is the first person whom we remember to have held that a man's testimony respecting a given species of experience is more credible if he was asleep at the time that he claims to have had it, than if he was awake. He states that dreams "in some instances have brought us information as to occurrences before unknown to us, but subsequently proved to be true," but the same is asserted in respect to waking apparitional experiences on exactly as satisfactory evidence, in many cases. He accounts for the wonderful stories we hear in respect to waking apparitions, and discredits them on exactly the same grounds that others account for and discredit his dreams. The fact is that, with Dean Hole as with many others, the personal equation is operative. He believes in coincidental dreams because he himself has experienced them and knows that he is not guilty of exaggerations in recounting them, nor can he see how natural causes can explain them; he never has had a waking apparition, and therefore is inclined to conjure up guesses as to the inaccuracy and inveracity of those who have—guesses which he would resent if they were applied to himself.

But the Dean's testimony is one matter, his opinions or prejudices another.

Incidents Reported by Serjeant Ballantine

Serjeant William Ballantine (1812-1887) was one of the foremost lawyers in England, noted for his skill in cross-examination. He was counsel in the Tichborne claimant case, one of the most celebrated in the history of the English courts, and in the equally famed trial of the Gaekwar of Baroda. The incidents which impressed him are to be found in Ballantine's Some Experiences of a Barrister's Life, pp. 256-267.

"I do not think it will be out of place whilst upon this subject to relate a story told of Sir Astley Cooper.[22] I am not certain that it has not been already in print, but I know that I have had frequent conversations about it with his nephew.

"There had been a murder, and Sir Astley was upon the scene when a man suspected of it was apprehended. Sir Astley, being greatly interested, accompanied the officers with their prisoner to the gaol, and he and they and the accused were all in a cell, locked in together, when they noticed a little dog which kept biting at the skirt of the prisoner's coat. This led them to examine the garment, and they found upon it traces of blood which ultimately led to conviction of the man. When they looked around the dog had disappeared, although the door had never been opened. How it had got there or how it got away, of course nobody could tell. When Bransby Cooper spoke of this he always said that of course his uncle had made a mistake, and was convinced of this himself; Bransby used to add that no doubt if the matter had been investigated it would have been shown that there was a mode of accounting for it

---

[22] Sir Astley Paston Cooper was perhaps the most famous and influential surgeon of his time in England.

from natural causes. But I believe that neither Sir Astley nor his nephew in their hearts discarded entirely the supernatural."

Mr. Ballantine added an incident which some may think is accounted for by a telepathic impression followed by auto-suggestion which lowered the mental alertness of the player.

"There was a member of the club, a very harmless, inoffensive man of the name of Townend, for whom Lord Lytton [the novelist entertained a mortal antipathy, and would never play whilst that gentleman was in the room. He firmly believed that he brought him bad luck. I was witness to what must be termed an odd coincidence. One afternoon, when Lord Lytton was playing and had enjoyed an uninterrupted run of luck, it suddenly turned, upon which he exclaimed, 'I am sure that Mr. Townend has come into the club.' Some three minutes after, just time enough to ascend the stairs, in walked that unlucky personage. Lord Lytton as soon as the rubber was over, left the table and did not renew the play."

Ben Jonson's Premonition by Apparition

This eminent dramatist, contemporary of Shakespeare (1573?-1637), visited the Scottish poet, William Drummond, who took notes of his conversations which he afterwards published in the form of a book. One incident which Jonson related and Drummond recorded may be found in The Library of the World's Best Literature under the title, Ben Jonson.

"At that tyme the pest was in London; he being in the country—with old Cambden, he saw in a vision his eldest sone, then a child and at London, appear unto him with the mark of a bloodie crosse in his forehead, as if it had been cutted with a shord, at which amazed he prayed unto God, and in the morning he came to Mr. Cambden's chamber to tell him; who persuaded him it was but ane apprehension of his fantasie, at which he sould not be disjected; in the mean tyme comes then letters from his wife of the death of that boy in plague. He appeared to him (he said) of a manly shape, and of that grouth that he thinks he shall be at the resurrection."

Rubinstein's Death Compact

A pupil of Anton Rubinstein, the great pianist and composer (1829-1894), tells this story. It may be found in Harper's Magazine for December, 1912, under the title A Girl's Recollections of Rubinstein, by Lillian Nichia.

"One wild, blustery night I found myself at dinner with Rubinstein, the weather being terrific even for St. Petersburg. The winds were howling round the house and Rubinstein, who liked to ask questions, inquired of me what they represented to my mind. I replied, 'The moaning of lost souls.' From this a theological discussion followed.

"'There may be a future,' he said.

"'There is a future,' I cried, 'a great and beautiful future. If I die first I shall come to you and prove this.'

"He turned to me with great solemnity.

"'Good, Liloscha, that is a bargain; and I will come to you.'

"Six years later in Paris I woke one night with a cry of agony and despair ringing in my ears, such as I hope may never be duplicated in my lifetime. Rubinstein's face was close to mine, a countenance distorted by every phase of fear, despair, agony, remorse and anger. I started up, turned on all the lights, and stood for a moment shaking in every limb, till I put fear from me and decided it was merely a dream. I had for the moment completely forgotten our compact. News is always late in Paris, and it was in Le Petit Journal, published in the afternoon, that had the first account of his sudden death.

"Four years later, Teresa Carreno, who had just come from Russia and was touring America—I had met her in St. Petersburg frequently at Rubinstein's dinner-table—told me that Rubinstein died with a cry of agony impossible of description. I knew then that even in death Rubinstein had kept, as he always did, his word."

Here again, we are at liberty to accept the testimony regarding the remarkable and complex coincidence, and to disregard what is really an expression of opinion in the last sentence. Whether Rubinstein remembered his compact in his dying hour, or the impression produced upon his far-away pupil was automatically produced by some obscure telepathic process, the dying man having in his mind no conscious thought of his promise, or some intervening tertium quid produced the impression, could never be determined by this incident alone.

Previsionary Dream by Charles Dickens

This incident in the experience of Charles Dickens (1812-1870) is to be found in the standard biography by Forster, III, pp. 484-5 (London, 1874). On May 30, 1863, Dickens wrote:

"Here is a curious case at first-hand. On Thursday night in last week, being at my office here, I dreamed that I saw a lady in a red shawl with her back toward me (whom I supposed to be E—). On her turning round I found that I didn't know her, and she said, 'I am Miss Napier.' All the time I was dressing next morning I thought

'What a preposterous thing to have so very distinct a dream about nothing!' and why Miss Napier?—for I never heard of any Miss Napier. That same Friday night I read. After the reading, came into my retiring-room, Mary Boyle and her brother, and the lady in the red shawl, whom they present as 'Miss Napier.' These are all the circumstances exactly told."

I can imagine the late Professor Royce saying thirty years ago—for I much doubt if he would have said it twenty years later—"In certain people, under certain exciting circumstances, there occur what I shall henceforth call Pseudo-presentiments, i.e., more or less instantaneous hallucinations of memory, which make it seem to one that something which now excites or astonishes him has been prefigured in a recent dream, or in the form of some other warning, although this seeming is wholly unfounded, and although the supposed prophecy really succeeds its own fulfillment."

Apply this curious theory (which has probably not been urged for many years) to the incident just cited, and see how loosely it fits. What was there about three persons, one a stranger coming to Dickens after he had finished a reading from his own works, to "excite" or "astonish" him, make his brain whirl and bring about a hallucination of memory, an illusion of having dreamed it all before? It was the most commonplace event to him. Besides, as in most such cases, he had the distinct recollection of his thoughts about the dream after waking, thoughts inextricably interwoven with the acts performed while dressing! Besides, a pseudo-presentiment should tally with the event as a reflection does with the object, but in the dream Miss Napier introduced herself, while in reality she was introduced by another.

www.ingramcontent.com/pod-product-compliance
Lightning Source LLC
Chambersburg PA
CBHW010401310726
48979CB00017B/2807/J

* 9 7 8 1 6 3 6 3 7 2 7 3 0 *